ELSA BLOODST

I leapt forward and sideways ... into an aerial even as I pulled out one of my throwing knives. I flung it toward the attacker who'd tried to ambush me from behind. It dropped the thorny branch it had been carrying and clutched at its face, squealing in agony.

Two more ratmen who'd followed it ran at me. I jabbed the first one in the face with my nicely pointy shovel, making it recoil. Then I pivoted and walloped the second one across the side of the head so hard it fell to the ground in a heap, motionless except for the occasional twitch. Before the first one could recover, I pulled out my machete – matte black and sharpened to a monofilament edge – and swung, smoothly separating its head from its body. I walked over to the one that was still rolling around squealing and, with a single well-placed stroke, silenced it too.

I straightened up and shook the blood off my machete. "Well," I said, staring around the darkness with a bright smile. "I do believe this party's started now."

ALSO AVAILABLE

MARVEL HEROINES

ELSA BLOODSTONE
BEQUEST

CATH LAURIA

ACONYTE®

FOR MARVEL PUBLISHING

VP Production & Special Projects: Jeff Youngquist
Associate Editor, Special Projects: Caitlin O'Connell
Manager, Licensed Publishing: Jeremy West
VP, Licensed Publishing: Sven Larsen
SVP Print, Sales & Marketing: David Gabriel
Editor in Chief: C B Cebulski

Special Thanks to Nick Lowe and Jake Thomas

© 2021 MARVEL

First published by Aconyte Books in 2021
ISBN 978-1-83908-072-2
Ebook ISBN 978-1-83908-073-9

Cover art by Joey Hi-Fi

Distributed in North America by Simon & Schuster Inc, New York, USA
Printed in the United States of America
9 8 7 6 5 4 3 2 1

ACONYTE BOOKS

An imprint of Asmodee Entertainment Ltd
Mercury House, Shipstones Business Centre
North Gate, Nottingham NG7 7FN, UK
aconytebooks.com // twitter.com/aconytebooks

For Damian, who believes I can do anything and celebrates every milestone, and for Janet and Jes, who are stellar mentors and even better friends. I hope you all enjoy Elsa's fantastic adventures.

ONE

Glasgow Cathedral's City of the Dead was absolutely lovely in the moonlight.

That was the first thing that struck me as I looked out over the rising hillsides of the necropolis, thick with marble tombs and monuments to people who were only remembered for their historical headstones these days. The burial ground glowed beneath the full moon, with various memorial spires and their stone-faced angels reaching up to heaven as if trying to coax it into their hands and capture it for their centuries-old corpses.

To be fair, the place was quite lovely during the daytime, too. Glasgow Necropolis was a proper old-fashioned Victorian cemetery that embraced its identity as a repository of not only the dead, but also of art, beauty, and faith. The city had done a rather good job of keeping it up, I thought as I scanned the shadows, looking for the slightest hint of movement. This was a top-notch place to be interred. Anyone who tried to tell you there was nothing good about being dead had clearly never visited Glasgow.

Right now, however, it was a less than ideal place for a dirt nap if one was looking forward to eternal rest. A clan of ratmen had recently installed itself in the City of the Dead, taking over tombs, desecrating memorials, and generally leaving their filth everywhere. I turned my face into the wind and inhaled deep. Yes, there it was – a rotting garbage-heap sweetness that shouldn't be there. Ratmen were nowhere near as fastidious about cleanliness as their vastly smaller rodent cousins, and the ever-increasing stench had been the first tipoff to the people who ran the place that something wasn't right. Ratmen claimed territory in stages, and stage one was spreading their filth about and seeing if anyone noticed.

The second tipoff had been the poor guide who'd gotten a bit too close to the nest the dirty grubbers had made inside a stately grave along the main tour route. One moment he was chattering away about "architectural influences from Jerusalem that account for the repeating pattern up there, d'you see the pattern?" and the next moment a snarling ratman bashed him over the head with an old iron cross pilfered from one of the other tombs.

People had proceeded to run about screaming, and two more visitors were injured in the melee – one bitten, while the other one tripped over her own untied shoelace and sprained her wrist when she hit the ground. One thing led to another, and a few days later the necropolis was closed for "restoration" while the archbishop of Glasgow got ahold of me.

It was rather flattering, honestly, if a bit below my pay grade. I hunt *monsters*, the bigger and badder the better, and ratmen are an annoyance at best. But the old gent who'd rung me up had asked so politely, and they were as generous with their stipend as a group operating on donations could be, so I'd agreed. Blast my bleeding heart.

Hmm. Nothing to be seen from here other than a flock of rather atmospheric ravens sitting in a tree about fifty meters away. I sauntered deeper into the necropolis, shouldering my shovel in a casual-ready position that wouldn't cause alarm. It felt rather strange, walking into a fight without my customary firearms. Back in Britain or not, I was resourceful enough to get my guns into just about anywhere, but the church had begged me not to bring them into the cemetery.

"Think of the statuary!" the gentleman in charge of running the place implored with tears in his eyes. "You might be responsible for destroying something that's nearly two hundred years old! Not to mention endangering the Cathedral, which is far older! How would you live with the guilt?"

"I've taken out plenty of things a lot older than that for kicks," I'd blithely informed him. "Like vampires," I added when the man looked at me in horror. "Some of those blokes have been around for millennia, you know."

Jokes were never as fun when you had to explain them.

Regardless, now I was walking into a melee with a shovel over my shoulder, a machete under my trench coat, and several smaller knives stashed here and there, just in case. And one, just *one* tiny little P90 semiautomatic rifle filled to capacity with hollow points. As a last resort. In my profession it paid to have backup plans.

The ground crunched slightly beneath my boots, the stiletto heels scraping along the path. I wasn't trying to be quiet. Quiet wasn't the point, after all, and it wasn't exactly my strong suit to begin with. I hummed a bit of the song that had been playing on the radio as I'd driven in – and I'd clearly spent too much time in America lately, because driving on the correct, left-hand side of the road had felt a touch awkward – and absently touched the bloodstone choker at the base of my neck. It seemed to pulse as I petted it, the stone as warm to my fingertips as my own blood.

I didn't need to be holding it in my hand to access its power – keeping it around my neck was just fine – but it felt nice to give it a nudge every now and then as I was walking into a situation. It was almost like promising an old friend that we'd meet up for a pint later when things were less busy.

Ah, there. That was the smell of ratmen, carried over to my hypersensitive nose on the night breeze once more. It might have been filtering in from miles away, given how huge the necropolis was, but no, this was fresher than that. More immediate. Ratmen could hide, but they couldn't stop smelling like a skunk had fallen in love with a dirty diaper and they'd shacked up in an old garbage can together.

Bin. It's a bloody bin! Lord, I'd been in Boston for so long that Americanisms were infiltrating my vocabulary. Before long I'd be "pahking the cahr in Hahvahd Yahd."

I wasn't going to waste my time following the ratmen's rather nasty trail of breadcrumbs when I could simply call them out to face me. Ratmen were rather simple creatures, but there was still a touch of intelligence within those beady eyes, and they were sensitive to matters of hierarchy. And me? I was here to royally disrupt their current leadership model. And look amazing while doing it, thank you very much.

I tossed my long, vermilion ponytail over my shoulder and pulled a chocolate bar wrapper out of my pocket.

"Right, you lot," I shouted into the night. "I understand you've decided to claim the City of the Dead as your own. Lovely thought, but there's just one problem – I don't acknowledge your claim." I dropped the chocolate wrapper on the ground and stepped on it a few times, so the crinkle of the silvery paper could be heard. "I think I'll be taking over this place, starting right here in front of me. Do any of you prats have the stomach to step up and do something about it?"

There was complete silence for a moment before a raven croaked in the distance. A second later the whole conspiracy of them flapped noisily out of the tree they'd been settled in, perching all over the necropolis on different tombs like they were guests at an ancient Roman coliseum. *Ready for some bloodshed, boys?* They'd be getting their fill of entertainment before long.

"Come on now, you overgrown vermin, I don't have all night." I pulled out a battered old cloth I used to clean my guns and threw it a few feet away. "Are any of you going to bother putting up a fight, or will I be hunting you down while you cower like the frightened little mice you are?"

A low growl resonated against the nearest tombs, harsh and angry. I smirked. Finally. "There we are, that wasn't too hard," I cooed. "Honestly, I thought I'd have to start insulting your mothers before one of you useless, slack-jawed, dull-fanged excuses for a proper ratman would gather your nerve. Come on then, let's have a look at you, hmm?" I took my last bit of affrontery ammunition, an hours-old banana peel, already dark brown and rotten-sweet, and waggled it in the air. "Or you could just run like a bunch of baby bunnies back to your hidey holes." I flung the banana peel into the air ahead of me, and–

Snap! Whip-quick jaws snatched it out of the air before it hit the ground. The ratman responsible for eating my challenge stalked forward through the shadows, slinking low along the ground before finally stepping into the light. It was tall for a ratman, and its head came up to my shoulder. It had a set of claws on both front and rear paws that were half as long as my machete. Its bared teeth gleamed yellow in the moonlight, and the pair of rudimentary pants and torn, stained vest it was wearing clearly indicated it as the alpha of the pack. Only the smartest ones figured out how to wear human clothes, and they used their special knowledge as a bludgeon against the lesser rats. Perhaps literally in this case – the ratman alpha held a three-foot wrought iron spike in its hands. Its eyes gleamed maliciously.

I grinned. "Oh yes, we will have fun, won't we?" Two meters behind me and thirty degrees to the left, I felt the air shift a little. Clever things. "Good boy," I whispered. "What's your name, then?"

It snarled something unintelligible. The hairs on the back of my neck stood up as whoever was behind me crept closer and closer. "What was that, love? Gnar-shnar-grawr-ugh? You'll have to tell me again. I'd hate to have the wrong name inscribed on your very own tombsto–"

Whoosh! I leapt forward and sideways, throwing myself into an aerial even as I pulled out one of my throwing knives. I flung it toward the attacker who'd tried to ambush me from behind, and the knife went right into the smaller ratman's left eye. It dropped the thorny branch it had been carrying and clutched at its face, squealing in agony.

Two more ratmen who'd followed it ran at me. I jabbed the first one in the face with my nicely pointy shovel, making it recoil. Then I pivoted and walloped the second one across the side of the head so hard it fell to the ground in a heap, motionless except for the occasional twitch. Before the first one could recover, I pulled out my machete – matte black and sharpened to a monofilament edge – and swung, smoothly separating its head from its body. I walked over to the one that was still rolling around squealing and, with a single well-placed stroke, silenced it too.

I straightened up and shook the blood off my machete. "Well," I said, staring around the darkness with a bright smile. "I do believe this party's started now." I could see more of them now, sliding out from behind decorative crosses and obelisks en masse. Their dark, muddy fur rendered them almost invisible against the ground, but the power of the bloodstone not only made me stronger and quicker than any ratman out there, it sharpened my senses considerably. Anyone who thought they could sneak up on me with impunity would pay for their assumption with their head.

I cast a quick look at my boots – ugh, arterial spray, of course right after I'd gotten these all polished up. This job would be so much simpler if I could just shoot everyone from a distance. "Bloody period architecture." Well, there was nothing to be done but carry on.

"Right, who's next?" I pointed my machete at the alpha rat, who still hung back, his constant sputtering snarl making him sound like an old lawnmower about to run out of fuel. "How about you, your highness?" I ran toward him, but swiftly found my way blocked by a trio of large, imposing ratmen, all wielding tomb decorations – or rather, desecrations, as the case was now. "Ah good, I do so love a volunteer."

Three were more challenging to handle than two, but only by a hair. They tended to get in each other's way and didn't bother to charge as a group, waiting for me to make a move before any of them reacted. The simplicity of such killing should have been a relief, an easy job to help pay the bills, but really it was all a bit… well, *boring*.

Then again, that was life lately, I reflected as I smashed the flat of my shovel into the belly of one ratman while executing a pirouette that left the other two without their right and left forepaws. I finished all three of them off with a flourish of my blade, then moved on to the next clump of excrement-scented enemies.

Boring. What I would give for a decent fight with a monster that thought with its brain instead of its claws. Another bout with Fin Fang Foom would set me up for weeks! Or some eldritch horror climbing out of a Manhattan sewer who only wants to see the world end in a rain of blood and terror – now that would be invigorating!

"Instead I get you lot," I grunted, thrusting my machete through one ratman's head as I walloped the one trying to sneak up behind me with the point of the shovel. It warbled a pained howl and fell over onto its face, clutching its groin. "Just like a man," I tsked. "One good shot to the crown jewels and you're down for the count. It's not that I don't appreciate the consistency, really–"

A smaller ratman flung itself at me from a twelve-foot high monument. I kicked my right foot into the air and speared the wiry creature right through the throat with my stiletto heel. *Ugh. Efficient, but so messy.* I shook the body off and continued, "But the bollocks are always going to be an issue for gents. And nice try, you blighter, but you'll have to do better than that to get the drop on me."

The falling ratman had distracted me for a moment, though, and the rest of the clan took advantage of that time to tighten their ranks around me, armed with pieces of marble, nail-studded boards, and whatever else they could find. The closest ones hesitated in their approach, which made sense given they were stepping over the bodies of their brethren to get to me. Those behind them insistently pushed them forward, though. They'd made a ratman snare, and I was square in the middle of it.

"Bloody hell, you lot multiply faster than real rats." I grinned, showing all my teeth in a dominant display. "Perfect."

I swung into action, widening the circle around me with a looping swing of my shovel, then leapt straight up into the air as the horde charged. The first layer of ratmen toppled into one another, and then I was back in the middle of the fray – or above it, rather, using their heads and backs as stepping stones as I hopped over the mass of them to the outer edge of the circle.

Every footstep evoked a fresh cry of pain from my living sidewalk. "Enjoying the physics that result from me putting fifteen hundred pounds of pressure per square inch on your spine, pet? Isn't science glorious?"

The challenge with foes like ratmen was simply in handling their numbers. They weren't innovative or challenging fighters one-on-one, but even a swarm of butterflies could be a problem if they landed on you all at once. As long as you could avoid being surrounded, you had options.

"Of course, this would have been so much bloody simpler if I could just shoot you all." Every jostle of the P90 beneath my coat was like a siren's call, but I was determined to handle this the old-fashioned way. I'd promised, after all, and the statuary *was* rather lovely, if overwhelmingly morose.

"Come on, then," I shouted into the churning fray as the clan tried to regroup, shuffling around to face me once more. "Where's your alpha gone off to? Is this proper behavior for the leader of a clan to engage in, hiding behind his people like a baby? Where's Big Daddy Ratman, hmm?"

Two of the clan toughs lunged toward me, and I dispatched my throwing knives with alacrity, taking each of them in the gut and doubling them over. Lovely. Two ratmen rolling about the ground in pain was just the thing to make the ones behind them give me a bit of space.

"We don't have all night," I added. "Truly, we don't – I don't know about you, but I intend to get at least eight hours' beauty rest before I'm back on a plane to Boston tomorrow, and whoever in the clan survives could put that time to good use running back to the highland hole they crawled out of." I paused dramatically, then said, "Unless you don't want *anyone* in your clan to make it. You've already lost, what, a dozen or so of your best fighters? Are you going to start throwing the mothers at me next? The adolescents? Is that how you want your clan to end?"

The was a rumble of discontent in the crowd of ratmen. A moment before I shrugged and began indiscriminately slicing again, the alpha slithered out of the shadows, stepping forward to face me. It swung its iron spike in a fast circle around its body, the bar practically blurring with speed.

"Someone's watched a few kung fu movies, I see."

It was a rather impressive display – for a ratman.

"But anyone can sling a bit of metal around and intimidate the masses. Let's see if you can actually use it." I brought my shovel up in an *en garde* position.

The ratman bunched down as it gathered itself, then shrieked a garbled war cry and leapt into an attack, spinning its spike perilously close to my head. I reached out to parry with the shovel and finish the thing with the machete, and–

Blam! A bullet punched straight through the ratman alpha's head, destroying its tight, predictable arc and sending its body slumping down to the ground – nearly right on top of me. *What the bloody hell is going on now?* In the distance, I heard a marble frontispiece shatter.

"Right, who brought a gun to a shovel fight?" I shouted, even as I took cover behind a nearby tomb. A ratman was already there, crouched down on all fours and trembling from nose to tail. It took one look at me and bolted away. A short burst of gunfire followed, telling me quite a bit about the party crashers who'd just arrived.

First, it was a group of them. At least three, judging from the sound of the gunfire, but quite likely more. Second, they weren't here for the ratmen – if they had been, they'd have continued firing at the monster I'd briefly shared shelter with until it dropped, but I was pretty sure it had gotten away clean. So, if the church wasn't cheating on me by hiring other killers to take out their monster trash, then my third conclusion could only be that the newcomers were here for me.

"Bloody inconsiderate timing," I snapped. I stared at my shovel for a moment, then threw it to the ground and pulled out the P90. "At least I tried," I said, briefly checking the magazine.

A few bullets hit the back of the long, rectangular headstone I was hiding behind, then the guns went silent. I could hear multiple footsteps moving on both sides of me, though – not the clawed ratman kind, but the heavy boot kind. A flanking maneuver, how original.

"Can't say I didn't give historical preservation a go, but I was outvoted on the subject."

The sound of people moving intensified on my left. I didn't pause to take a look, just whirled out from behind the headstone already firing. I had fifty rounds in the magazine and no spare, thanks to my bloody bleeding heart, so each bullet needed to count. The first shot got my target to instinctively duck, even though it was nowhere near him. The second one cut off his attempted escape behind another marble edifice nearby through the expedience of blowing a healthy chunk of it off. The third one took the lucky bloke square in the head. A hollow point round did wonders against an unarmored target, but could fail against body armor – and these people were wearing body armor. That meant the head was going to be the best option.

The man slumped to the ground, dead in an instant, and I nodded with satisfaction. Yes, headshots were definitely the way to go.

I shifted before my ambushers could nail me down, throwing myself into a roll that took me behind a long, low-laying tomb. Bullets followed, chewing into the granite right behind me. Rather than emerging into a firing stance on the other end of the cover, I leapt up and into a backflip, craning my neck to spot my opponents before they could get me back in their sights. *Nine o'clock, ten meters away – BLAM BLAM! Two o'clock, fourteen meters away – BLAM BLAM BLAM!* Both of them were down before my feet touched the ground.

BANG! A heavy-caliber bullet shattered a cross two feet away, and a chip from it cut through my cheek, leaving a thin, bleeding line. The wound was gone in the time it would have taken for me to wipe the blood away, but it was still rather annoying.

"Are you lot American?" I shouted as I darted in the direction of the shooter, laying down a spray of covering fire to keep Mr Big Gun from trying anything rash. "You're American, aren't you? Who else would be so cavalier about firing a gun at someone?" There, two graves away, trying to hide behind the black marble obelisk. I grinned. "Other than me, that is."

I fired a brief burst into the obelisk itself, then leapt into a sidekick and struck the weakened edifice hard enough to crack it in two. The top half slid backward onto the ground behind it, followed quickly by a pained, "Hrrghuh!"

"Down and out then, love?" I ducked so I could use the bottom half of the obelisk as cover and glanced around it at the attacker I'd just flattened. "Oh, rather. Well done, me."

The obelisk had settled right over his midsection. Scrabble as he might trying to push it off, he didn't have the leverage – or the wind – to move it anywhere. The man wheezed. Still alive. "Perfect," I said. "You stay right here. I'm going to have some questions for you later."

Enough of reacting. It was time to take the fight to the enemy. A nearby grave was decorated with an actual metal shield set into the stone. It was iron, no doubt, and brittle from age, but I didn't need it to last long. I braced against the grave and got my fingers around the edges of the shield. One good wrench, and – ah! It came right off in my hands. I felt very Captain America in that moment, not that I was going to be throwing this old thing at anyone.

I hoisted the shield with my left arm, pointed the P90 with my right, and ran north, in the direction that the closest attackers had come from. Two shots zinged out of the darkness. One hit the shield, the other hit a stone cherub, taking out its fat little foot. I fired on instinct – *blamblamblam* – and was rewarded with a man crumpling to the ground from a nearby alder tree.

Four down. How many of you are left?

I crouched suddenly as a spray of bullets chewed into the graves in front of me. Two hit the shield, shattering the iron. I flung the shards away and fired my P90 as I rolled to the right, finding new cover behind an absolute monolith of a tomb. Either someone important was buried behind this one, or the gent – and judging from the sheer size and *pointiness* of the memorial, it was definitely a man who'd been interred here – wanted his death to tell a different story from his life.

Either way, I was happy to use this monument to self-aggrandizement as a convenient place to shelter.

"Elsa Bloodstone!" a voice called out.

"Oh, are we finally ready to use our words instead of our guns?" I shouted back, noticing for the first time a fresh bullet hole in my lovely long coat. Bloody hell, I just had this thing mended! "Right, go on then, lay your terms on me."

Attacks from monsters were easy to understand, for the most part. Attacks from people like this? It generally meant that either some rival had put a kill bounty on my head, and this was the unlucky pack of mercenaries who'd taken the contract, or someone was after my bloodstone shard.

"Hand over the shard!"

Spot on, called that one. "Ooh, let me think about it," I said as I ducked my head out for a quick glance. No one was immediately visible, but there were only two tombs big enough to hide behind in the direction the gunfire had been coming from. If my attackers had come in as a single strike team, then there probably weren't more than four of them left. No wonder they finally wanted to try talking it out. Eight against one was hardly fair – four against one is a massacre. "I'm going to have to go with absolutely not on that one, pet, thanks for asking."

"We have you surrounded!"

I rolled my eyes. Bloody idiots. "You've got anywhere from two to four blokes hunkering down behind the mortal remains of some wealthy Victorians!" I shouted back. "Unless you're about to get necromantic, I'm rather assured that you *don't*, in fact, have me surrounded." Nevertheless, it wouldn't do to stay here for too long. There was no sense in making finding me easy on them, even if I was pretty sure at this point that I didn't have much to fear from the stragglers.

"Comply or die!"

"Is it rhyme time, then? Here, I've got a nursery rhyme for you."

The tomb on the left was closer, only eight or so meters away, and there were plenty of smaller graves I could hide behind on my way there. I checked my ammo. Twelve shots left. It's time to finish this. "How about this one… 'Here comes a candle to light you to bed.'"

I rolled to the side, coming to rest behind a simple marble headstone. Bullets followed me, spattering turf and gravel. All of a sudden, the gunfire stopped. I heard an insistent *click-click-click!* Ah, lovely – someone had run out of ammunition, and, even better, no one else had taken over firing practice. Perhaps they'd brought fewer mercenaries along than I'd reckoned. *The fatal price of idiocy.* It was time to move.

I stood up and ran, shooting one round of covering fire for every footstep I took. I reached the nearest tomb in eight long steps and leapt onto the top of it in a crouch. The black-garbed man behind it was fumbling a magazine into his pistol.

"'And here comes a chopper to chop off your head!'" I fired two shots through the top of his helmet, and the man dropped instantly.

"You ought to have practiced reloading under pressure," I informed his corpse, hopping down beside him. I was down to two bullets. Should I bother finishing the reload job and using his gun?

Nah, I didn't know what sort of state it was in. Bloody fool who couldn't even load it probably wasn't meticulous about keeping it clean enough to shoot without jamming at the worst possible moment. "How many of you are left, then?" I called toward the other big gravestone.

"More than you know."

"Hmm." That meant just one, in all likelihood, two at the most. If there'd been more of them then the man at my feet wouldn't have been back here by himself. I glanced toward the tomb. Was that… a *knee* sticking out on the side? Eh, worth finding out. I fired one shot at the bump just barely visible around the worn marble edge. My reward was a plethora of foul language and a sudden barrage of gunfire that, just like with my unlucky gravemate here, turned into *clicks* after about ten rounds.

"Ooh, that doesn't sound good," I laughed. "I rather doubt you can run away at this point either, hard lad. Now that we've established that you're well and truly in it, why don't you tell me who sent you?"

"Go to hell!"

"You first." It hardly mattered if he talked or not. I had another assailant waiting in the wings, patiently held in place by half a helpful obelisk. Let's get this over with, then.

I crouched, ready to spring out and close the distance between me and my final attacker, then... "Oh, *sh–*"

I leapt back to the far side of the heavy tomb as soon as I saw the object lobbed in my direction. I crouched down and clapped my hands over my ears just before a *BOOM* rocked what felt like the entire cemetery. The air itself seemed to quiver for a moment, mimicking the ground beneath me.

I took a breath and immediately regretted it as grave dust infiltrated my nose, making me cough uncontrollably for a moment. The stone behind me trembled – the blast had nearly broken the monument apart. *Good lord, overkill much?* Good thing I'd had a blast wall handy.

One thing was for sure – the craven arsehole cowering behind the other tomb was going to get what was coming to him. Dust filled the air, so it was as good a time as any to run over and put a bullet in my problem.

Three seconds later, I was disappointed to find that the last man standing – probably more like hunkered down in agony, more like – had somehow escaped. Where had he crawled off to?

"Not the time," I reminded myself. I had someone else to interrogate, and then a very good explanation to come up with for the archbishop. *Ah well, it could have been worse*, I consoled myself as I headed back to the broken obelisk. *I could have ended up empty-handed.*

"Right, then," I called out as I got close to my prisoner. "Let's see what you have to… Oy!" I fired my last bullet at the cluster of ratmen hovering over the fallen merc. They scattered. "Oh, you dullards better not have… *ugh*." Yes, they had, they'd eaten all the available and unsquashed parts attached to my source of information. There'd be no prying anything out of *that*.

"Brilliant. Just… bloody… brilliant."

TWO

Bloody-minded bureaucrats! God and good sense save me from ever doing another job for the church. They get unreasonable over the smallest details. Admittedly, I hadn't followed the *absolute* letter of the agreement I'd made with them, considering that twelve of their largest and most impressive historical graves had been demolished in my search for cover. But that certainly wasn't my fault! I hadn't been the one to start that fight, after all – I'd just been the one to finish it.

In the end, a job that should have taken an hour, tops, took me nearly *eight*. Not because it was that difficult to hunt down the ratmen who remained, but because my most immediate employer, Mr McDonnel, head of the Friends of the Necropolis group, took one look at the damage done to the cemetery and fell over in a dead faint. After I roused him with a few gentle words and several invigorating slaps, he outright refused to pay for my services. In the process, he called me so many vile imprecations that his salty vocabulary would have put a sailor to shame. We ended up bringing in the archbishop to mediate, who promptly paid me, thanked me for my services, and told me never to contact them again.

"You approached me about this job, not the other way around," I pointed out, rather miffed.

"I know. And I'd never have done it if I'd known you were the subject of a manhunt. Good *day*, Miss Bloodstone."

The cheek of it. And after all that, after I was up all night and well into the next day, I ended up having to fly commercial home. What good is it being friends with some of the world's most notorious billionaires if you can't catch a lift in their private jets every now and then? Sometimes I thought I was the universe's version of a joke played on myself. Given my spotty memory and the fact that hopping from one reality to another wasn't exactly unknown among my set, it was entirely possible that some other Elsa Bloodstone was watching my exploits and learning an object lesson about being thankful that she wasn't me.

I couldn't let myself think in circles like that for too long. That way lay nothing but madness. All I could do was put one gorgeously shod foot in front of the other and carry on. In this case, I carried on to the airport, checked my luggage (one suitcase, one guitar case, both loaded with weapons), and prepared for the flight back to Boston.

I could have taken a side-trip to visit my younger brother Cullen, off working hard at Braddock Academy – at least he'd better be, if he knew what was good for him – but decided against it. I was tired, I was filthy, and for now I wanted nothing more than to be in my own house, in my own bed. Oddly domestic for a woman who does the world's dirty work for a living, but there you go.

The flight got underway, and the attendant came around to get drink orders and hand out hot towels. I might be flying commercial, but at least I was flying first class.

"Ooh, yes, I'll take all of those," I said, divesting her of her tray and digging into the layer of dust I could still feel caked against my face and neck. I'd changed out of my soiled set of work clothes and triple-bagged them in my luggage but had been denied anything more than a washup in a sink from the denizens of Glasgow Cathedral, those wankers. "And a pot of Earl Gray."

Nothing beat a fresh cup of tea when you were feeling out of sorts. So many of my contemporaries used alcohol as a coping mechanism, but I wouldn't be falling into that trap, not so long as there was a decent cuppa to be had.

Considering the fact that I lived in America most of the time, that wasn't always a given, but I did my best.

I spent the rest of the flight trying to doze, but it was useless. I couldn't stop thinking about the attack. The more I mulled it over, the stranger the circumstances seemed. The number of people I'd told about going to Scotland I could count on one hand, and none of them would have spilled that news willingly. It was possible the archbishop or Mr McDonnel had told someone, but who would they be speaking to that might be interested in sending a team of mercenaries after me? I couldn't recall any enemies who were blatantly Catholic, and God himself, I assumed, wouldn't bother with all that indirect, secondhand rigamarole. He'd just smite me and be done.

I wished I'd been able to get a picture of the mercs with my phone. Unfortunately, I hadn't had it with me during the fight. I'd destroyed too many of the flimsy things that way. I'd texted Adam the broad strokes of what had happened before boarding the plane, and he was quite good with research, but I doubted there was much he'd be able to find. After all, they'd been so painfully bland: majority Caucasian, all in high-end black body armor that nevertheless wasn't custom and so couldn't be tracked that way, armed with weapons they could buy in any gun shop in America, curse the place. No visible tattoos, jewelry, or other symbols declaring their allegiance to a particular group or ideal. *Useless.*

How had they found me? Had they tracked the bloodstone somehow? Could they do it again?

It didn't matter. If they were really desperate to get their hands on my bloodstone shard, then they were welcome to try once more. I'd send the next group packing much the same way I had with those poor toerags, and hopefully send a message that I wasn't remotely to be screwed with.

Getting back to Boston at last was a relief. I would never

say it out loud, but there was a part of me that missed the old homestead while I was away. Bloodstone Manor was an immense old Victorian estate located on the outskirts of the city, surrounded by a fair bit of grass-green acreage. It wasn't the same place I'd first learned to love – that version had been mostly torn apart when Cullen went a bit berserk while possessed by a Glartrox, unfortunately. The rebuild was nearly identical though, save for the vastly updated bathrooms, kitchen, and security systems. Also, I'd had the house repainted in colors other than earth-tone drab, exchanging gray and brown for sky blue and rose pink. That had gotten some squawks from the local historical society, which I silenced by pointing out that I was making the residence *more* historically accurate by giving it some color, not *less*. Nowadays, Bloodstone Manor was home sweet home, and Adam was its undead caretaker.

He met me at the door, reaching out automatically to take my bags. Adam had a good foot and a half of height on me, and I was no slouch in my heels. His skin had a gray, deadened look to it, and the bright black stitches across his forehead, cheeks, and chin practically glowed by comparison. He must have just redone them. He wore his usual monochrome outfit – dark gray pants, a gray turtleneck sweater, and comfortable shoes that were so long they might have fit a yeti.

"Cheers, Adam," I said, wearily, giving him a nod before heading straight for the stairs. "Don't bother opening those unless you're committing to doing my laundry, because therein lies a mélange of such foulness it might even be capable of knocking *you* out."

"Elsa–"

"I already cleaned the guns, of course, they're in the guitar case, and the knives were simple enough, but we might have to get a professional to see to that particular coat." I was going to salvage it come hell or high water. It was my favorite trench coat, a custom fit, and I wasn't made of money like some of my peers. I didn't keep a dozen more just like it on hand.

"Elsa…" Adam closed the door but didn't move away, shifting back and forth in the physical equivalent of dithering. "Um… there's a–"

Wait, was that a puddle forming in my foyer? "Oh lord, is it leaking?" I marched back over and hoisted the bag – yes, it most assuredly was leaking. "I triple-sealed that filth! The *effluvia*, I don't know why it always surprises me given everything I've seen and smelled, but *every time*, something ends up getting the better of me, and I–"

"Elsa!"

The low, bass shout reverberated through the front hall, making the chandelier shudder. I turned to face Adam, putting my hands on my hips. He hunched his shoulders, a trifle shamefaced, but held his ground. "There's someone here to see you," he said.

I was in no mood to see anyone right now, thank you very much. "Tell them to come back tomorrow, at a more reasonable hour."

"I think … I think you're going to want to meet with her, Elsa."

Oh, a *her*, was it? Had the lady caught Adam's eye? Was that why he hadn't followed protocol and kept her out of my manor house after business hours? The "Bloodstone Curios" part of this sprawling place, those items from my father Ulysses Bloodstone's personal artifact collection that I felt comfortable sharing with the public in a makeshift museum, was on the far side of the house, and it had been closed to visitors for the past hour. "And why," I asked acidly, crossing my arms and tapping one dirty toe on the flagstone floor, "am I going to want to do that?"

"Because I have information about the men who attacked you."

I whirled toward the parlor door, where a woman – who apparently could move more quietly than a mouse – was standing, her hands folded demurely in front of her. There wasn't a trace of demureness to be found on her face, however; nothing but sheer determination in that clenched jaw. She was an older woman, at least sixty, with long dark hair streaked silver that had been pulled back into a braid, and crow's feet at the edges of her eyes and mouth. She held herself rigidly upright, her lifted chin making her look as haughty as a queen, despite the simple black skirt and blouse she wore. Her eyes were a dark deep blue, sparkling like gems under the glittering light of the chandelier.

She was an intruder, and I wanted her gone. "Right. Lovely. You couldn't have, oh, sent a text? A ruddy email?

I'd even have taken an actual phone call, archaic as that sort of thing is, rather than have you show up unannounced and uninvited at my home."

"Now, now, Elsa." She had a trace of an accent – not British, perhaps Slavic judging from the even tonality of her sentences. "Is that any way to speak to your sister?"

You could have knocked me over with a feather. I wasn't too proud to admit that I gaped at her. My jaw dropped in pure astonishment. That was just about the *last* thing I expected to come out of her mouth right then. "Bloody ever-loving infernal abyss, you can't be serious."

She frowned. "Why can't I be serious? Is it so hard to believe that we share a father? The man didn't live as a monk, you know. I am Mihaela Zamfir, daughter of Katya Zamfir and Ulysses Bloodstone."

"But this… it… How could he…" *It doesn't make any sense!*

Oh, stop lying to yourself, Elsa. It wasn't that it didn't make sense, it was that I didn't want it to make sense. Ulysses Bloodstone was a larger-than-life figure whose exploits stretched across thousands of years of human history. It was inevitable that he'd shagged a lot of people along the way. I was evidence of that. Cullen was evidence of that, and he'd been hard enough for me to swallow. But another one? Good lord, had the man in all his years never figured out the concept of birth control?

"Right. Well. You're going to need to prove that." Any random passerby could say they were the spawn of dead old Dad, but I wasn't taking verbal assurances as anyone's gospel truth. "I don't suppose you have a bloodstone shard?" That would certainly help assure me of her veracity.

Her lips thinned. "I did have one. It was taken from me not twenty-four hours ago, by a group of black-garbed men with guns."

"Mmhmm. Convenient." I crossed my arms and leaned against the door. "And now I suppose you're here to beg for me to help you get it back. Very convenient. It's an interesting cover story you've come up with, but I wouldn't be surprised if this was all just a ploy to–"

"Elsa," Adam interjected, his face pained. "It's not a ploy. I've known about Mihaela for a long time." He paused, then added, "Your father mentioned her to me."

"Ah." Ulysses *had*, had he? Hadn't bothered to give me the same courtesy, the old rat fink. He'd left all sorts of notes and texts behind when he died, but drop a line letting me know about my siblings? Apparently that hadn't even occurred to him.

And I still wasn't sold on this woman's identity. "Fascinating. And did you ever meet her in person?"

"Well, no, but–" Adam started.

"Ever see a picture?" I pressed.

Adam heaved a sigh. "No. But you have the same nose, and she has your father's eyes, and–"

I cut him off. "Then again, I'm going to need more than just a name and a nasal profile analysis to believe that you–" I pointed a finger at Mihaela "–are anything more than a gold-digging con woman looking to take advantage of a family connection to insinuate your way into my life."

"Because you clearly have such a good life," she said disdainfully, waving a hand in front of her nose. "But fine. I will prove our connection, and then you will listen to my story. Agreed?"

"Agreed." This ought to be good.

"Very well." She folded her arms and stared at me. "There are several artifacts in this house that you consider too valuable or too bizarre to be on display. For instance, I know that our father owned three shrunken heads, but there are only two up in the museum. The third one, he felt, bore a strange resemblance to someone he used to know before he carried the bloodstone, and he could never bring himself to reveal it to others for that reason."

Stone the crows. That was what the note next to the thing had said, certainly. *I* couldn't see much of a resemblance to anyone who'd ever been alive in the sad, tiny thing, but who knew what strange connections had been made in the mind of a man who'd lived for ten thousand years? Still... "Keep going," I said.

Her lips pursed with irritation, but she continued. "There are rumors out there that you own a magic lamp capable of transporting you anywhere in the world. Although personally," she said with a haughty sniff, "I find this one quite hard to believe. A genie in a lamp? Pure fairytale. Not to mention, you've just gotten off an airplane. If you had an artifact that would let you travel the globe without having to use normal transport, I don't see why you wouldn't use it."

"Right, that one's utter bunk," I agreed, glad she hadn't been able to confirm that the lamp, in fact, really did exist. Now that was an artifact that didn't bear any resemblance to anything in the public collection. I kept it absolutely secret – not just because it was a rather unreliable mode of transport that nevertheless could be handy every now and then, but because people were so stupid about things like genies and wishes. They never, ever, *ever* worked out the way you hoped they would. Genies were akin to the most cunning contract lawyers on the planet, and quite possibly off the planet too. You'd never get the better of them, but people were certainly willing to try.

"I also brought security footage from near my own home in Bucharest, where my bloodstone was stolen from me." She reached around the back of her neck and removed a chain, then handed it over to me. A tiny thumb drive dangled from the end of it. "This should prove that I'm telling the truth. If you don't believe me after seeing this, then you can go to seven different kinds of underworlds."

Well, my goodness. Perhaps we were related after all. I handed the drive to Adam, who looked at it with resignation. "Fine. Cue that up in the media room, if you please," I said to him. "I'll watch it, but not before I get a hot shower and a fresh cup of tea."

"You do smell rather pungent," Mihaela said, as though I wasn't aware of my own personal *eau de monstre*.

"Right." I pointed a finger at her. "You wait here. No wandering about, no poking into things that don't concern you. If I find you looking for secret passageways, I'll show you one that leads straight to the sewer, got it?"

She didn't seem perturbed by my warnings. Another reluctant point in her favor. "I'm quite content to sit and wait for your better judgment to prevail."

"My *better judgment* would have me toss you outside no matter who you're related to," I said quite honestly. "You're a complication that I have neither the time nor the inclination for, but I'm not the sort to turn my back on someone who comes to me for help." Not even when it was a potential sibling singing a song of bloodstone thievery, which would strain anyone's credulity. I turned back to Adam. "I won't be long."

Lord, though, how I wanted to linger under the hot spray of the shower. It refreshed and revitalized me in a way only a luxury like hot running water and sweet-smelling soap could. I wasn't sure how many of my memories were real; the bits and pieces I recalled of being with my father were quite possibly implanted. Even if none of the scenes from my childhood involving his training methods were real, though, I'd still been through enough since coming into my own as a Bloodstone to value every moment of peace, quiet, and comfort that I could get. They were so rare, it made having them all the more valuable.

My mum had suggested to me, more than once, that I could leave the life of a monster hunter behind. Settle in as the caretaker of Bloodstone Curios and Museum, go back to school and finish my degree. Live a normal life. Mum was a dear, but she didn't understand the imperative I felt inside me to hunt down the things that went bump in the night. It was more than a job for me, it was a calling. Whether or not I'd inherited that impulse from my father or come into it all on my own, I wouldn't change it for the world.

I could love the little luxuries and the calm moments in life, but I could never be happy with just those.

I turned the water off, got out of the massive shower enclosure, toweled myself dry, and put my hair back. Then I picked out a comfortable set of clothes that nevertheless had special pockets for my favorite knives and a reinforced waistband so a holster wouldn't just pull my trousers down about my ankles. In deference to Adam's sensibilities – he got quite miffed if I insinuated in any way that I wasn't safe within the manor, his demesne – I added my smallest gun to the ensemble, then headed back downstairs to the media room. Adam and Mihaela were waiting for me there, and so was a fresh cup of tea.

"Thank you," I said to Adam, sitting down in a comfortable lounger in such a way that I could see the screen and Mihaela at the same time. Was she about to attack me? Almost certainly not, but if you didn't plan with the exceptional in mind, you didn't live long in this business. I picked up the tea and blew on it for a moment, then sipped. Perfect temperature. "All right, go on then."

Adam turned to the projector controls, and a moment

later a grainy black and white video showed up on the far wall. A woman – Mihaela, judging from the squared shoulders and prim but purposeful stride – was walking down the sidewalk of some minor metropolis, alone except for the occasional passing car. She remained alone for exactly five seconds, before a van stopped right beside her. The sliding side door opened, and three men poured out of it, converging on her.

I had to give her props – the woman fought like a demon, kicking, scratching, and clearly shrieking her head off even though the video had no soundtrack. Two of the men eventually managed to subdue her, one holding onto either arm while the third pried something off her wrist. Even in the faint light, it had a familiar glint to it. You could always tell a bloodstone.

As soon as it was off her wrist, the Mihaela on screen seemed to lose her mind, as well as all her inhibitions. She wrenched her arms free and kicked the man holding her bloodstone right in the fork. He crumpled, but one of the other men grabbed him and dragged him to safety while the third held Mihaela's mad charge off long enough for them to get back into the van and get away. The figure of Mihaela ran after them for a few seconds, waving her arms frantically. A moment later a man ran out of a shop to join her, and after that the video ended.

"You see?" Mihaela gestured sharply toward the wall we'd just been watching on. "I told you the truth."

"At least part of it," I agreed, pausing to sip my tea. "I'm still not entirely sure what you expect me to do about it. Losing your bloodstone like that is sad for you, but I don't see what it has to do with me."

She seemed taken aback. "They also came after you, didn't they? They wanted to steal your bloodstone as well."

"Mmm, they did. Didn't succeed, though." I gestured to the choker still sitting firmly around my neck. Mihaela's eyes followed it, avid – nearly too much so. "And now they've got yours, so there's no reason to think they'd try to take this one again."

Mihaela huffed and crossed her arms. "That's an inane assumption. Neither of us knows what these men wanted the bloodstones for. It's quite possible one isn't enough for them. Are there any others in the manor?"

"No."

"Are you sure?" Mihaela pressed. "Because it's clear to me you don't know everything about the bloodstone gems, despite being the keeper of our father's legacy."

That stung, a bit. What did this stranger know about my father's legacy? She might be a child of his, but she clearly didn't have an iota of my training.

"I want my bloodstone back," she continued, getting to her feet and starting to pace. She moved with a smooth, easy stride that almost looked out of place on a woman in her sixties. "It is my only keepsake of our father, and I'm not going to give it up without a fight."

I'd heard enough. I didn't have time for someone else's vendetta, not when I had more than enough of my own to go around. I stood up as well. "Enjoy the fight then, darling, but I've got bigger monsters to fry than hunting down a lot of humans."

"Don't be a fool," Mihaela snapped. "This is your chance, possibly your only chance, to get ahead of them. If they truly want your bloodstone, they'll come after you again with twice as many people."

I smirked. "I'm not intimidated by size."

"Perhaps you are not, but is our brother?" she asked, her voice going sly. "Is anyone else out there with a bloodstone shard more vulnerable than the vaunted Elsa Bloodstone? Will you leave our father's legacy to be stolen away by these *banditi* and used for whatever nefarious purpose they have in mind?"

I glared at her puffed-up expression. "There are no other bloodstone shards out there!"

At least, I didn't think there were. Then again, I hadn't known about Mihaela's existence until tonight, much less the fact that she'd carried a piece of the bloodstone. Could there be more shards out there, in the hands of people who didn't understand what they had? Or perhaps there were more hidden in my father's old bases. This manor house had been his primary home, but he'd kept hideaways all over the globe. I thought they were mostly just weapons caches – I'd never even been to any of the others. Ulysses Bloodstone had been gone for a long time, and I was content to let the past lie buried along with him.

Perhaps someone else was not.

Lord, it was intensely irritating to be agreeing with this woman. "You might have a point," I amended. Grudgingly.

She looked distastefully smug. "*I* knew that. So now we must—"

"*We* must nothing at all," I cut in. "Firstly, while you might have a point, I'm not sure what my next move is going to be. I'm certainly not going running after suspicious-looking vans willy-nilly. If the bloodstones are the draw, then I could just wait around for them to come after me and let that lead to its own investigating." She opened her mouth to speak, and I cut her off again. "And yes, I know that doing so might mean others are being drawn into this mess, so no, it's not my first option. What I need is information." Information about my father's past, a history that stretched so far back no one alive was completely sure of the origin of it.

Perhaps I needed to seek help from the undead, then.

"I'll make an appointment with Barnabus tomorrow morning. The family lawyer," I clarified when Mihaela looked confused. "He might be able to shed some light on the subject of our father's old haunts and bloodstone shards."

The light would be shed metaphorically only, of course, given that Charles Barnabus was a vampire, but he was a font of information. If anyone could help, it was him.

"You can stay the night. Adam will show you to a guest room," I said.

"And tomorrow?" Mihaela asked insistently. "What about tomorrow?"

Tomorrow I had every intention of sending her packing back to Romania, but I wasn't going to pass that along yet. "We'll see." I smiled and aimed a finger-pistol at her. "Off to bed with you now."

And off to bed with me. My catnaps on the plane hadn't done me much good, and if I was about to embark on an adventure of some sort, I was going to need my beauty rest while I could get it.

THREE

Barnabus was kind enough to call on us the next morning, which was an arrival above and beyond for a vampire as far as I was concerned. I'd offered to meet him at his office – it was only polite – but after I explained what I was looking for, he decided it was better for all of us if he came to me. "Safer for both you and your guest not to travel if you don't have to," he said.

The only reason I didn't call him on the ridiculousness of worrying about my safety was because he might have a point when it came to Mihaela. She was tough, but she was also unpowered and elderly, and I wasn't about to hand over any of my weapons to up her chances. Those were *custom*, and if she wanted something to wield, she'd have to prove to me that she could use them first. Admittedly, it wasn't impossible that she knew more about weaponry than first glance would suggest, given her parentage. Still, it was something I hoped to avoid altogether unless Mihaela absolutely insisted on having something to do with this bloodstone puzzle. Which she wouldn't, if she knew what was good for her.

Adam let Barnabus's car through the gate, then opened up the ramp to the underground parking structure. It had ostensibly been built as a place for visitors to the museum to park, but the truth of the matter was that I occasionally hosted a guest who preferred to avoid the sunlight.

"He is… a vampire?" Mihaela said with some surprise as she watched the specialized security feed with Adam and me, observing Barnabus emerge from his heavily tinted Mercedes and head for the elevator, carrying an oversized briefcase in one hand.

"Good eye," I replied. "Not everyone can spot it." Perhaps it was the unnatural grace that gave him away to her. Being Ulysses' daughter, Mihaela was bound to know some of the hallmarks of supernatural creatures. It came with the territory.

"I've always been good at identifying f… monsters." She seemed to stumble over the word. Was he really disconcerting her so much? "I just didn't think you'd allow one into your home like this. Aren't you supposed to be the world's foremost monster hunter?"

I couldn't help myself. I rolled my eyes. It was juvenile, but in this moment I didn't much care. "Is there or isn't there a seven-foot tall bloke sitting in the chair right in front of us?" I asked pointedly.

"I thought he had to be the exception to the rule. A monster hunter who tolerates such creatures? It seems out of character."

"Honestly, I don't understand why you think you know enough about me to make that sort of judgment," I snapped. It wasn't polite, but to hell with it. I'd slept like a great white shark in a goldfish tank last night, my mind constantly running into walls and turning me in new, pointless directions. I felt tired and bruised this morning, despite not having a scratch left on me from my sojourn in Glasgow. "There are plenty of people out there who happen to bear monstrous forms, and I've worked with many of them over the years. Barnabus is one of those."

Honesty compelled me to add, "Certainly, the vast majority of vampires are bloodsucking murderers who should be staked out in the sunshine and left to play bonfire, but I believe in doing my due diligence."

Mihaela raised one thin, elegant eyebrow. "And what does due diligence look like, in your case?"

Was she doubting me, straight to my face? What a wench. "It starts with information gathering and ends with finding out whether or not they attack me as soon as they get close to me. If I bother letting them get close at all. That's the beautiful thing about modern technology, isn't it? I've got guns in this place that can shoot around corners. I don't even have to look my targets in the eye if I don't care to."

I took a step closer to her, enjoying the way my heels gave me half a foot of height on her. "But I always *do* care to. I like to be close enough to watch them die, to see them look at me and realize that I'm the reason their dangerous ways are coming to an end. I like to be the last thing they ever see, because the real reason that I do this work? It's not because of our father and his legacy. It's because I like it and I'm good at it, and nothing in the world is more satisfying to me than practicing my craft while ridding the world of darkness." I smiled brightly. "Does that clear things up for you, love?"

The elevator dinged. Adam got to his feet so fast his chair almost tipped over. "I'll just, uh… go and get… Mr Barnabus. Please excuse…" He charged out of the room like his coat was on fire. I chuckled as I watched him go.

"God forbid he gets caught in the middle of a catfight, poor delicate thing," I cooed.

"I am not a cat," Mihaela pointed out indignantly.

"No, you're not." She was my half-sister, which was so much worse. "Let's go meet with Barnabus, shall we?"

Adam had already closed all the blinds in anticipation of Barnabus's visit – solid metal blinds that could handle a strike from most grenade launchers, because if you were going to rebuild your home you might as well do it right – and the halls were illuminated solely by the dimmed, soothing light of the wall sconces. Adam had insisted on keeping those, old-fashioned as they were, but at least they didn't hold actual torches any more. I walked briskly toward the sitting room, expecting Mihaela to struggle a bit to keep up with me. Instead, she kept to the exact pace without a hint of challenge, despite our height difference.

Hmm. Had she been trained as a dancer, perhaps? Did she have some sort of martial background that I wasn't aware of? Had our father actually spent *time* with her, showing her how to track and stalk her prey, how to shadow it so that the two of you stepped in perfect rhythm?

I wasn't jealous. I'd long ago ceased being jealous of anything pertaining to Ulysses because, frankly, I had it the best out of my little family when it came to legacy, but I was… curious.

Barnabus was standing and speaking quietly with Adam when Mihaela and I entered. He glanced our way, and then looked at us, putting effort into his scrutiny. After a moment he said, "Ah. It's true, then."

That was my dear lawyer, always forgetting the proper segues. I swear, the vampire spent more time speaking to himself in his head than he did talking out loud in the real world.

"Charles," I said brightly, coming over to shake his hand. His skin was cool – undead cool, he was a very traditional sort of vampire – but his grip was firm. "Thank you for coming out on such short notice." I indicated my reluctant companion. "This is Mihaela Zamfir, a relative of Ulysses'."

Barnabus extended a hand to her, and she took it readily enough. Not afraid to shake hands with a vampire, then. Good.

"The pleasure is mine," Barnabus said politely to her

before taking his hand back and looking at me. "And I was quite pleased to take on this assignment." He brushed a long, strand of hair back from his face. Long black hair, black suit, even the black briefcase – Barnabus wasn't exactly subtle when it came to his supernatural nature, again if you knew what to look for. "It's been a long time since I looked at these documents, and what I found within was most interesting. Your father was a man of considerable means, and luckily for us he also believed in doing things legally whenever he could. That meant paperwork, which I will supply to support the claims I'm about to make."

"Proper paperwork makes you happy as a clam, doesn't it?" I said, sitting down on the loveseat across from him as he opened the briefcase and began to pull out stacks of papers. Ugh, just the thought of having to go through every single one of those made me want to claim a headache and go to the manor's subterranean gun range just to get my focus back. Mihaela, to my annoyance, sat right next to me on the loveseat, her hands folded neatly in her lap, her expression far more interested than mine.

Barnabus smiled briefly. "I know it makes you think you'll break out in hives, Miss Bloodstone. Don't worry, I won't ask you to do anything onerous today. Most of this is redundant, copies made for you to have on hand should you need them."

"You could have just emailed them to me," I suggested.

"How often do you check your email?"

He had me there. "Fair enough. So. Is there anything in

those reams of paper to suggest that my father might have stashed more bloodstones out there?"

Barnabus shrugged slightly. "It's unclear. The likelihood of a bloodstone going unfound for so long after your father's death is small, given their value and reputation, but Ulysses was something of a packrat when it came to preparedness. He had multiple bases set up all over the world, six in total that I could find, just in case he found himself in need of something. It isn't impossible that he could have hidden shards in some of those locations."

"Why would he be the one to have all these shards in the first place?" Mihaela asked.

Barnabus nodded. "A relevant question. Ulysses Bloodstone's gem originally came from a meteorite, one shard of a larger piece. That piece was supposedly reassembled briefly before his death, and the gem that Elsa now bears was thought to be the whole of it. That doesn't mean other shards don't exist, or that there couldn't be other pieces of the original meteorite that are still extant, or at least not joined to this gem."

"Such as the one her brother carries," Mihaela said.

"Exactly," Barnabus agreed. "And the one that you yourself must have carried just a short time ago."

She twitched, startled, and I stared at Barnabus. "Did Adam tell you that?" I demanded. Because Charles being my lawyer or no, if he had, I was going to have a talk with my butler about proper channels of information and bloody boundaries.

"Not at all," Barnabus said, while Adam just huffed, looking offended where he stood by the sideboard. "It was simple extrapolation on my part. Miss Zamfir, you bear more than a passing resemblance to Miss Bloodstone, and you've been rubbing your right wrist on and off since you sat down. With the introduction you were given, I presumed that you were one of Ulysses Bloodstone's children, and that he'd saved a shard for you as well." He looked pleased with himself.

"Yes, yes, you're so smart, naff off about it." I leaned forward. "Let's get to the heart of the matter, then. You can't tell me that our father definitely had other bloodstone shards hidden here and there, but you can't rule it out either."

Barnabus inclined his head. "Correct."

"But if they do exist, they're bloody valuable, and exactly the sort of thing that could get a person into trouble if they don't know how to handle them."

"Also correct," he said.

I glanced at Adam. "What do you think? Is it worth going on a wild goose chase on the off chance we get to some shards before our hypothetical treasure hunter does? Or should I hunker in my bunker and prepare to take all comers if they want to try for my shard again?" Mihaela shifted beside me, clearly wanting to interject, but I ignored her.

Adam shrugged. "If they want it bad enough, they'll come. We could hold off an army in this place, but the same isn't true for Cullen."

Right. If someone was after my shard, they'd likely be after his too.

"He's got safety in numbers as long as he's at school, but the risk to him gets higher and higher the longer whoever is stealing bloodstones is free to prepare for such an assault," Adam continued.

Oh, what a way to put it. Cullen and I weren't close, not by a long shot, but I wasn't about to leave my brother to be attacked by some unknown assailant when I could potentially put a stop to it just by gallivanting about the globe for a while. Although… Cullen ought to be able to handle himself at his age. It might do him some good to be tested instead of coddled at school like he had been ever since that git Arcade had made off with him and his friends and stuck them in a kill-or-be-killed free for all Murderworld. It seemed to me that any man who took such glee in creating entire habitats for their victims to fall afoul of had far too much time on his hands, but who was I to tell the "heroes" how to pick their villains of the week? Anyhow, Arcade was dead now and Cullen was not, so I counted that as a win.

I very nearly slapped myself for falling into the familiar old mindset of "That which doesn't kill you makes you stronger." *That's your father speaking, not you.* I'd had more than enough of that in my life, and it was one more aspect of the family legacy that I would do my best to spare Cullen as I could.

Mihaela shifted next to me, and I turned my head to

look at her. What did I owe this woman? Nothing, really – the fact that we were related by blood amounted to a hill of beans. Our father clearly hadn't cared enough to make sure we met up with each other under less dire circumstances. And she, at least, had known about me and our connection since long before now, but had never bothered to introduce herself until she needed something from me.

It annoyed me. Worse than that, it made me angry, which in turn annoyed me even more. I wasn't going to get upset just because my half-sister hadn't wanted anything to do with me until I became an opportunity for her. I didn't care. I had other family members, and I had plenty of friends. I didn't need her approval.

Mihaela noticed me staring and frowned. "What?" she demanded.

"Nothing." *Absolutely nothing.* I looked back at Barnabus. "Talk to me about these bases of his. Where are they located?"

Barnabus opened a manila file folder and pulled out a folded piece of paper, then spread it out on the coffee table. It was a map of the world, with six bright red dots placed hither and yon on it. "This house, of course, is one of his bases of operation," he said, pointing at Boston. "There is another in New York City. In a bar, I believe."

I grinned. "Well, at least we could have some fun there while digging for lost treasure." Judging from the beleaguered sigh to my right, Mihaela didn't approve of my sense of humor. Oh, too bad, so sad. "Where else?" I asked, pushing my fringe back from my face.

Barnabus indicated the dot in East Africa. "This one is less than a day's journey outside of Mombasa, Kenya."

"Lovely place, and I have some contacts in the area." I inspected the map more closely, then groaned. "Oh, no. Tell me he didn't have a base in the Savage Land."

"He didn't have a base in the Savage Land," Barnabus said obediently. Then he added, "He had a base somewhere outside the Savage Land. I'm not sure of the exact coordinates of it, I'm afraid to say."

Adam chuckled. "All the inconvenience of Antarctica without the tropical temperatures of the Savage Land itself. Sounds like Ulysses."

"God, why was he such a colossal git?" Antarctica, honestly. That was going to be a delight to get to. "What else have we got? Where's this one?" I tapped the dot in Russia. "Moscow?"

"Near there, yes. I'm afraid I don't have a precise location for that one either, yet, but I'm working on it."

"Well, at least the drinks will be good." They would invariably be vodka – Russia was nothing if not committed to its national beverage. "Hopefully he picked a bar there, too. Where's the final one?"

"That one–" Barnabus tapped the dot located in the eastern part of the Caribbean "–is Bloodstone Isle. It was nearly granted sovereignty by the United Nations before your father's death. He spent a great deal of time there and made quite a homestead out of it. While it's been attacked numerous times over the years, it's also undoubtedly the most extensive of his bases."

I nodded. "So there might be some nooks and crannies that other people have missed."

"Indeed." Barnabus smiled. His sharp teeth gleamed in the light. "And I have an original blueprint of the facility your father built, which should help you ensure that your search there is thorough."

"You think of everything, Charles."

He inclined his head. "A lawyer wouldn't be good at their job without understanding the importance of diligence."

"Still, this is rather above and beyond. I quite appreciate your efforts," I said.

If he could have blushed in that moment, I think he would have. "Well. We're… friends in addition to my role as your lawyer, aren't we? I wouldn't want to let down a friend in need."

"You haven't," I assured him, giving him a smile and a wink before turning my attention back to the map. "Now, the question is… which one do I visit first?"

"You mean 'we.'"

I glanced over at Mihaela. She held herself rigidly upright, and I was a little surprised her spine wasn't creaking under the strain of her perfect posture. "Nooo," I drawled. "I mean 'I.' I'm the one who's equipped for this sort of work, while you're better suited to minding the home and hearth until I have news."

"Unacceptable. I need to accompany you." She lifted her chin pugnaciously.

"You absolutely do not need to accompany me, and you won't be accompanying me." What part of this was hard to understand? "You are a non-combatant. I won't be responsible for keeping monsters off your back or mercenaries from taking you out while in the middle of defending myself and whatever else I might find out there. If you're truly worried about your wellbeing, you can stay here with Adam, but I don't cater to tourists like you when I'm working, do you understand?"

Mihaela glared at me for a long moment, then stood up. "Where is your shooting range?"

I frowned at her. "Beg pardon?"

"Your range, the place you shoot your guns, the private place you test out all the weapons you own." Her face was stiff, her expression cold. "I don't believe for a moment that someone who spends so much of her time in battle doesn't have the means of readying herself *for* that battle on her own property. Or are you more careless than I thought?"

I stood up to face her and put my hands on my hips. "Of the two of us, which one still has her bloodstone? And you think I'm careless?"

"I think you're brash and prone to making decisions too quickly," Mihaela replied. "I know that I can be an asset to you on this quest, and I want you to give me the chance to prove it. If you don't, then perhaps you're more like our father than you want to believe."

How. *Dare*. She. I didn't say anything for a long moment, knowing that if I opened my mouth too soon, I'd probably just affirm all her petty accusations, and also quite possibly give into the urge to slap her so hard I knocked her unconscious. I was *not* like my father, though, not in the ways it counted. He'd died alone, the bloodstone pried from his chest by a madman. I could work on a team. I'd worked on plenty of teams.

And did any of them ever want to work with you again?

Shut up, you.

"Fine," I said in clipped tones. "You want to prove you're more than just a victim? You'll get your shot. Adam, Charles, please stay up here."

"Perhaps I should go along," Adam ventured. I turned my glare on him, and he shrank in on himself as much as an undead behemoth of a monster could. "Just… to make sure no one gets… that tempers don't… that…"

"We'll be quite all right, thank you *ever* so much for your concern." I turned back to Mihaela. "Come on, then."

I stalked out of the room at a brisk pace, annoyed anew when she fell in step next to me without even making it look like she was working hard. I led the way to the elevator for the parking garage, got inside, and pressed my entire hand against the down button. The metal facing glowed for a moment, then the elevator dropped us a level. Instead of the doors opening up, though, the back wall of the elevator slid aside, revealing a slender hallway lit with fluorescent lights.

"This way." I walked down the hall, pleased that it was narrow enough she had to follow me this time, and stopped at another door a few meters down. I pressed my hand against the pad beside it, then lowered my face for another green-light scan. "Tea's up," I said, and the lights around the door blinked three times. It opened for me a moment later.

"Tea's up?" Mihaela asked wryly as she followed me onto the range.

It was more than just a range, though. It was where I worked out the kinks in my custom weapons, including all the explosives and specialized ammunition I used. It was vast, expanding well beyond the footprint of the manor above, and it was built to withstand a huge amount of firepower. There were blast marks here and there on the walls, and the whole place smelled slightly of cordite, but for me it was the most relaxing room in the entire manor. There was a bunker-like observation center at the back, where the controls were for all of my training programs, as well as the weapons locker. I went there first.

"A password should be something that makes you think pleasant thoughts, in my opinion," I said, responding to her implicit critique. "Tea is one of the few things that consistently improves my day."

I flung open the door of the weapons locker with a grin. I had all sorts of delightful things in there, from several custom double-barreled shotguns to energy weapons that would do everything from stun to dissolve, based on the genetic makeup of the lifeform I was firing on. For this, though, I thought it best to stick to the purely ballistic sort of firearm.

I considered my selection, then considered the likely strength of Mihaela's arms and pulled out a Smith and Wesson M&P. Only fifteen rounds in this particular version's magazine, but if she needed more than that to get through the scenario I was about to throw at her, she'd have failed anyway. "Here." I tossed the gun in her direction and she caught it fluidly, which was a surprise all on its own.

"You shouldn't throw a loaded firearm!" Mihaela scolded me. "It's dangerous."

"Is that right?" I said, pressing a hand to my cheek in mock surprise. "I would never have guessed such a thing, given that I'm *clearly* a toddler. Do check the weapon before chiding me."

She checked the chamber and the magazine, and a dull flush spread across her pale cheeks. "Ah."

"*Ah*, indeed." I tossed her a full magazine and watched her load the trim gun. "Now. Look down-range and get ready to fire."

"Fire at what?" she asked, hoisting the pistol and taking a shooting stance as she squinted into the distance. I closed off the observation room, securing myself behind the transparent, bulletproof walls just in case Mihaela got carried away.

I smiled beatifically at her. "At whatever comes your way. No reloads, by the by, so take care not to exhaust your ammo too quickly." Then I entered the code for my custom

"By Land, By Air #3" training scenario and prepared to watch some quality flailing.

The lights dimmed. At the other end of the range, a creature slowly crawled into view. It was a hologram, of course, not the real thing – I didn't keep a bloody monster menagerie on hand for training purposes, that would be far too much work. It would respond to bullets the same way as the real thing, though. The beast was large, bigger than her and me put together, and had six limbs protruding from its abdomen. The face was vaguely humanoid, and when it opened its jaws to hiss at Mihaela, it put rows of internal fangs on display.

A rorgg. One of my favorites. Strong, brutal, casually superior, but easy to take out if you know the right spots to target. Not that Mihaela did. I waited, expecting her to begin firing wildly the moment it started to scuttle across the floor. It had to be decades since she'd trained with our father, despite her decent firing stance.

The virtual rorgg charged, weaving back and forth with a jittery, bug-like pace. It was disconcerting, even to me, but Mihaela narrowed her eyes and held her ground until the rorgg was within twenty feet of her – nearly enough for it to jump the distance. As it bunched itself up to attack, she fired three shots: front right limb, front left limb, and as the rorgg shrieked and collapsed, the final shot went right into its gaping mouth, blowing the bottom half of its jaw off.

"Fatal hit," my program scrawled across the screen, and the rorgg vanished. Mihaela looked satisfied with herself.

"Not done yet, sassy pants," I muttered. A moment later, two moth-like beings appeared in the air. At the same time, a heavy-bodied, bipedal giant with whiskery protrusions poking from the top of its head began to lumber toward her. It wasn't fast – zzutak were like tanks, slow but steady – but it would certainly take the more firepower to down, so the question was where she would choose to concentrate first. The skreel were nothing to ignore either, honestly. They were less deadly, but if they got you in their claws – worse yet, if they ganged up on you and got you into the sky high enough to make the drop fatal–

Bang! Bang! Mihaela spent one shot on each of the skreel, sending the creatures wailing down to the ground, then focused her fire on the zzutak. It picked up the pace, roaring, and brushed off the first few bullets that she sent at its head. *Too heavily armored there. Where will you try next?*

She shifted her target to the groin. *Ooh, good choice!* I had to cross my arms to hold back the urge to clap. The zzutak was particularly vulnerable there, with large arteries sitting just below the surface of their thick skin. It took her three bullets to penetrate, and then the zzutak managed to go another three meters before the bleeding slowed it down enough for her to get a bead on its eye and fire straight into its brain. It fell over with a *crunch*, right on top of one of the writhing, squawking skreel. That particular one was finished, but the other crawled toward her now, fangs extended, claws groping for her. If she was out of ammunition…

Bang! She fired right between its wings, which severed the spinal cord. The skreel slumped over, dead. A second later, the holograms disappeared, and the lights came up. "Program completed," my computer told me. "Four fatalities. Perfect score."

"Yeah, yeah," I muttered. Anyone could get a perfect score on an easy, breezy program like this one. I *was* impressed, however reluctantly, with the way Mihaela had kept her cool. I came out of the observation center. "Not bad," I said.

She pulled the magazine out. "Two bullets left," she said, and threw it to me. I caught it, and the gun that followed. "Is that enough proof that I'm not without my own abilities? You won't have to worry about protecting me. I was taught how to protect myself." The last was said fiercely, like it was something to be proud of. And, to be fair, it was. But then…

"Why did those mercenaries get the drop on you so easily, then?" It was bothering me now. The woman in the video had been fierce, but not skilled the way Mihaela was proving herself to be.

Mihaela scowled and looked at the floor. "I have gone to a great deal of trouble to appear as nothing more than a *bună*, a grandmother, in my town. I want to be a normal person to them. I want to be thought of as *one* of them. That is my goal. It has been my life for many decades. When those men attacked me… I was not thinking 'kill these fools', I was thinking 'don't let them expose you.'" She sighed. "I should have fought harder from the start. I might have my own bloodstone shard right now if I had taken them out... or they might have sent more people after me, better people, and killed me for it. I don't know."

"If you want to be normal so badly, why bother hanging on to a bloodstone?" That part didn't make sense either. The bloodstones attracted attention, always, and usually not the good kind.

"I hid it well," she said, rubbing her wrist again. "As much as I want to be normal, I didn't want to let go of my last token of our father. It is clear you don't like him, and I don't judge you for that, but for me..." She looked blankly at the far wall. "I didn't know him as a little girl, but as a young woman he came back for me at the darkest moment of my life and he... he *saved* me. He couldn't bring back my mother, but he prevented me from following her into darkness. For that I owe him a great deal. The time he spent with me, training me, making sure I would be safe, it was one of the best times of my young life."

A kernel of pain blossomed inside my chest. She had seen a side of Ulysses Bloodstone that I never had, and never would. "Well, then." I smiled, but it felt brittle. "I suppose you can come along, as long as you continue to look after yourself. We'll make for Bloodstone Isle as soon as I can find a friend with a plane who's willing to fly us there." I put the gun down on a nearby table – I would clean it later, when I was alone – and headed for the hallway back to the elevator. After a moment, Mihaela followed me.

I was careful not to look at her. I didn't want to see whatever expression was on her face. I had no patience for pity and no tolerance for empathy. It was time to get down to business.

We had places to go, bloodstones to find, and enemies to fight, after all.

FOUR

There weren't many things I loathed more in the world than heart-to-heart chats, but commercial air flight was right up there with them. Unfortunately, none of my wealthy acquaintances could spare a plane to head to a tiny speck of land east of Andros Island – and, in their defense, there was no way a plane would be able to land there. Looking over an old supply list of my father's revealed that he'd made most of his approaches by sea, using a skimmer craft to evade the treacherous rocks and reefs around the narcissistically named "Bloodstone Isle." Unfortunately, all of those skimmers had been sunk for years.

"Fabulous," I snarked. "Just delightful." If I couldn't fly directly in, then I'd sail in. "Adam, if we fly into San Salvador, can you make some calls to have a skimmer available for us to take from there?"

"Of course." Adam had as many connections in the field as I did, or more. I knew I could trust his word.

"Wonderful." One of these days I was finally going to bite the bullet and get my pilot's license so I could fly myself all over the world. There were other methods of travel available to me as well, rather more mystical methods, but I preferred not to pull those out unless I had to. They either involved asking sorcerers for favors, which was rarely a good idea, or relying on the beneficence of a genie, which also tended to be in short supply. "Right, then. Let's make it happen," I said.

Mihaela was surprisingly amenable to the plan, which essentially consisted of: get ourselves to Bloodstone Isle in as direct a manner as we could, spend no more than a day investigating the ruins of our father's base, and move on to the location outside of Mombasa after that. It would be a rather grueling schedule, but I trusted she'd let me know if it proved to be too much for her.

Well no, in fact, I trusted that she'd grit her teeth and bear the pain rather than admit to me that she was suffering. That was frankly the *least* she could do after forcing her way into this escapade.

"I know it's hard," Adam told me as he packed my fourth suitcase into the car that would take us to the airport, "but try to be kind. She's an old woman, after all."

"She is a gimlet-eyed harridan who happens to reside in a slightly feebler frame than mine," I said, patting my pocket for my passport. Bloody paperwork. "She'll be fine, or she'll be left behind."

"What is all this?" said gimlet-eyed harridan demanded as she brought her own single bag out to the car and stared at the bulging trunk. "How are we supposed to travel fast when you're hauling so much luggage around?"

"Do you want to run out of bullets?" I snapped. "I certainly don't want to run out of bullets. That's nobody's idea of a good time."

"You have four bags dedicated to bullets?"

"No." I patted the leather bag on top. "This one is fresh clothes and personal necessities, because I'm not inclined to be mistaken for a frat boy on a weeklong bender. This one underneath has my favorite shotgun, a rifle, several handguns and, yes, a decent stock of ammunition. That guitar case over there has my Uzi, and the one right here has my *other* Uzi."

She frowned. "Why on earth do you need two Uzis?"

What kind of a question was that? "Because it's a terrible thing to need an Uzi and not have it available." I smiled insincerely. "Shall we go, then?"

"I'm not helping you lug those around," Mihaela warned me before getting into the car.

I stared at Adam. "Who's right?" I asked, my tone mild, but I was on the verge of grinding my teeth to powder. "Tell me which of us is bloody right about her now."

If Adam's undead cheeks could have flushed, I think they would have. "Good luck out there," was all he said, but he didn't meet my eyes. Coward. "I'll be ready if you need backup."

"Excellent. Check in on the family for me, would you? I promised Mum I'd be round this week for dinner, but that's obviously off now." As much as I loved my mother, our lives had inexorably bifurcated after my introduction to my father's world. We chatted weekly on the phone, and I saw her on all the major holidays, but that was it.

Given how topsy-turvy my life had been lately, keeping my distance from my mother was a benevolent action on my part.

Praise be, somehow the pair of us managed to make it all the way to the tiny island of San Salvador without bloodshed. Adam had *so* thoughtfully gotten us both first-class tickets, sitting right next to each other the whole way down, or at least until we transferred over to a puddle jumper and had to sit one behind the other for the last flight. Getting off the plane and out into the island air was shocking, a wet, hot slap to the face from the humidity. I shrugged off my overcoat and was fine, but Mihaela appeared to be struggling a bit in her high-necked shirt and long pants, both in gray. She didn't sweat, didn't even glisten, but she did appear to wilt a bit, like the world's most boring flower slowly curling in on itself.

"You could always stay here," I suggested as we gathered our luggage right there at the plane. It was all very casual and convenient. I liked it. The fewer scans I had to put my bags through, the better. "The airport lounge might even have air conditioning, and I can't imagine I'll be long."

She scowled at me. "Stop asking me to stay behind. What if the men who stole my shard are there?"

"What if they are?" I asked. "We're not on the lookout for *your* shard right now, we're looking for *any* shard. If those blokes are on Bloodstone Isle, their presence will be a good sign for us and a bad one for them. In other words," I hoisted one of my Uzi bags meaningfully, "we'll take care of them."

Mihaela rolled her eyes. "I don't know why it still surprises me that your first and only solution to a problem is shooting it."

"Better than rolling over and showing my belly." I motioned to a cabbie as we walked out of the airport, and within moments we were headed for the dock where Adam had arranged for our skimmer to be located.

It had probably been a nice dock, once upon a time. It was large and concrete, with yellow and blue paint that was almost entirely flecked off now. A dilapidated clubhouse sat on the hill beside it for whoever owned the place to keep an eye on things from, or for visiting sailors to grab a drink. Now it was a dump, but the skimmer moored at it certainly wasn't.

"Lovely," I said as I got in, casting off the spring line and running my hands over the inlaid mahogany sideboard between the seats in the back.

Mihaela sniffed. "It looks like it belongs to a drug dealer."

"That's entirely possible." I laughed at her expression. "What? Wouldn't you rather we use it than they do? And even drug dealers are allowed to indulge in a little luxury."

"Do you have any moral lines?" she demanded as she climbed into the skimmer and stood straight as a pin behind me. "Any places you won't go or people you won't use to get the job done?"

If this entire trip was going to be an unending stream of criticism, I was going to have to gag her at some point. I turned on the skimmer and jetted us forward a few meters, sending Mihaela sprawling onto her arse in one of the leather-covered back seats. "Whoops!" I said. "Sorry about that! Goodness, you might want to strap in so you don't break a hip."

"I'll break your – *whoa!*"

High rates of speed worked even better than a gag.

Finding Bloodstone Isle was a bit more difficult than I'd anticipated. The pictures I had of it were all from the Seventies, and showed a small, rocky enclave with a mansion in the middle of it, surrounded by massive defensive towers. I knew from subsequent satellite imagery that the towers were mostly gone now, but I had thought there would still be remnants here and there, piles of debris if nothing else. But no – there was literally nothing remaining of any of the above-ground structures that had featured so prominently in my father's pictures.

"What happened to it all?" Mihaela shouted from by my side. I'd finally slowed the skimmer down, the better to navigate the challenging shoreline, and this was the first time she'd spoken to me in an hour. The silence had been glorious.

"Targeted nuclear strike," I shouted back. Her eyes bulged comically, her mouth dropping open. "Or so I've heard," I said, slowing down to dodge a section of rough, seaweed-blanketed reef. This place was nothing like the surrounding islands. The water wasn't clear and blue, the shores weren't sandy, and no palm trees waved at us from inland. Everything here was either the color of dingy green algae or black heat-blasted rock.

"Does that mean it will be radioactive there?" Mihaela asked.

I slowed further, pulling out my binoculars to inspect the shoreline we were coming up on. There had been a decent dock here at one point... was any of that left? "Quite likely."

She blinked with surprise. "Is that safe?"

"It's not a problem for me, and likely it won't be a problem for you in the short term," I said, as honest as I could be about it. "I mean, tourists go to Chernobyl all the time now, so..."

"That is not comforting!"

"No," I agreed. No dock. We'd have to anchor and splash in. "It's not. But we won't be here for long. I mean, look at this place. It's practically been wiped clean. I can't imagine there will be much left there."

This section of rocky shoreline was as good a place as any to park. I turned off the skimmer and dropped anchor, then opened up one of my guitar cases. "Hello, darling," I purred at the Uzi as I took it out. "It's been too long."

"You are disturbing," Mihaela informed me as she pulled

out her borrowed Smith and Wesson. "Do you sleep with them too?"

"Only when I'm abroad in hostile territory surrounded by people I can't trust, which is most of the time." I added a few more weapons into my array, then hopped down into the thigh-deep water and began to wade ashore. "Do keep that gun out of the salt water."

"Not an idiot," she muttered, but I noticed that she held the gun above her head as she followed me. *Good.*

Once my toes were dry again, I started off for the middle of the island where the castle fortress Ulysses had spent so much time in had formerly been. I didn't bother checking the crumbled outer perimeter. If the defensive towers weren't there any more, as powerful and bulky as they'd been, then it wasn't likely that anything else would remain either. The center, though...

While nuclear war might have been a novelty in the final chapter of my father's long and eventful life, there had certainly been destruction on a similar level all the way through. The meteor which had brought the Bloodstone Gem to Earth in the first place was the catalyst that had destroyed his village and everything he'd ever known. He'd been lucky to survive, even luckier to end up with a shard of the bloodstone embedded in his chest – if being cursed to a near-immortal existence could be considered "luck", which I wasn't at all convinced of.

Ulysses had seen utter ruin, complete and tragic devastation. He'd been exposed to the worst of the worst that humanity, and others, could wreak. If he had something he wanted to keep protected, *really* wanted to keep protected, then he might have assumed something like a nuclear strike was possible. It wasn't outside the realm of possibility that he'd secured a part of his base here so well that it had survived.

Mihaela was breathing hard by the time we reached the top of the hill, but she didn't ask for me to slow down. I paused anyway, just to get my bearings, and pointed out the landmarks that I recognized. "The near corner of the base was there," I said, indicating a deep indentation in the rock that had once housed part of the building's foundation. "We can get into the guts of the place that way."

"It's so…" Mihaela looked around, not focusing on the ruin but beyond and around it. "It's so barren here. This is the Bahamas, I thought it would be more…"

"Verdant? Beautiful?" I suggested.

"Alive," she finished.

"Yes, nuclear bombs will do that to a place." She had a point, though. Even Chernobyl had recovered better than this. "Perhaps it was like this before he died." Ulysses Bloodstone had never made a decision based on creature comforts. "He might have wanted a place that was less hospitable in order to make it more defensible."

"He wouldn't have wanted to build a place he was staging for conflict where other people lived, either," Mihaela said. "This island was probably uninhabited before he got here."

Goodness, that was a leap. "You think so," I said flatly.

She scowled at me. "He wasn't a monster, no matter what you seem to think."

"He wasn't half as good as some of the monsters I've met, either." I didn't want to get into it with her right now, despite the fact that I knew she was wrong, wrong, wrong. Beating her opinions down would only make her irritable, and I didn't care to deal with a petulant, fussy bit of baggage right now. "Come on, let's get going."

Despite the bomb, I could still make out the footprint of the base. It was huge, and while the general outline of the foundation was visible, it had collapsed here and there, filled with rocks and debris and fallen walls. Checking this place out for shards would be a challenge, especially if we wanted to be thorough. I could lift just about anything I came across, but Mihaela wouldn't be able to. "Stick close to me," I said before jumping off the rocky edge of what used to be a wall into the broken foundation.

I didn't watch her get down, but I heard her exasperated sigh. "I'm not a child."

"You're not superhuman either." I began to pick my way through the wreckage, looking for signs of a safe or vault, something that would have been extra insulated against attack. "Tell me if you see something likely and I'll help unearth it."

It was both depressing and interesting, wading through the detritus of my father's former life. I'd thought I knew as much as could be gleaned through his rather exorbitant sense of decoration and architecture thanks to the manor, but this place was completely different from what I was used to. Either one of the women in his life had taken a liberal hand with redecorating in Boston before I got there, or Ulysses was a very changeable man. Being down here was like stepping through a portal into the 1970s. God, was that faded avocado green paint on the ruined walls? Was I going to find goldenrod Formica countertops around here? Psychedelic posters featuring The Beatles and The Grateful Dead?

"Help me lift this up," Mihaela called out.

I turned back toward her and saw her standing over a fallen corner of cement wall, one that was thicker than the surrounding pieces. There might be something in it, or he might have just wanted to reinforce the edges of the property, but either way it was something to do. I walked over to her, bent at the knees – proper posture and lifting technique had been drilled into me by *someone*, even if I wasn't entirely sure who – and heaved the massive chunk of concrete up and back. It came to rest upright against the rock behind it.

There was no big hole in the wall that might have indicated a safe was once there, and certainly no telltale metal door with a handy knob sticking out of it waiting to be exhumed. There was, however, a shattered picture still dangling from its nail. The image was terribly faded – I had no idea how it had survived over the years – but I could still make out a woman in there. Not my mother, that was for sure. This was a blonde, lovely if rather stern looking, like she was daring whoever had taken the picture to *try it again, buster.*

Mihaela leaned closer. "Who is that?" she asked, peering at the picture with interest.

"I don't know." It certainly wasn't either of his daughters. "His flavor of the week, I suppose."

She shook her head. "You don't give him enough credit."

"I give him the credit I feel he's earned." Which, for my part, was very little. "Let's move on."

"Elsa…"

"Or do you want to risk spending the night on a radioactive island?" I tossed my hair and turned away. "Let's get this done."

We picked and pulled our way through far too many square meters of fallen building, much of it ground into so much indistinguishable rubble, some of it still bearing the hallmarks of the wall or column or ceiling it had been. It wasn't until we reached the halfway point that I learned we were pursuing a dead end.

"Well, blast it," I muttered.

Mihaela looked over from where she was patiently scraping through a pile of gravel with her boot, as though there would be anything in it other than mildew and a few intrepid insects. "What is it?"

"We're not the first ones to come to Bloodstone Isle lately."

She stopped scraping and came over to my side. "What do you mean?"

"Look down."

She looked, and a moment later she let out a presumably Romanian swear word as she saw the shining pair of bullet casings. "They might not be *that* recent," she said after a moment. "It takes some time for brass to tarnish."

"I can still smell the powder on them." Faintly, but a good rain would certainly have washed that telltale sign away. "I doubt they're more than forty-eight hours old." That meant someone with a rather nice rifle had been through here recently. Probably several someones, if we were dealing with the same people who'd gone after our bloodstone shards.

Mihaela looked alarmingly distressed, the creases beside her mouth deepening like she was holding back sobs.

No, no, don't cry! I don't know what to do when people bloody cry other than offer them tea, and I don't have any tea.

"It's not the worst thing ever," I said, trying to be bracing and probably failing miserably. "Honestly, what are the chances that there was a shard here after so many years, in one of Ulysses Bloodstone's most notable haunts? They probably came up with nothing, same as us. We've likely got more and better intel on our father's old bases than they do, though, so the advantage will shift our way now. There's still a lot of ground to cover."

"I'm not sorry they were here," Mihaela snarled, pulling her lips back from her teeth like a dog about to bite before stomping on the casings so hard they deformed. "I'm sorry that we missed them, because I have a score to settle and

I won't be able to wring the location of my shard out of people who aren't available for interrogation!"

Goodness, she was quite sore about missing out on possibly having her shard back. "Why is it so important to you?" I snapped, tired of having her bad mood taken out on me. "Honestly. If it's nothing but a memento to you, why not just settle for a less-dangerous replica? Something that won't lead mercenaries to attack you in the streets?"

"It wouldn't be the same," she protested. "I grew up in a world that only valued me for the labors of my body and mind. There was nothing special about my existence, nothing to make me stand out from the crowd. Our father's attentions to me, his gift ... it was all I had to remind me that I was more than another gear in the machine of the state. I will not give up the only thing that helped keep me ... keep me sane in my youth."

I sighed. If Mihaela was bound and determined to be foolishly sentimental over her shard, then I wouldn't be able to pry her away from this quest with a crowbar. I felt for her, I did, but there was nothing I could do about it other than enable us to press on as quickly as possible. "Then let's get back to the airport and be on our way to Mombasa," I said, turning back in the direction we'd come. "Perhaps we'll be lucky and get ambushed on the way."

She huffed and followed. "You are hopeless."

"I'm not the one taking out my angst on innocent bullet casings," I reminded her, then suddenly stopped. Mihaela ran into me.

"What are you–"

"Ssshhh!" I held up a hand to emphasize the importance of her not moving, and she settled in behind me as I focused on the ruins around us.

My bloodstone shard did a lot for my personal toughness and healing ability, there was no doubt about that, and enhanced senses had been part and parcel of the bloodstone package. I wasn't as good at detecting every little thing as, say, Wolverine, but I did all right for myself. In the case of something like the ratmen, finding them was pretty easy – you followed the trail of garbage. Right now, I wasn't sure what had triggered my sense of wariness. It could have been a smell or a sound or just a sixth sense that came from experience, but I knew I needed to be still. A minute later, my patience paid off.

Soft as a mouse's footfall, a creature appeared over the edge of the rubble in front of us. It revealed itself like an ink-black wave, spilling over the pitted concrete and coalescing into a vague, slug-like shape a few meters away. I couldn't make out its eyes – I'd never seen a monster quite like this before, I didn't know where the eyes would even be – but I could certainly make out its mouth. The entire front half of the thing seemed to be nothing *but* mouth, flat and wide like a frog's. When it opened that mouth, I saw it was filled with rows upon rows of teeth that wouldn't have looked out of place in a great white shark.

"*Maaagic,*" it murmured, its rumble surprisingly articulate. "You come here with more *magic.*"

Perhaps I should have been firing upon it already, but I could practically feel the tension in Mihaela at the mention of something magical. A bloodstone shard? Some other artifact of our father's?

"More?" I asked, soundlessly flicking the latch on my guitar case even as I made conversation. "Was there magic here before?"

"Magic...maaaagic."

"Yes, love, magic, hurrah. Get to the point."

"There was *magic* here, for a long time. Many years, much *magic.*"

"Indeed." Of course there had been, Ulysses had been a packrat of the first order. I could only imagine the sorts of things he'd stowed down in the basement, locked away out of casual view. "What did that have to do with you?"

"It... made us."

Made us, eh? It was good to know that there was more than one of them, but where were the others? "How did it make you? Where?"

"Deep... underground. *Magic* fed us, made us big, strong... then it burned, but we fed on the burn. We fed, so good, for so long. Then it was gone, all gone, and we slept. But they brought more."

"Who brought more?" Mihaela demanded, moving up beside me.

Ugh, I could have slapped her. You didn't interrupt when someone had a rapport going – it was elementary negotiating. Not to mention, if that thing hadn't known there were two of us – and without eyes it was entirely possible it hadn't known that – then it knew now.

"More… from footsteps, many footsteps, in boots. Not much." The be-fanged blob inched forward. "Just enough *magic* to make us… hungry." It oozed another few meters. "So hungry, we're always… always hungry. Give us your *magic*." The terrible, wide mouth split into a parody of a smile. "Be our friend. *Shaaaaare.*"

Oh, that was the way this thing was going to play it, hmm? Like a so-called "nice guy" slipping into your girls' night out, only to get offended when no one would let him buy them a drink. Only this particular "nice guy" probably had more in common with a tar pit than any of my unfortunate encounters at bars. "Sorry, but I never share magic on the first date," I said.

Predictably, the monster didn't like being told no. It surged forward, rising from its nearly flat position on the ground to become taller than me. Its mouth gaped wide, serrated teeth glistening with slimy purple saliva. It looked like it was going to fall right over onto us.

Time to get serious, then.

I threw the guitar case to the side, hoisted my Uzi into a firing position, and let loose with the entirety of my extended magazine right into the creature's maw. Teeth shattered, gore spattered everywhere, and by the time my fiftieth round was spent, the slug-like thing had hunkered back down close to the ground, whimpering and looking pathetic.

"Peace, peace!" it whined, staining the floor dark purple as it writhed about. "Just hungry, so hungry! Keep your *magic* if you must but give us peace. All we want is peace!"

"Elsa!" Mihaela shrieked from behind me. I turned around in time to see another, smaller monster envelop her foot with its pointy mouth, jerking her off her feet. It bunched itself up as though it was about to begin crawling up her leg, merrily munching all the way as she tried to bring her gun to bear in a way that wouldn't mean shooting herself.

I shot the glistening, meaty back of the thing, high up enough that I was confident I'd missed her foot. It let her go with a squeal, rolling so that its wounds were against the ground. I was about to attack it again, but Mihaela got there first, shooting with a familiar grim, focused expression. The smaller monster shriveled beneath her barrage, and I turned my attention back to the first one, which had steadily crept closer to me while my attention had been split.

"Peace!" it screamed as soon as I turned around, shrinking back a few feet. "Don't you want peace?"

"Oh, I love peace, darling," I snarked as I slammed a fresh magazine home in my gun. "But I'm afraid I left it in my other guitar case – this one only has my Uzis." I fired into the creature's center of mass, blasting a hole in it so wide I could see right through it to the cracked concrete on the other side. The monster fell with a flop and a moan, but I didn't trust it. I never trusted anything that could handle a full magazine from my Uzi and not be very dead.

"We need to get out of here, now," I said to Mihaela, who was back on her feet again, if standing a bit gingerly on the left one. "Didn't finally break that hip, did you?"

"I'll show *you* a broken hip," she snapped, and began climbing the nearest fallen-down bit of masonry that looked like it would lead back up to the surface of the island.

Not to be outdone, I ran for a few steps, crouched and jumped straight up and out just a few meters ahead of her. I offered her a hand for the last steps. She batted it away with a scowl and made it out to stand beside me on her own.

"Well," I said, looking down into the pit that was once a part of our father's massive lair. "That was a disappointment, there's no gainsaying it, but we have learned a few interesting things."

"Like what?" Mihaela demanded. "There are no shards here! This entire trip was a waste of time."

Interesting priorities. It wasn't the first time she'd spoken in such a way, putting regaining a bloodstone shard over finding out who'd done the stealing in the first place, but it was quite a shift from how she'd leveraged her way into this mess with me back in Boston. I'd have to think more about it, but first, I'd have to put her in her place with *logic*, nonetheless. I called that personal growth.

"The fact that there aren't any shards here is secondary. We know that a team of people was here recently. We know that they brought something magical here with them and, either accidentally or deliberately, used it to wake up these beasts. We know that the interaction wasn't entirely a

positive one, thanks to the shell casings they left behind."
I nodded decisively. "This has been in the nature of a
confirmation stop. Not exciting, but it tells me that we're
on the right track."

"Elsa…" she said slowly.

*No, no more doom and gloom, no more interrupting me
every other second while I was trying to keep us alive.* "And
really, while we're on the subject of the right track, it would
be quite a bloody boon if you would focus a bit more
on keeping your spirits up. I don't have the time or the
inclination to buck you up every step of the way."

"Elsa."

Mihaela seemed agitated now, but to the land of the
undead with it, I was on a roll and I wasn't in the mood to
stop just because she felt the need to interrupt. "I mean, it's
one thing to take this all seriously, that's fine, no complaints
here, but there's serious and then there's pretending our
situation is dire, and I think we're a long way from that, so
if you could do your best to control your urge to grumble
and shout, I'd be–"

"Elsa!" She pointed desperately at the edge of the
subterranean base, which was slowly filling with…

Oh, hell. Every hell, all of them. The basement was filling
with black ooze, a morass of creepy crawly creature coming
in on its own tide. Mouths – not one mouth, many mouths,
each of them a new level of horrifying, some of them had
bloody *tentacles* coming out of them – appeared in the
thick, oily surface, snapping like hungry piranhas.

I didn't have sufficient artillery to handle some Cthulhu-wannabe right now. This particular monster would have to wait until we were done looking for shards.

"Right, we're off." I grabbed Mihaela's hand, turned, and ran for the skimmer. She tripped several times, but I jerked her back to her feet after each stumble. We ran until we were at the edge of the water. The messy magic-eating ooze behind us was picking up speed. I didn't know if it could travel through water, but I didn't want to find out the hard way either.

"In." I practically threw Mihaela into the craft before pulling up the anchor. "Here." I put her at the controls. "You start backing us up while I guarantee our escape route."

"I don't know how to drive a boat!" she protested, hovering her hands over the wheel like it was going to bite her.

"Figure it out!" I was shoulder-deep in one of my bags, looking for my stock of custom grenades. Fire fed the nasty blighters, from what the one had said about taking a nuclear strike, which, no matter how small the nuke was, should hurt. So, setting them on fire probably wasn't the best bet, but…

Ah, the frag grenades, those might do in a pinch, given how the monsters had reacted to getting shot. I straightened up as the boat lurched forward, almost sending us onto the rocks. "Reverse, reverse," I shouted, pointing at the button before throwing my first grenade into the creeping wave of goo. One of the mouths caught it with a grin, and–

Foom! That part of the monstrous mess was blown apart, raining chunks of purple gunk spotted with the occasional tooth down in the water, and onto us as well. The mass of creatures stopped, undoubtedly startled and hopefully scared. I threw two more grenades as Mihaela finally backed us away from the island. The first one sank a few inches into the monster and produced another rain of gore, but the moment the second one hit, the monster modified its surface somehow, making it glassy and hard. The grenade didn't penetrate, just rolled down a few feet before exploding. It still did some damage, but not on the scale of the first two.

So, it can learn to defend itself against projectiles. That's… interesting. I wasn't a big fan of monsters that changed up their technique on the fly. I mean, good for them in the long run, evolution and the survival of the fittest and all that, but it made killing them less a hunt and more a guessing game. I was a monster hunter, not a scientist. If I wanted to play "answer the hypothesis" with my work, I'd have gone into cryptobiology.

The bottom of the skimmer scraped the top of a reef, too close for us to avoid. I looked down and saw that, like a lava flow, the creature was spreading out underwater, following us out to sea. "Damn it," I muttered, then turned to Mihaela. "Drive faster."

"What's going on?" she asked, her hands clenched around the wheel as she tried to steer clear of rock formations. We were still too close to the island to use a lot of speed.

"Oh, you know, just ..." No, there was no way to sugarcoat this. "It swims," I said succinctly, rummaging through my bag for a different type of weapon. Frag grenades were out, they wouldn't work well underwater anyway and this thing had already learned to protect itself against them, but what about... Ah-*ha!*

I pulled out my find and looked down into the water again. The blackness of the monster's body glittered as the water filtered the light, turning it into a parody of a starry sky. Said sky abruptly split in half, revealing a mouth the size of the entire skimmer. It began to close the distance, ready to swallow us whole.

I pulled the pin on the concussion grenade and dropped it into the water. A few seconds later the water erupted in a mighty splash right behind us, pelting us and the boat with seaweed and tiny chunks of reef. Far more satisfying was the scream that simultaneously erupted from every single open mouth in the creature, the entire mass of it writhing in agony as the sonic reverberations disrupted it. The mouth drawing close to us vanished, the blackness in the water receding back into its land-self faster than my eyes could track.

"Oh, lovely," I said with satisfaction, hands on my hips as I stared after the retreating monster. "Better than I expected. Job well done, us." I looked at Mihaela to make sure she wasn't crying or anything. There were no tears, just a certain set to her face that spoke of slight shock. Well, I couldn't blame her for that. Not everyone was used to staring down their own mortality in the form of sentient, passive-aggressive ooze that wanted to eat them alive. "All right, then?" I asked.

"Fine," she said mechanically.

"Really? Because you were limping on our way to the skimmer."

"You were tugging me along so fast I thought my legs might fall off, who would not limp?"

"Nevertheless, better let me take a look at that foot." We were in open water at last, and I reached around her and set the skimmer to autopilot, then detached her hands from the wheel. "Come on, that thing had teeth like can openers. I don't care how good your boot is, it couldn't have been enough to protect you."

She jerked her hands out of my grasp. "It was fine."

"You say that now, but even the tiniest scratch could cause an infection that you *don't* want to have to fight." I had learned that the hard way. Bloody zombies.

I led her to one of the plush back seats and tipped her over into a sitting position. It wasn't hard – which definitely meant that shock was taking place, because before this she'd been quite careful about portraying herself as my equal, rather than someone I would be taking care of. I tried not to let that worry me, and certainly didn't let any trace of concern enter my voice as I knelt down to get her right boot off. Ugh, yes, there were definite puncture marks all through the leather. I was surprised I hadn't run into any blood yet.

"I mean, that creature grew up on a wholesome diet of magic and radioactivity, do you really think it was carrying anything even remotely benign in its microbiome?" I carried on blathering as a distraction while I unlaced the boot. I could have just ripped the entire thing in two, but I didn't need to contribute to her sense of discomfort right now. Mihaela was so stern and forbidding it was hard, at times, to remember that she was only human, and a somewhat elderly human at that.

I set the shoe aside, then pulled back her sock. Still no blood. Perhaps higher up… I examined her foot, ankle, and the bottom half of her calf, and was astonished to find that in fact she hadn't suffered a single scratch. Her foot was clammy and cold – not surprising given that she was dealing with shock – but there were no wounds at all. "You *were* lucky," I said once I made sure that I hadn't missed anything.

"I told you," she said. I looked at her and met her gaze, her face distant and expressionless but with a hint of something vulnerable lurking in her eyes. What was she thinking?

Bless, what was I doing? I didn't go in for this kind of stuff, this woo-woo, oh-so-delicate checking in, this roundabout sentimentalism. If she were my actual family it would be different, but she wasn't. I had to remember that. She wasn't my mother, she wasn't Adam. She wasn't even as close to me as Cullen, and my closeness to him generally came from being occasionally on the same continent, not from a sense of camaraderie. Mihaela was nothing more than an interested third party, and I needed to remember that if I was going to maintain my professionalism. Besides, nothing about her seemed to indicate that she wanted anything other than that out of knowing me, so why should I be the one to stick my neck out?

"Right." I got up and turned back to the controls, not bothering to hand back her sock and boot. She wasn't hurt; she could do it herself. "Back to San Salvador."

FIVE

We were booked on the first flight out the next day, with a series of hops scheduled to take us to Mombasa after that. I had a general idea of where Ulysses' base might be, but "general" wasn't good enough. I wanted to get in and get out, not wander along the coast like a lost tourist. I had set Barnabus to the problem before leaving Boston, and that evening, once we were back at the hotel and Mihaela was in the shower, I called him up.

"Tell me you know where we're going," I said as soon as he answered the phone.

"Well, broadly speaking–"

"No, no, give me an address, Charles."

Mombasa was an enormous city, and Ulysses hadn't been active there for a long time. It would take forever to track down people who'd known him from before, and we simply didn't have that kind of flexibility in our schedule.

"I'm afraid I'm not capable of that level of specificity," he said apologetically, "but I've been reading through some of Samantha Eden's old articles, and she mentioned your father in conjunction with activities along Mtawpa Creek several times."

"Samantha Eden?" The name was vaguely familiar.

"An investigative journalist who was particularly active in the 1970s. She did a number of interviews with your father and was invited to Bloodstone Isle at one point. She also wrote a comprehensive article on him several years ago, which is where one of the references to Mtawpa Creek is found."

Interesting. "Send me that article, please. And anything else by her that you think might be relevant."

"I'll do my best, of course." He paused, then asked, "And how is Ms Zamfir faring?"

"She's fine." Filthy as sin, if the fact that she'd been in the shower for the past forty-five minutes was any indication, but fine. "We got off the isle unscathed, thankfully. I'll be going back there once we're done with this, though." And I'd be packing enough sonic weaponry to drive the goo monster of Bloodstone Isle so far underground it would never dare show its hideous face on the surface again.

Charles hummed thoughtfully. "I'm glad to hear that. Please keep me updated on your search. Adam sends his best – he would come, but he's in the middle of a tour."

"Naturally." Adam was a born showman, and although one might think it was a bit of a comedown for a creature as illustrious as Frankenstein's Monster, he relished taking visitors through the manor, showing them the creepy bits and bobs of a life that spanned centuries of activity in the paranormal world. I was convinced it was the real reason he'd stuck around with me after all this time. Lord knows no one else had, other than Mum. "I'll let you know how it goes," I said.

"I'd be most gratified." He ended the call, and I leaned back on my hands on the bed, tilted my face toward the ceiling, and pondered where the best place to get my hands on a sonic cannon was, and how big an ultrasound machine I could lug to the island on a skimmer and put directly into the water. Pretty blasted big, I bet.

"What are you smiling about?"

I glanced over at Mihaela as she came out of the bathroom. She was wrapped up so tight in her nighties and bathrobe she looked like a mummy – and I was friends with N'Kantu the Living Mummy, I knew wrappings when I saw them – but seemed refreshed after her marathon shower. Her complexion had more color than when she'd gone in, and some of the lines creasing her cheeks and the corners of her mouth were fainter. "I was just thinking about some targeted annihilation," I replied, just to make her frown. "Nothing serious."

"How can you say things like that and not take them seriously?" she demanded, going over to her bed but not bothering to sit down. She crossed her arms over her chest and glared at me like I was a rude child, or perhaps a naughty puppy. No, definitely a child – no one would stare at a puppy with so much disappointment in their eyes. "Is mayhem and death and annihilation just a joke to you?"

"Of course," I said, and I meant it. This part was obvious, and I suddenly wanted – no, I needed – for her to get it. "Everything is a joke. My existence is a joke, and so is yours, and so is Cullen's. We're the result of a silly game our father played, toying at being happy families and settling down before getting back to what he was meant to do. We shouldn't exist. If he was smarter, we *wouldn't* exist." I certainly hadn't taken any chances myself. Unwilling implantation of monstrous parasitical children by the brood of Goram didn't count. Ugh, I still couldn't step foot in Prague without shuddering.

I spread my hands in a "what can you do" kind of gesture. "I'm certainly not sad to be alive, but I'm absolutely determined that as far as the Bloodstone legacy goes, I won't be continuing it. I'll be a monster hunter and nothing else for the rest of my life – not a wife, not a mother, not an academic – because if I didn't hunt monsters, by this time I'd be one. Not just a monster, but a mother of monsters."

I could still remember how it felt to be carrying those hideous parasites before the bloodstone served up its eviction notice. It had felt so alien, and yet something about it had felt so right, too. It would be too easy to slip into the role of a monster if I wasn't careful, so bugger it, I was going to *be* careful.

"I won't be a monster, but I won't pretend I'm not a bit of a cosmic punchline, and neither should you. Although," I added, "seems like it's less of a joke for you, since you managed to avoid the family business before now."

Mihaela held still for a long moment, staring at me like I'd grown an extra head.

"What?" I finally said.

"Just…" She stared a moment longer, then turned away. "Nothing. But you should know, my life has not always been free of monsters."

Indeed? "Any you'd care to tell me about?" I was always interested in a good beastie hunt.

She shook her head, though.

"Fair enough," I said. I couldn't say I wasn't disappointed by her reticence, but whatever. I didn't need her to be my friend, much less my family, but perhaps it wouldn't be the worst thing in the world if we could be decent companions, at least. After all, we'd just faced down a rather intimidating monster together, and it undoubtedly wouldn't be the last one we had to deal with on our inadvertent adventure.

"Right." I got up and grabbed my pillow gun out of my weapons bag. It was a lovely HK USP Compact, small enough not to leave me with a sore neck but hefty enough that whatever came at me in the night would regret it for long enough for me to get my big guns, at which point they'd really regret it. I put the pistol under my pillow, which I gently fluffed, then set my Bowie knife on the bedside table, right next to the hotel's cheap alarm clock I'd already set to wake us up at four.

"Best get some sleep, then," I said. How was this woman not falling-over exhausted already? *I* was even tired, and we'd barely had any sort of fight today at all. Actually, that might be part of the problem. I tended to be energized by conflict rather than fatigued by it, unless I was dealing with a *lot* of conflict. Our fight with the goo monster had hardly even tipped the scale, although that bit at the end had been adrenalizing.

"Another big day tomorrow?" Mihaela asked wryly, finally sitting down on her bed and unwrapping her hair from the towel it was bound up in. It looked darker in the lamplight, less gray and more black. For a moment there, I could picture her as a young woman.

I scoffed. "Another day spent mostly on an airplane. We'll get to Mombasa by midday and see what can be done to find the base, but we might not be able to resolve things there until the day after."

"Wonderful," she said with a grimace, putting one hand on the small of her back. Ah, there was the cantankerous old wench I was getting used to. "Aren't you rich? Why don't you have a plane?"

"There are a hundred and one reasons to have my own plane, and a hundred and two reasons not to. The biggest reason not? Midair battles." I rolled my eyes. "I've lost enough vehicles to monster attacks. I'm not about to get drawn into a fight in the sky where I'm also meant to be flying the bloody plane. Besides, I can only imagine how it would feel to regenerate after falling to the ground from twenty thousand feet."

"Oh." She fell into silence, hopefully a thoughtful one because I knew I'd made a good point, even if it wasn't one she'd considered before.

Not that I cared if she thought I'd made a good point or not. No, of course not.

I turned off my bedside lamp without another word and settled in for a night of very light sleep. Amongst my various enhanced abilities was a super-sense for feeling the presence of people around me. I knew every shift and stir she made would wake me up, and I was resigned to that. Separate rooms next time, I promised myself.

After she settled in, though, I didn't hear a thing – not even the rustle of her breathing. Falling asleep was the easiest it had ever been outside the manor.

I didn't quite know what to make of that.

SIX

If there wasn't yet a religion that specified airports as a special level of Hell, or at least Purgatory, I was going to start one. I simply spent too much time in the bloody places not to feel like I was slogging about on a journey through the underworld, trying to escape and perpetually failing. It was even worse while having a sidekick along. I still didn't like having my likes and dislikes exposed in ways I couldn't control.

Damn it, this was why I didn't tend to stay on teams for long. Well, this and the fact that any team where the blokes spent more time looking at my chest than reading my lips didn't deserve me.

Actually arriving in Mombasa was a respite, and even better was the message on my phone that was waiting for me once I turned the thing back on. "Ah," I said with satisfaction as we headed for baggage claim. "Azizi is here!"

Mihaela, who seemed to wilt as soon as she emerged from the plane into the equatorial heat, brushed a lank strand of hair out of her face. "Who is Azizi?"

"An old friend of mine," I said airily as I stalked down the wide corridor. There were people of all types flying into this metropolitan city – Mombasa was the second-most populous region in the entire country, after Nairobi – and all of them parted before me like rain sheeting off an invisible umbrella. There was a lot of power to be had in a particular type of walk, and I had studied with the best.

In a twist of fate that proved that the airport was in fact *only* Purgatory, our luggage arrived quickly. I led the way out to the front of the airport. Mihaela still managed to match my brisk pace while complaining about my lack of explanation.

"–can't go making all sorts of decisions that affect both of us without talking to me first," she snapped as we stepped outside.

I paused to bask in the sun. It had been damp in Glasgow, rainy in Boston, and cloyingly humid in San Salvador and Bloodstone Isle. Mombasa was a port city, built to take advantage of the sea, but a strong breeze blew off the water right now, enough to make the heat bearable.

"Well?" Mihaela demanded, putting her free hand on her hip.

"Hmm?" I turned to her. "Did you say something that was an actual question in there?"

If looks could kill, I would be a bug beneath her boot

heel right now. "Why," she said through grinding teeth, "should I trust this Azizi?"

"Because if you want to get anything done with any sort of rapidity in this part of the world, Azizi is one of the best people to know," I replied. "He's got connections all over the monster-hunting world. I've worked with him on and off for years now, and he's never let me down."

"Why do we need to work with someone else at all?" Lord, she was like a shark on a seal with this. "Don't you know where the base is?"

If I'd had a pair of sunglasses, I would have pushed them down my nose and given her a stare over the top of them. As it was, my normal dismissive glare had to suffice. "I really don't know where you get all these delusions about our father. That he was careful about how he used his powers, that he cared about his children, that he was in any way organized..."

"He *was* organized!" At least she didn't try to come at me on the second one. "The stories he told me when I was young... He had an incredible memory for everything that happened in his long life!"

"He might have had a great memory, but that didn't translate into anything outside of his own head," I said. "In places where he had to worry about things like paperwork, organization happened simply because it was easier to do it than to not. Boston, Bloodstone Isle, possibly the place in New York... but here? In Mombasa?" I shook my head. "There's been so much property theft here over the years by white people, why would another big, blond asshole throwing his weight around stand out? Who would go up to Ulysses Bloodstone and make sure he paid property taxes, or followed building codes, or any of the like?"

"I know someone who would have," a voice to the right said. I turned with a grin to greet the newcomer. He was a Black man a few inches shorter than me, with a bald head and a red and white patterned pagne shirt over black pants. He wore a necklace with a fang set in gold around his neck, but other than that there was nothing particularly flashy about him. He could have been any one of a number of taxi drivers waiting to take travelers into the city.

I, of course, knew better. "Azizi! What, were you waiting for the mood to be right before coming over here?"

"Just wanted to be in time to stop a fight breaking out," he said smoothly. "I thought you might need me, given the way you ladies were speaking."

"It was only a simple, friendly conversation," I said. Azizi gave me a look. "It was! Do you see knives out or guns drawn?"

"Since when have you ever needed a knife or a gun to get into a fight?"

I heaved a sigh. "It was one time, and he should have known better than to take that tone with me while I'm wearing my stilettos. My God, the threat is right there in the name."

"Be that as it may…" He paused meaningfully, and I

realized I was a bit behind in the schedule of social niceties. I waved a hand at my half-sister.

"Azizi, this is Mihaela Zamfir, a client with a mercenary problem. Mihaela, this is Azizi Kimachu, the man I go to whenever I have a job that brings me to the area."

Azizi held out his hand. "Jambo, Ms Zamfir, welcome to Mombasa!"

She paused, then took his hand briefly. "Thank you," she muttered, looking more and more like a drooping, gothic houseplant by the second. "Shall we be on our way, then?"

Azizi looked taken aback. "Already? Neither of you have even checked into your hotel. And you have *quite* the luggage with you." He glanced meaningfully at the stack of bags beside us. "Not the sort of thing you want to leave out in the open, I'd say."

"I would rather begin by finding the base immediately," Mihaela insisted.

Azizi glanced at me, and I in turn assessed Mihaela. She still looked a bit deflated, but she didn't seem ill. If anything, she seemed the opposite – more energized now than she'd been this morning, and correspondingly antsy. I wondered, the idea crystallizing in my mind for the first time, if perhaps she'd experienced an addiction of some kind to her bloodstone shard. Perhaps that was why she was so insistent about finding it when it was meant to be nothing but a memento. Perhaps what I was seeing now was the result of her going into withdrawal.

The last thing I needed right now was to deal with a

woman in detox while I was trying to get a job done. I was tempted to say that we should go to the hotel right now, even more tempted to tell her to stay there, but I knew she wouldn't listen to me. Leaving her alone was a recipe for disaster, which would doubtless fall squarely upon my head when I least needed it to.

This is what you get for being such a soft touch and letting a bloody tourist come on a job. Next time – ugh, no, there would be no next time, and now Azizi and Mihaela were both staring at me.

"Fine," I said after a moment. "We'll try to find the place now, but–"

"Finding the place won't be a problem," Azizi assured me. "I've done some legwork there. It was easier than I thought, once I talked a few things through with your friend Mr Barnabus. I haven't seen the base myself yet, but I've verified its location. The problem will be getting there. It's not so far out of the city, but the workday is ending, and..." He shrugged. "Traffic, it's a problem everywhere. Tomorrow morning would be much more expedient, but–"

"We should get started immediately." Mihaela hoisted her bag. "Where's your car?"

He'd brought a van, a rather nice Mercedes in point of fact. "I see we're traveling in style," I said as I placed my bags in the van where the middle seat would have been. It functioned quite well as convenient storage space.

"Only the best," he agreed, heading around to the front of the car to get into the right-side driver's seat – the proper side, in my opinion. I got in front with him, leaving Mihaela to perch in the far back seat like a solitary crow.

"So, where are we headed?" I asked as we pulled out of the airport parking lot. As soon as we passed the enormous dolphin statues and got on the highway, our pace slowed. There was certainly plenty of traffic, and I heard Mihaela huff in frustration in the back.

Yes, it's not all kicking arses and taking names. A great deal of time on the job gets spent simply traveling from one bloody place to the next. I did have the means to avoid a lot of the tedium of travel, but using that particular artifact was always a double-edged sword, so I limited myself whenever I could. There was nothing about this job so far that required instantaneous travel, so I wasn't going to slop a heap of additional risk on top of what was already in store for me.

Lo and behold, I could be reasonable about danger at times. Take that, everyone who said I'd get myself killed before I was twenty-five.

Azizi swiftly changed lanes before replying. "The place you're looking for is in the Mtawpa Creek tidal zone. It's not heavily farmed, there's too much flooding for that, so we don't have to worry about frightening landowners. What we *do* have to worry about is, unfortunately, the flooding. We've had more rainfall than usual these last few weeks, and Mtawpa Creek is overflowing its banks. The coordinates for this base of yours were very close to the creek's original route, which means–"

"We might be digging around underwater." *What a delight.* "We'll need gear, then."

"I have it in the back. Most likely, you won't need to get in any deeper than your waist, but..." He shrugged. "*Mtaka cha mvunguni sharti ainame.*"

I chuckled.

"What does that mean?" Mihaela asked.

"It means you do what you have to do to get the job done," I told her. "More literally, it translates as 'He who wants to fetch something from under the bed must bend over.' Which right now means bending over to get through this awful traffic."

"Ah." Mihaela nodded. "When we get there, I'm going to do the work underwater."

I turned in my seat to stare at her. "What about that prospect could possibly appeal to you?"

She looked at me serenely. "I'm a very good swimmer, and I'm excellent at holding my breath."

"Are you excellent at fighting off things that come at you in the darkness and murk and taking them out with a speargun? Because that's the weapon you fire underwater if you want to have any effect whatsoever."

"Actually," Azizi interjected, "I have an amphibious rifle in the back."

I eyed him. "An ADS?"

He winced. "APS. Still Russian, though!"

My jaw dropped. "Are you joking? You might as well hand me a bloody Lancejet and prepare my funeral dirge!"

"I can use an ADS," Mihaela said in an oh-so-helpful tone of voice from the back.

"How do you have experience firing a Russian-made underwater rifle?" I demanded.

She smirked at me. "I'm Romanian. Where do you think we got any of our weapons from?"

That was... quite a good point. It didn't answer the larger question, though. "And where did you have the opportunity to acquaint yourself with the technical ins and outs of amphibious rifles?"

She raised one eyebrow at me, as if to say, *where do you think?*

Hmm. I turned around, opting not to pursue the obvious line of questioning at the moment, but now that I was on the hunt I couldn't keep my mind from working at it. I'd read the dossier Adam had compiled on Mihaela the night before we left, and it had been incredibly mild, and likely incomplete. She'd lived in the countryside for the earliest decades of her life before heading to university at the age of twenty-three. She'd studied archeology and ancient languages in school and proceeded to have a long career as an academic who frequented digs of mostly Dacian sites. She'd never married, never had children, and retired from her working life two years ago. She was... normal. Utterly normal. Mundane even, considering the circles I ran in. So, what was the purpose in learning how to fire guns underwater? What was the purpose in learning to fire guns at all?

Did Ulysses Bloodstone need a purpose beyond training his children for the worst imaginable outcome? *He was bad with Cullen, and God only knows what went on with you.* What kind of steps might he have taken with Mihaela, who was born during the Cold War?

It was tempting to blame everything that ever went wrong in my life on my father, and I did so frequently. Was this just more of the same, another example of his over-zealousness? Perhaps.

Or perhaps Mihaela was full of it and letting her anxiousness get the better of her. Either way, we'd find out. She wanted to go mucking about underwater looking for shards or booby traps or whatever else might be in one of our father's old bases? She was welcome to it.

"Right, then," I said at last. "You're up. Just don't come crying to me when you end up chewed to bits."

"I'll try to contain myself." Her voice was as dry as the air was humid.

Azizi glanced between the two of us, opened his mouth to say something, and, after a second of contemplation, closed it again. "Smart," I said to him, then settled back so that my head rested between the window and the head rest. "Wake me up when we get there."

I didn't actually fall asleep. I closed my eyes and listened to the sound of the engine, hearing it change as we sped up and slowed down. I felt the change in the vibrations of the tires as we turned from a main road onto a smaller, less maintained one. I heard the murmurs of conversation that passed between Azizi and Mihaela, mostly mindless pleasantries, but a few gems.

"How long have you known her?" Mihaela asked at one point.

"Oh, quite some time now. Ever since her first break from college."

"She went to college?" Mihaela didn't even bother to couch her disbelief in politeness.

"Indeed, indeed. Was a good student too, from what I understand, but the pull of the craft became too much for her to bear. It's hard to look on from a distance and watch people suffer when you know that you could be doing something about it, after all. She approached me for help on a case concerning, what was it… inkanyamba, I think. A giant, man-eating eel," he elaborated for the sake of Mihaela's presumably puzzled expression. "Usually found in South Africa, but this one had been sold on the black market and got free in Lake Victoria." I could practically hear him grin. "There's a good reason she doesn't care to work underwater, and an equally good reason I make sure she can, just in case."

There was a pause, and then, "You're a good friend to her."

"I don't know about that, but I do my best for her when she's here. Same as she does for me." Azizi sounded fond. "We work well together."

That was the heart of my entire approach to relationships. Azizi was someone I considered a friend, but for me, *friend* was really the same thing as coworker that I trust a bit farther than I can throw him or her. I didn't have friends in the classic sense – no real casual confidants or the like. I had family, and then I had "professional acquaintances" who became "friends" for as long as I was in the area. We didn't exchange birthday cards, never called each other for the holidays, but we were there for each other when it counted.

In my opinion, that was a better definition of friendship than any buddy-buddy acquaintance ever could be.

I "woke up" when the van slowed way down, finally coming to a stop at the dead end of a dirt road surrounded by grassy, overgrown fields on either side. "We'll have to walk in from here," Azizi explained as he shut off the engine. The sun was noticeably closer to the horizon than when I'd last looked. We had an hour, maybe an hour and a half before twilight.

I wasn't going to have Mihaela paddling about out here after twilight. I'd pack her off into the van and have Azizi sit on her while I did it myself, if it came to that, no matter how capable she thought she was. "Right, then." I got into the back and began to pull my first-choice weapons for uncertain terrain like this out of my bag. Amphibious rifles were all well and good, but I wanted something with stopping power in both the air and for firing into the water. Overprepared, thy name is Elsa. My double-barreled shotgun with a round for every occasion in my bandolier fit the bill quite nicely. I took my pistol and Bowie knife as well, just in case, then looked down at my gorgeous boots. I'd already done such terrible things to them on Bloodstone Isle, and I hadn't brought a second pair. Mucking about in them for hours on end would certainly finish them off.

I sighed. "OK, where are the bloody waders?"

Thank whatever god was laughing over us that there were no bystanders watching me wade into a swamp looking like a vastly overprepared fisherwoman. Mihaela came behind, lugging her specialty equipment without a peep. She'd accepted the mask, wetsuit, and high-powered flashlight but declined the air tank, preferring to hold her breath and surface whenever she needed a fresh lungful.

More and more, I was convinced that we weren't going to get anything out of this particular site. By the time we reached the only building visible in any direction, the water was up over my hips. If this really was Ulysses' base, he should have planned better for the rainy season. The base itself wasn't very tall, the ceiling no more than two feet above my head where it hadn't collapsed into the water entirely. It was a fairly long, simple affair, and just one story as far as Azizi knew. "None of the locals gave it much heed," he explained as we mucked through the field that housed the base. "They said they got bad feelings from it, said too many monsters were drawn to it."

"Monsters, drawn to it! You see?" Mihaela turned to me with a smile on her face. "That could mean there was something powerful luring them in! There could be a shard here."

"Or there *might* have been one once upon a time," I said, more than ready to disabuse her of the notion, but surprisingly, Azizi stuck up for her.

"No, as far as the people say, dark and dangerous creatures still come here often – too often to make farming the area safe for them."

Mihaela raised her chin slightly, like a queen waiting for her court jester to bow down.

I'd be having none of that, thank you very much. "Well, then." I waved my hand at the dark, open doorway of the building. Water lapped gently at the reeds and tall grasses that surrounded us, the light breeze making it ripple. Something small crawled over the foot of my wader, but I didn't bother to look down – the water was too murky to make out anything that low. "You'd best get started. Give us a shout if you find a pot of gold, all right?"

She sniffed and turned away, pulling her mask down and turning on her flashlight so she could see deeper into the water. With the light in one hand and the rifle in the other, she waded through the doorway, then ducked down into the water to get around an obstruction. In less than a minute, her light was out of sight.

I'd expected to stand around shooting the breeze with Azizi for a while, perhaps give a shout if more than ten minutes went by without me hearing from her. Instead, only a moment later, a hideous shriek split the silence into a thousand quivering pieces. It was as though a mountain lion was mating with a crocodile in surround sound. A second after that, a shadowy bat-winged creature burst through the fractured top of the base, flying straight up into the air. It gripped Mihaela by one of her ankles, and was flinging her about as it rose and fell, rose and fell, never getting more than twenty or so feet away.

"Popobawa!" Azizi shouted, going for his gun. I stopped him.

"Regular ammunition won't work on a popobawa. We need iron!" Fortunately, I had iron rounds on my bandolier. Accessorizing: it was always a good idea. I slammed two cartridges into the gun, sighted, and fired in less time than it took me to exhale.

I winged it. Bloody thing was fast and I only caught the edge of it – it screamed that awful scream again, but it wasn't moving any more slowly. Mihaela had gotten her wits about her enough to start firing her own rifle at the beast, but the flechette rounds didn't even phase it.

I reloaded, then gathered myself and leapt out of the water onto the edge of the old concrete building. The whole rotten thing was on the verge of crumbling. Then again, what could I expect after over forty years? It would hold me long enough to get this next bloody shot off, though. *Bam-Bam!*

This time I hit it in the torso, right where I'd expect the shoulder to be if I could see around its scythe-like claws, each one twice the length of its arms. How had Mihaela not been shredded to cabbage already just from being held by it? The popobawa screamed again, jerking and twisting but not flying away, not seeking shelter. It didn't bother to land, either.

"Looking for a fight?" I snarled as I loaded a new type of round. "I'll give you a fight, you bastard." This time I sighted with less care. I was firing salt rounds this time, after all – it would hurt Mihaela if it hit her, but not mortally, whereas it would make this thing as sick as swine flu. *Bam-Bam!*

Mihaela jerked, but I couldn't tell if it was because I grazed her with a round or because I hit the popobawa square in the face. It let go of Mihaela, who fell through a section of roof with a crash, immediately followed by a splash.

"Get after her!" I called to Azizi as the popobawa, trailing blood-tinged shadows from its wounds, focused all its furious energy on me.

I'd fought a popobawa before, after a rising wave of hysteria had afflicted town after town in northern Tanzania. Azizi had called that one in to me, and the fight had been a learning experience that had gone on for fifteen minutes before I finally offed the thing. Now I knew better how to handle them, but I was also balanced on the edge of a crumbling building in water-logged waders as the sun set ever lower, making the shadows of this creature almost indistinguishable from the shadows of the nearby trees.

Good thing I had exceptional balance and better than 20/20 eyesight. The popobawa charged me, its wings flaring out behind it like a cloak, claws extended four full feet in front of it like a handful of spears. I leapt sideways, clear to the other side of the building, as I loaded another two iron rounds into the shotgun. The moment I landed, I fired.

One round missed, the popobawa rising into the air with incredible speed. The other round hit one of its grotesque, oversized feet, which practically exploded with the force of the shot. The monster screamed and shot straight up–

And just as quickly came back down, loosing what I was sure was the popobawa's version of a long list of very dirty swear words. Its behavior was so odd. Clearly it wanted to escape and not get shot to bits by me and my beloved shotgun, but it never went more than twenty feet away. Some sort of compulsion, perhaps? Or overwhelming hunger?

Eh, didn't matter either way. "Think I've got your number now, pet," I said as I loaded for the kill shot. Iron filings mixed with a salt round – good for all sorts of beasties, and I was sure it would make a meal out of this one, too. I raised the shotgun and took aim at the loathsome creature…

Crack! The grinding crunch beneath my feet that had begun the moment I'd jumped up here became a rumbling crash as the wall I stood on tilted and fell, tipping me forward as it plunged into the water. I stumbled for a moment before recovering enough to jump for a new section of wall, but that stumble was all the opening the popobawa needed. It plunged back to earth and, after drawing one hand back like it was about to throw a punch, flung its hand – and its massively elongated shadow claws –

straight at me. I ducked and rolled, but not quickly enough.

The claw that speared me felt like acid being poured straight into my thigh, and once the creature had me, it held on. I ground my teeth and gripped the edge of the building to keep from being jerked any closer, but it was a near thing. The popobawa, wounded though it was, was still immensely strong. It tugged for a few more seconds, then appeared to give it up as lost and used the claw as a reel for itself instead, crossing the distance between the sides of the building in the blink of an eye. It landed beside me and reached for me with the other hand, its red eyes glowing with hunger and its mouthful of fangs opening in a satisfied snarl.

At which point I slashed it across the face with my Bowie knife. The popobawa reeled back with a stunned shriek, and I grinned fiercely before bringing the knife down on the edge of the claw still jutting from my leg and severing it. I tugged the claw out, and a moment later the wound began to mend with a familiar, almost comforting pain. A regular steel-bladed knife wouldn't have fazed the beast, but what sort of monster hunter would I be if I didn't plan ahead? I had silver, iron, and copper inlaid on the edge of the blade, as well as a section lined with granules of obsidian glass. Every dollar paid for the creation and maintenance of my weapon was repaid ten times over as I watched the popobawa writhe and clasp its hands to its face, utterly forgetting for the moment that I was still there.

And that I had a shotgun.

From my a sitting position, I fired the first shot. *Bam!* Straight into the monster's gut. It doubled over, a burst of reddish-black shadow blood erupting from the wound like I'd just cut a line in its belly and neatly disemboweled it. As I fired the second round straight at its head, the popobawa threw itself at me, mouth open and aiming for my throat. I shot it a millisecond before it hit .

We fell backwards into the water outside the rotting base, tangled together. I kept my mouth shut against the muddy water and fought to free myself from the monster's dead weight. Its arms, which had fallen to either side of me, were tremendously long, and I scratched myself several times with the claws as I worked to get out from under the enveloping corpse.

I finally surfaced, feeling like a boat that was on the verge of capsizing. My waders were more than waterlogged now, they were their own micro-climates. I wouldn't be surprised to find a fish swimming around in one of them. I wiped my sodden bangs back from my face, pulling a clump of scummy grass away as I did. "Ugh."

"Elsa!"

I turned toward the exhortation and saw Azizi and Mihaela making their way toward me. A surprising surge of relief went through me to see Mihaela unharmed – or at least unharmed enough to be making headway through the water faster than Azizi, who was younger than her by a good twenty years. "Oh, good," I said as she got closer. "You're still alive."

"And kicking," she confirmed, looking at me with something like anxiety in her face. "Are you all right? I thought I saw you get injured in the fight."

Oh lord, that little scratch? "I'm fine," I assured her, raising my leg so she could see the hole in the upper part of the wader and my healed skin underneath. "It barely perforated me. You're the senior citizen who got dropped through a rooftop. Still no broken hip, I take it?"

She shook her head. "The roof was rotten, and the water was right below. It was practically as good as landing on a feather bed."

I laughed. "You must have some interesting feather beds in Romania!"

"We lay them over a bed of nails at night, to give ourselves a reason to get up in the morning," she said slyly. For a moment, just a moment, I felt an actual sense of kinship with this bizarre woman who happened to be my sister. "As long as you're well, I'm going back in," she said a second later.

"There's no shard in this base!" I told her, exasperated beyond all measure at this point. "Look at the state of it! I sincerely doubt the old man hid any heavy-duty safes in these walls, and if this flooding is a regular thing then everything that was once tucked up on a shelf or under a cot has been washed away."

Mihaela's shoulders stiffened. "Nevertheless, it would be wasteful of us not to make certain of that after coming all this way. After all, we found that creature here." She pointed at the carcass of the popobawa, of which all we could see were the tips of the wings. "Perhaps it's like the monsters back on Bloodstone Isle, attracted by magical residue."

"Mapopobawa don't work like that," Azizi put in. "They're attracted to easy victims, not someone or something that might be strengthened by magic."

Mihaela's jaw was beginning to jut forward, a sure sign she was heading into a strop. I held up a hand. "You know what? Fine. Go ahead, wade on in there again and see what you can see. I certainly won't be going after you if you roust another monster out of its den, but please, make yourself content."

"I will, thank you very much." She turned her glowing flashlight back toward the entrance of the base and ducked inside again.

Azizi leaned in close. "Elsa, it isn't safe for her to–"

"She'll be fine," I murmured, feeling around under the water for the popobawa's limbs. "We're right here if she has a problem with an aggressive minnow. I need to check something out on this creature." Right wrist... right ankle, ha, practically no foot remaining, which was more than it had deserved... left ankle – *ah*. I hoisted the oil-black body part out of the murk. "Bring your light in closer." I said to Azizi.

"What are you looking for?" he asked, shining the beam of light where I indicated.

"Something was wrong about this entire attack," I said, inspecting the popobawa's skin for tears or abrasions that

I wasn't responsible for. "Why wouldn't a creature of such strength, one with wings no less, simply grab Mihaela and fly off? Why hover here, even when it realized it was outmatched?" Because it had realized that, decidedly – the moment it ditched Mihaela, I knew the popobawa was thinking of running. But it hadn't, it had gone after me instead, a decision which was, at best, poorly thought out.

Perhaps I was checking the wrong limb. Perhaps… Wait, no, it was here, just a little higher up, wrapped around the knee. I saw the burn line, as smooth as though it had been cut into the creature's skin with a laser, and grinned. "Clever. Expensive, but clever."

"Feel free to share any time," Azizi grumbled.

"This monster," I said, hoisting the popobawa's knee up farther so the uniform line was more clearly visible, "was bound by a dwarven chain."

Azizi looked blankly at me.

"Like the one that bound Fenrir the Wolf? Made of the sound of a cat's footfall, the root of a mountain, the… look, it doesn't matter. The point is that you can get them on the black market for a lot of money, if you have the right – or perhaps, the *wrong* sort of connections, and they can hold anyone, whether they're human, monster, or god." This was an odd use for such a valuable item, binding a popobawa to a place like this. Seemed like a waste of a good booby trap to me, unless whoever was behind the mysterious mercenaries in black had far more money than sense.

Given the fact that whoever it was seemed perfectly

happy to throw their human capital at problems with little regard to their prospects for success, it seemed reasonable that they might be a wealthy sociopath. Truly, sending a single mercenary team of fewer than twenty people after me was just... audaciously hopeful on their part. Or was our mysterious enemy as titillated by death as he was by the hunt for the bloodstones?

Well... I couldn't prove the popobawa was connected to them. There were plenty of people with power in this area, and even more people who had grudges against Ulysses. This could have had nothing at all to do with Mihaela and me. That was where the logic took me, but my instincts were clanging a different bell. Still, if I couldn't prove it or gain anything useful from the knowing, then why pursue it?

Because I hated unanswered questions, that was why.

"Would you do me a favor?" I asked Azizi, who was still inspecting the wounds with interest. "Would you see if you can source a dwarven chain locally? It might have come with whoever put the beast here, but I'd like to know if there's someone in the area with a line to items like this."

"Of course. I'd like to know for myself, as well."

"Naturally." Who wouldn't like to know where to find mythical dwarves who made magical artifacts that were some of the highest caliber in the entire bloody multiverse?

A swamp witch emerged from the water a few meters from us a second later. Spluttering, her hands clawed, her filthy hair covering her face, she spewed a spray of water straight toward us before beginning to hack.

"Oooh, shouldn't have gotten it in your mouth," I said, coming over and smacking her between the shoulder blades. Mihaela, whose face was barely visible under all that hair, winced. "So what did you find, O intrepid explorer?" I asked.

"Nothing," she snapped at me, shoving my hand away like it was a poisonous snake. "Nothing at all. Does it make you happy to be right, to get the better of me again?"

Honestly it did, a bit, but I had the sense to know that that sentiment wouldn't fly right now. I wasn't a complete muppet. "Let's go," I said instead, turning to Azizi. "And unfortunately, we have to bring this thing and burn it." I prodded the popobawa's corpse. "Do you think we can fit it into the back?"

"In *my* van?" He raised his eyes to the sky and heaved a huge sigh. "I will never get the smell out. Never."

I folded my arms. "It's that or we burn it here, and after all the ruckus we just made I rather think we'd be noticed. Unless you have a better idea?"

He thought about it for a moment, then grinned. "Actually, I do."

SEVEN

Azizi's plan consisted of wrapping the monster up in a tarp and tying it to the top of his van. I was acutely aware of the fact that we had a legendary beast known for powering hysterics in entire countries bound right above us, one loose knot or flapping corner of cloth away from being exposed, but as Azizi had pointed out, it fit better up there, and he wasn't wrong about the smell. Besides, it was dark out now, and people here transported livestock and more on top of their vehicles every day. A single indistinct bundle of ineffable darkness wasn't all that strange.

We drove to a lovely house with private beach access, right beside Old Town. "Your Airbnb," Azizi indicated with a flourish as he parked the van. "If I remember, there is a good spot for bonfires on the beach. We can dispose of the creature there."

"Fantastic," I said as I got out of the van and reached up

to work the corpse free. "Can we order some food, too? I'm starving."

"How can you be hungry after that?" Mihaela asked disgustedly as she got out of the car. I thought it was a rather funny question, given that I'd barely ingested a thing other than airline pretzels, tea, and a much-deserved gin martini in celebration of the noisy man in the seat behind mine finally succumbing to fatigue on the flight over.

"What can I say?" I gestured at myself in all my filthy glory. "It takes a lot of energy to fuel a body as magnificent as all this, especially after healing a wound."

"Nyama choma?" Azizi offered as he pulled out his phone. "Lobster? Prawns? I can get some–"

"I want steak," Mihaela snapped. "Rare. Where are the keys to this place?"

"Um… here." He took them out of his pocket and barely extended them more than an inch before she grabbed them out of his hand and stalked off toward the front door, limping slightly. Perhaps the witch had strained a knee during the festivities.

That was no reason to be rude, though.

"Don't offer to help carry the body or anything!" I hollered after her. Only after she was gone did I realize that the front door of one of the neighboring homes was open, and an elderly Black woman was standing there looking at me like I was mad. "Just a joke," I assured her, and waited until she'd quickly shut the door before I lugged the popobawa off the van and threw it over my shoulder. "All right then," I said to Azizi. "Let's get our burn on."

In the end, the popobawa was one of the easiest monsters I'd ever had the pleasure of setting fire to. Its flesh seemed to catch and hold the flame, and it hardly took any effort at all for the entire thing to erupt in a blaze of light. Even I had to step back a few paces, the temperature got so intense so quickly. It burned hot enough that the smell wasn't much of an issue, which was delightful. I wasn't in the mood to explain to any nosy neighbors why we were polluting their pristine shores with what amounted to some *very* toxic waste.

I moved my bags in from the van – no bloody thanks at all to Mihaela – and cleaned up, then joined Azizi just in time for our dinner to be delivered by a young man driving a yellow and black tuk tuk that advertised onboard wi-fi. *Mmm,* hot skewers of spicy goat meat, fried potatoes with tomato gravy, roasted prawns and even a packet of bright red achari mango were available. There was also a separate box with the rather European offering of a baked potato and steak so rare it was sitting in a pool of its own blood.

Mihaela seemed displeased with it, though, barely picking at it with her utensils before pushing it aside. "You ought to eat that," I said around a mouthful of potato. "You were thrown through a building earlier, after all. I'm sure your body could use the energy."

"I'm fine." She did look fine, actually – she didn't sit with any hint of discomfort, despite the fact that her sixty year-old back had taken significant impact when she hit the roof.

The firelight danced across her face, rendering it a mosaic of light and shadow, hard to peer into and see much of anything, let alone pain. "I ate on the plane."

"That was hours ago," I pointed out.

She scowled. "Stop *parenting* me!"

The *beep* of an incoming message on Azizi's phone saved me the trouble of having to slap my annoying sister across her annoying face. He checked the message and beamed a smile at me. "Auntie Z send her best and wants you to know 'sounds like a decently done job, for a Bloodstone.'"

I chuckled, the tension broken. "Tell Zawadi that she's more than welcome to join me on a hunt if she cares to come out of retirement."

"Ah, I've tried time and again," Azizi said regretfully. "Once made up, her mind is set, I'm afraid. She keeps up with the news, though. Told me the only source she knows of for dwarven chain right now operates out of Latveria."

"Latveria," I mused. "That's an awfully long way from here."

"It could have been an older artifact, perhaps, not newly bought?"

Perhaps, but... "It still begs the question why someone would use it now, though, even if it's not newly forged. I don't see that being the act of a local."

"Nor do I. Auntie Z says the same."

Mihaela frowned and held up a hand. "Hold on. Who is Zawadi?"

"She's a former teammate of Ulysses Bloodstone, and

my aunt," Azizi said, sounding proud. As well he should be – Zawadi was the only one of the monster hunters that our father had run around with in the Fifties who'd had the good sense to get out of the game before she was killed.

I'd been introduced to her by Jacob Hathaway, the son of the man who used to run the Explorer's Club in New York, where Ulysses had met most of his crew. Jacob had been keen to encourage us to get the band back together, so to speak, but Zawadi was happily retired in a lovely house at the border of Wakanda, and I wasn't about to start slowing down. Besides, as today's episode had clearly illustrated, I worked better when I didn't have to worry about anyone but myself.

Zawadi wasn't just anyone, though. She'd gotten her hands on a dose of the famous heart-shaped herb of the Wakandan kings, and, surprisingly, it didn't kill her. With the boost it gave her, she could give me a run for my money in the toughness department. Ulysses had certainly been impressed by her, if his few journal entries that mentioned her were to be believed.

"I can't believe you."

I blinked and looked over at Mihaela, whose body language had gone from slumped and fussy to rigidly furious in the space of a few seconds. "What?"

"You do nothing but denigrate our father to me! Ever since I have met you, it's been one bad word after another about him. But the more I learn about how you do your business, the more I see that everything you have, every connection, every resource, every skill – is the result of *his* hard work! The manor and your butler, your shard, even the few people you call friends – you wouldn't have any of them if it wasn't for him, and yet you use every opportunity you get to decry him." She shoved her chair back violently as she stood up. "You are such a hypocrite!" Then she turned and stomped back into the house, slamming the glass door so hard I was surprised it didn't shatter.

I watched her go, my eyes narrow. Her stiff knee seemed to have loosened up.

"Elsa, Elsa, Elsa." Azizi shook his head and reached for Mihaela's abandoned steak, cutting into it with gusto. "What have you gotten yourself into with this woman?"

"That's a good question." The longer I thought about it, the harder I wondered what was really going on with my half-sister. That she desired the return of her shard more than her own comfort had been obvious from the start, but the more time passed, the more her stability seemed to fracture. Two days ago, in Boston, she had been the picture of cold composure, utterly unflappable. Now, barely forty-eight hours later, she was unable to hang on to her temper.

We weren't going to get along in the slightest if both of us had attitude problems, and I'd already laid claim to that particular personality quirk.

"I can certainly see the resemblance between the two of you, though," Azizi went on, grabbing a pinch of achari and contemplating it between his fingers for a moment before popping it into his mouth.

"What resemblance?" I asked indignantly. "We're absolutely nothing alike!"

Azizi almost choked on his mango, he was laughing so hard. "Are you joking with me?" he demanded once he finally swallowed. "You're so alike, if you dyed your hair and ran forward in time for about thirty-five years, you would be twins! You're both prickly like porcupines, and fierce like honey badgers, and daring like cheetahs–"

"You're not selling me on a safari experience, Azizi, there's no need for all the animal comparisons."

He shrugged, his expression contemplative. "You both dislike being helped, but will accept it if it gets you closer to your goals. You're both very strong in your own ways, and skilled. Neither of you wants to show your soft spots to the other, for fear of being hit there."

"I don't have any soft spots," I said blithely, before biting a prawn in two.

"No person is made of adamantium," Azizi said. "Well, except for–"

"Yeah, he doesn't count," I agreed.

"You have your secrets," he continued. "So, no doubt, does she. I hope that they're secrets truly worth keeping, because I would hate for one of them to get the better of you."

Oh, please. I didn't have any secrets. I was an open book. My entire life was devoted to monster killing, and I did any and everything I could to support my efforts in that direction. Not everything I did was pretty, but I wasn't ashamed of any of it. I didn't hide anything because there wasn't anything to hide. My life was… rather empty, in a way.

Was Mihaela's life empty too?

I shook my head and changed the subject. "Did you get a chance to look at flights heading back to the States? Not that it hasn't been an absolute joy being here, but New York waits for no one."

"Ah." Now Azizi's expression was a bit regretful. "I looked, but a big technology conference downtown is ending tomorrow. All of the direct bookings were taken. There's a chance you'd do better if you tried flying out of Nairobi, but…"

"Technology conference?"

"The East African Robotics Symposium, yes. Rather specialized, but it's grown quite large ever since the Stark Corporation began sponsoring it."

"*EARS*, right, I remember reading something about that." I also happened to have an in with Stark Industries, and I was sick and tired of flying commercial. I pulled out my phone and shot off a quick text. Less than a minute later, I got a reply. "Ah, lovely," I said brightly as I put my phone away again. "No worries, Azizi. Mihaela and I are taken care of for the trip back."

He tilted his head. "Friends in… very fast places?"

"Rather, yes." Hitching rides on old friends' private jets didn't always work out, but in a case like this, where we were already in the same town and I promised I wasn't being pursued by anything eldritch or out for blood, I often got lucky.

After we finished dinner, Azizi left with his payment, my gratitude, and a promise to give his aunt my best. Rather than head inside and have to deal with Mihaela – even if she was already asleep, I knew she'd be lying there judging me, not something I cared to dwell on – I sunk back in my low, reclined beach chair under the stars and listened to the *sizzle-pop!* of the last bits of the popobawa burning down to ash. It was better than any lullaby I could think of. I put my gun in my lap, tucked my knife beneath my head, and fell asleep.

If my dreams were more turbulent than usual, with ghostly visions of my father haunting my every step and questioning my every move, well. At least my irritating half-sister wasn't around to interrogate me about them.

EIGHT

I would never describe myself as petty, but there was something satisfying about walking into the private hangar at the Mombasa International Airport the next day and hearing Mihaela catch her breath as she saw the shining red and gold Stark Industries private jet waiting for us. A steward welcomed us on board, helped us stow our bags without breathing a word about what might be in them, and immediately offered me a glimpse of their expansive tea selection. I picked a hearty Darjeeling and settled in for some overdue weapons maintenance. Mihaela sat down across from me and chose water for herself, declining any offer of food. Had she bothered to eat that morning?

Don't know, don't care. As she'd pointed out, it was clearly none of my business.

First, I read through the information Barnabus had sent me on Samantha Eden. Interesting stuff. I'd had no idea she'd run around with my father for a time, and she was just his type. Blonde and buxom. Then, I took out my cleaning kit and disassembled my Glock, inspecting each piece before and after I'd polished it up for signs of wear. I might die on the end of something's claw someday, but it wouldn't be because my bloody gun jammed at the wrong time.

The stiff-backed pillock sitting across from me shifted slightly. "I'm sorry."

I glanced over at Mihaela. "What was that?"

She huffed a sigh. "I said that I'm sorry, all right? For my behavior last night. I shouldn't have thrown your associations in your face."

No, she bloody well shouldn't have. I could understand why she had, though. "Apology accepted," I said after a moment, and went back to cleaning my gun.

"That easily?"

I snorted. "What, do you expect me to hold it over you for the rest of our expedition? That sounds like a waste of time and energy to me. I burn hot, but I don't hold a grudge." *Not normally, anyway.* "And being told off is hardly the worst thing a member of my family has ever done to me."

She nodded slowly. "You're referring to…"

"The Glartrox incident," I affirmed. "When Cullen turned into a monster that feeds on fear and anger and destroyed the manor in the process. You wouldn't think emotional control is something I excel at, to hear me sometimes, but I'm *exceptionally* good at it. If I'd let myself be angry with the Glartrox while we were fighting, or as an extension of it, Cullen, I might have been overwhelmed. Under circumstances like that, dispassion serves far better than fury or frenzy."

"How do you reconcile it all?" she asked, crossing one leg over the other. She looked oddly young right now, her hair loose and shadowing her face instead of in a tight bun like she'd sported when we first met, her hands soft on her knee. "All the things that have happened to you because of our father, or… or perhaps the things that didn't happen to you, that you're not quite certain about. Adam mentioned it," she added when I glared at her.

Adam was going to get a stern talking-to about appropriate topics of conversation with strange women. Not that my timeline travails were a secret in the super hero community. Frankly, they were hardly unique, but… I shrugged as I took one last look at the Glock, then began to reassemble it. "I don't try to any more. My mind doesn't know fact from fiction when it comes to my past. How much of what I remember happening to me is an implanted memory or a real one? How many of the things that make me the person I am today are a figment of my imagination, nourished by sociopathic forces beyond my control? I don't know, and thinking about it too much would drive me absolutely barmy, so I simply avoid it."

She shifted in her seat. "That sounds hard."

"It was, until I got used to it. Now it's just a way of life."

I put the Glock away and pulled out my shotgun. "What about you? How was it for you, growing up in the shadow of a giant like Ulysses Bloodstone?"

"It was different for me than it was for you," she mused, leaning her head back and gazing out the window. "It was another time, with different… expectations. My mother never had any illusions that our father would marry her – she was a brief stop in his journey across the world, and it didn't seem to bother her." Mihaela smiled for a moment. "My mother married a very understanding man in town right before I was born, so that I wouldn't come into the world without a father. They had two other children together, twin boys, but my mother always treasured me."

So she was the favorite child. Must have been nice. "When did you first meet him?" I asked. "Given that he wasn't around when you were a tot."

"Actually, I met him several times in my childhood. My mother never made a secret of who my real father was, although for my stepfather's sake we didn't speak of it often. He came through our village several times, always on the hunt for monsters. Each time he stopped by, he made a point of seeking me out and speaking to me. I'm not sure how he was so certain I was his, honestly, but he never denied it. He took me hunting once, when I was only five." She glanced at me. "For a deer, not a monster. He tracked it and aimed the gun, but he let me pull the trigger. When we brought it back to the village, I was so proud."

"Sounds idyllic," I murmured.

She laughed dryly. "Nothing was quite as idyllic as we'd been promised under Communism, but yes, we managed well enough for a while. It wasn't until later, when I was nearly grown, that things changed for the worse. There was a border skirmish… a small one, not the kind that makes the news, but it nevertheless cost many lives. My family were all killed." She briefly touched her fingertips to her throat. "I was nearly killed as well."

I wondered what she was remembering right then, as she traced the outline of a violent memory. I'd been damaged so often and recovered so quickly that I scarcely recalled most of my own wounds. Sometimes I wished that the scars had lingered for a while longer – did the experience still count as agonizing if I didn't feel the aftermath of torn muscles and gaping holes for longer than it took me to curse out all my exes? That was another slippery mental slope, and I bit the inside of my cheek to help me focus on what Mihaela was saying.

"I was alone for three days before our father found me. By the time he did, I was so out of my mind that I nearly took my own life. If he hadn't come when he did…" She shivered slightly. "He saved me. He healed me and taught me how to fight back. My training was nothing like as extensive as yours, but by the end of it I could hold my own against things I hadn't even realized existed before that. Before he left, he gave me a bloodstone shard set in a bracelet."

The hand that had been on her throat drifted down to encircle her right wrist. "He told me it was powerful," she said, so softly I could barely hear it even sitting right across from her. "He told me that its power would help keep me safe. And he was right. Other things came, people and monsters, and I evaded them all. I lived the life I wanted to, in the place I loved, and everything was as good for me as I could have hoped."

"Did you never have any desire to reach out to the rest of us?" I asked. I was a little surprised at myself for going there – it wasn't as if I'd wanted an older sibling. Blimey, I barely tolerated my younger sibling, although anyone with working senses could tell that was mostly because he was an epic pain. "You said you've known about me for a long time, back at the beginning of this. Did you never, I don't know... want to get in touch sooner? Compare notes? Because if you had, maybe I could have done something to help you before we got drawn into a trip seeking out moldering bases inhabited by various and sundry things that wish to kill us in faraway places."

"I didn't think you would want to meet me," Mihaela said simply, crossing her legs the other way. "At best I would be a reminder of a man you seem to despise. At worst, you might have perceived me as your enemy and..." Her voice trailed off, but it was too late – I already knew where she was going with this, and I didn't care for it at all.

"At worst I might have, what, succumbed to the lure of picking up another bloodstone shard for myself and offed you for the pleasure of owning it?" I felt mildly disgusted by the very thought of it. "Look, you might put your trinket on a bloody pedestal and think of it as nothing more than a pretty accessory to a normal life, but for me the bloodstone shard changed everything. It vanished any possibility of a normal life for me, and while I don't regret that, I certainly don't have some sort of fetish for hoarding them the way Ulysses did."

"He was trying to get them out of the hands of those who would misuse them," Mihaela argued.

"Was he? Or was he trying to increase his own power by having the most and biggest and best toys around?" I shot back. "He didn't need more shards than the one he already had – it had carried him on its back for thousands of bloody years! Who made him the keeper of all shards? What made him so much better than everyone else looking for them, that it was all right for him to storm around the world taking what he wanted and killing everyone who got in his way? Who says that's not misuse of a shard right there?"

"He killed monsters, not people!"

"Oh, records show that he killed plenty of people," I replied, bitter and not even trying to hide it. "And sometimes that's necessary, I understand that. But the legend of Ulysses Bloodstone is not a story of his mercy, or his benevolence, or his love for all mankind. The legend of our father is one of blood and rage and violence, of an ego the size of his own island, and a death as ignoble as he could be at times. That's what I inherited, Mihaela, and yeah, I like what I do and I'm bloody good at it, but I'm not going to do it like him."

I was absolutely positive on that score. "No more baby Bloodstones from me, no bequeathing my shard to my unsuspecting offspring, no one needing to implant memories of a wretched childhood in someone to motivate them to kill. I can't control what Cullen does," although if he got openly involved with someone who could have children all of a sudden, I'd be terribly suspicious, "but I can control my own actions, and they don't include continuing this for another generation." I smiled, and I didn't know what it looked like, but it was vaguely satisfying to see Mihaela blanch as she looked at me. "After all, who knows, maybe I'll live forever, just like he did. Or wait – not quite forever, but close enough, hmm?"

"I hope you do," Mihaela said, and it was closer to being a curse than a well-wish. Delightful. We were right back where we'd started, practically at each other's throats. She looked out the window and I looked down, finished up my Glock, then went to work on the shotgun, which was a right mess. I shouldn't have left it soaking in ooze after the last fight, but sometimes a lady has to prioritize cleaning up herself over cleaning up her accessories.

Once that was done, I checked my email, just in case Adam or Barnabus had come up with new information about the next mini-base we were trying to find. Nothing. *Bugger.* That meant we still only had generalities to go on.

The Manhattan bar had operated under the name Cliff's

Pink, it had been run by a rather large and intimidating gentleman named Billy Brand, and it had been a place that did business strictly by word of mouth. Seriously, there was no address associated with it, no number, no tax records. Only a handful of recollections from some seriously messed up people – they had to be if they'd frequented that place – had given us anything to go on. In each case it was generally something like, "Man, I don't know, somewhere on Second? Maybe First? I could hear the water from there, it was nice… kinda." Not ideally helpful.

Time to get another local's opinion. I called the last number I had for my least-dislikable contact in New York, Misty Knight. Once a badass NYPD detective, now a bionic-armed super hero who flitted from affiliation to affiliation and occasionally dated men who didn't deserve her, we'd worked together on hunting down a clutch of Brood hatchlings carrying out assassinations. She wasn't squeamish, I'd give her that. Misty and I'd both tried the team approach as well, but, like me, she wasn't really made for taking orders. Unlike me, she preferred to operate in one place: her hometown, New York City. Right now, her knowledge of the city could prove valuable on our hunt.

New York City wasn't a place I cared to frequent more than I had to – too many people in tights and capes living there, often with too much money not to get into trouble. I wasn't hurting for finances myself, but the way some of these heroes threw cash around you'd think they were celebrating the last day of their lives. Which, honestly, I didn't understand. The heroes were fine. Usually.

There was a brief pause, then a *beep*. "This is Misty's phone and you better have a good reason to be on it, because if this is another prank wasting my time, Danny, I will *end* you." *Beep*.

"Aren't you just a ray of sunshine on a dark and cloudy day?" I said lightly after the tone. "It's Elsa. I'm on the hunt for an old bar in Harlem that was associated with my father back in the Sixties and Seventies. The place is called Cliff's Pink, and while I doubt it's still around under that name, I'd appreciate an assist in finding out what it's become, if anything. The sooner the better." If the bloody bar had been bulldozed and turned into a skyscraper it was no skin off my nose, but the way Mihaela was fixating she'd probably insist we dig into the foundation, "just to make sure."

I ended the call and put the phone away, then poured myself another cup of tea and settled in for the long haul. It was another seven hours to New York. Hopefully by then Mihaela would be over herself enough that we could find Cliff's Pink without fighting, because so help me if she couldn't keep her opinions on my life and our father to herself, I would gag her and throw her back to the black ooze on Bloodstone Isle.

NINE

The Big Apple was a sweltering cesspool, the miasma of millions of souls in all their effluvia coming together to coexist in imperfect harmony. Not my favorite spot, no – not as good as Glasgow, that was for certain, not even as pleasant as London could occasionally be – but it had its charms.

One nice side effect of New York was the unexpected revelation that Mihaela's icy calm evaporated when she glimpsed the first poster for a Broadway show. "Oh..." she breathed, putting a hand on her cheek. "I've always wanted to see a performance on Broadway."

"Really? And do you have an extra evening to spare and a thousand dollars for a decent ticket?"

"Oh, *pfft*." She waved a dismissive hand at me. "You think to shock me with price? I know what these things cost. I had a trip all planned out for next spring. Tickets bought, events all planned. I was going to stay at the finest hotels, see all the sights, go to a different show every night. It was going to be glorious."

"Next spring is a long way off," I pointed out. "There's no reason you can't do any or all of those things, whether we're successful with our search for the shards or not."

She glared haughtily at me. "You understand nothing," she snapped, and hailed a taxi. To my annoyance, one pulled over immediately.

The driver was a woman with short blue hair who cracked her gum at us before asking, "Where you ladies wanna go?"

"Second and East 112th," I said.

"You got it." She popped the trunk so we could load our bags in, and a moment later we were on our way.

The cab smelled strongly of cheap air fresheners and watermelon-scented gum, but that was a welcome change from muscatel and gun oil after our plane ride. Mihaela certainly didn't seem to mind it. She'd practically pressed her nose to the window as she stared outside with an expression of wonder, even though all we were seeing for the most part were other cars leaving JFK. The ride along Grand Central Parkway was quite rapid, and before the hour was out, we were pulling up to a nondescript corner in Harlem.

I paid the fare, retrieved our bags, and the cabbie blew us a bubble, then a kiss before driving away. I rolled my eyes, but Mihaela seemed charmed. "What a fascinating place," she said, turning in a circle so she could take in everything around us – buildings, graffiti, broken sidewalks, and cars. And people. Lots and lots of people. *Thrilling*. "Will we see any super heroes while we're here?"

"Only if we're unlucky." Right, then. Time to start pottering around… unless Misty was there to give us a better idea of where to go. I tried her phone again and got shunted to her message immediately.

"Wench," I muttered. Fine. All the data Barnabus had been able to glean about the place suggested it was within a six-block radius of this corner, so a methodical search ought to turn it up. I hoisted my bags over my shoulders. "Let's start looking for a ramshackle old bar buried in Harlem, shall we?"

Perhaps sensing that I was in no mood for extra irritation, Mihaela stayed quiet as we set off down Second. We walked… turned… walked… looked… and walked some more. We walked for two bloody hours over miles of New York sidewalks, lugging our bags around and ignoring catcalls as we searched for our mythical destination, and found *nothing*. Not a sign, not a scrap, not even a memory. No one we spoke with or questioned along the way had ever heard of Cliff's Pink before.

"That's it," I finally snapped. Mihaela was wilting again in the heat, her enthusiasm for New York City drained after an afternoon of utter failure, and even my arms were getting a little tired of hauling my luggage about. "I'm done trying to pull a needle from a haystack."

"Are you going to call your friend again?" Mihaela asked

with a sigh. "It isn't as though she picked up the last four times, but perhaps the fifth will be the charm."

"No," I replied, although that had been my first idea. Fortunately, I thought of something much better. "We're going to the nearest senior center. If I recall, it's two blocks west of here."

"Oh joy," she deadpanned, but dutifully grabbed her suitcase and followed me down the street. After a moment of walking in silence, Mihaela asked, "Wait, did you just say *senior center?*"

"I did indeed."

"That's what I thought. But..."

I glanced over at her. "I'd think you of all people, and as a historian to boot, would understand the need to seek out original sources in order to get the proper perspective on a place or situation. New York City is gentrifying, and fast, but there are plenty of people who remember it the way it was when our father was active here. The easiest place to locate them is a senior center."

"That makes sense." She said it reluctantly, but I perceived a soupçon of a hint of a tremor of admiration there too, which straightened my spine for the last block of our walk.

The senior center was on the left, a brick building with a welcoming sign out front advertising "DAILY BINGO GAMES! $2 BUY-IN!" And weren't we lucky – there was one scheduled for right now.

I marched inside, greeted by the pungent smells of bleach, potpourri, and baked goods. An old lady sat behind a desk at the far side of the lobby, and she looked up as Mihaela and I entered with a smile on her face. That smile slid right off as she took in our general state of dishevelment, not to mention our enormous bags. "Oh dear," she murmured to herself, then called out, "Can I help you ladies?"

I smiled as I headed over. "You certainly can…" I glanced at her nametag. "Myrtle. I'm looking for the bingo game."

"It's, um… it's down the hall and to the right, last two doors, just follow the arrows, but… are you actually here to play bingo?"

"Canny question, Myrtle, and the answer is that while I wouldn't say no to some bingo, I'm here looking for some advice on where to have a good time." Oof, I didn't know a woman of her age could blush so quickly. "Thanks ever so much!" I finished, then turned to Mihaela. "Stay with the bags, if you please. I'll be back momentarily." I shucked mine to the ground, checked to make sure I wasn't forgetting any of my weapons – you could never be sure in New York, not even in a senior center – and strode down the hall toward the sound of spinning balls and a droning voice calling out "B-three. B-three, everyone, that's B… three."

I entered the gaming hall just as the gentleman holding the microphone at the front table looked up. He dropped the mic – literally dropped it – and stared at me as I walked down the center aisle, past tables of two covered with bingo cards and chips and surrounded by whispers.

"Holy smokes…"

"I didn't know ladies came that tall."

"Look at her *shoes!* You could kill a man with those things."

"Ya think she would if I asked her nicely?"

I bent down and picked up the mic, smiled at the gentleman who it belonged to, and said, "I need to borrow this for just one moment, please." He nodded shakily, and I held it up and turned around to face the crowd.

"Ladies and gentlemen," I said smoothly, "I have one simple question for you all and then I promise I'll let you get on with your game."

"No hurry!" someone in the back called out.

"My question is this: does anyone in here know where I might find a bar called Cliff's Pink?" I looked out over the sea of wizened faces, waiting for an answer. "It was run by a man named Billy Brand, also known as William Montague the Third?" I added.

"Billy's place!" a creaky voice in the third row called out. "Why didn't you say so sooner, missy?" A woman of indeterminate age – she could have been anything from seventy to a hundred or more – stood up with the help of a cane. Her hair, thin as it was, was meticulously curled, and she was wearing a cardigan edged with what looked like pictures of…

Ooh, switchblades! And was that a can of pepper spray I saw peeking just out of her purse? This was a lady after my own heart.

"I used to spend my evenings at Billy's," she went on, tottering down the aisle toward me. "The drinks were awful and the music stank, but it was the best place in town to make money hustling pool. I can take you there… for a price," she added, staring slyly at me from behind her spectacles.

I tapped my index finger against my chin. "What do you say I subsidize your next ten games?"

"Twenty bucks? Are you kidding me? I'm on a hot streak right now!" She leaned in, bracing herself on the table with one hand. "Make it fifty games."

"Twenty-five," I countered, because I might need this old lady, but I wasn't about to cut short the fun of negotiating. Besides, all eyes were riveted on her. She would be the queen of gossip in this place after today.

"Forty."

"Thirty."

"Done." She held out her hand and we shook on it. Then she called over her shoulder, "Ling, darling, play my cards for a few minutes, I've got to escort this young lady to a bar."

"Don't get too fresh with her, Phil, I don't wanna have to fight her for you!" an equally ancient lady with huge cats-eye glasses called back.

I laughed. "You are just the person I was looking for." I handed the microphone back to the still-stunned gentleman in front of the rotary cage full of balls. "Lead on, Phil."

"Let's get outta this place first," Phil said.

We made slow but steady progress back to the lobby, where Mihaela and Myrtle were engaged in a battle of unblinking cold stares. As soon as she saw us, Myrtle's glare became a gasp, and she pressed a hand to her chest.

"Philippa Dean, what do you think you're doing with that woman?"

"Oh, take the stick out of your butt, Myrtle," Phil snapped as she creaked toward the front door. "You'd think you've never seen a lady get an offer she couldn't refuse before. I'll be back in a jiff."

"You can't honestly be thinking of going with these... these... people! They just walked in like they owned the place and left their luggage here!" Myrtle looked somewhere between concerned and outraged. "What if they lead you astray?"

Phil just cackled as she hobbled out onto the sidewalk. Mihaela glanced questioningly at me, but I shook my head and shouldered my bags again. We followed Phil outside and turned toward the river.

"Cliff's Pink, Cliff's Pink," she muttered, meandering a bit as she made her way down the sidewalk but managing to avoid outright running into something. "Strange place. Why do you want to find it?"

"It's a point of family interest," I said.

"Family interest, huh?" She turned to look at me. "You related to Billy?"

"No."

"Huh. Ulysses, then?"

Well, that was nearly enough to make my jaw drop. "You knew him?" Mihaela asked before I could.

"Oh, everybody who ever entered the place knew about Ulysses Bloodstone. Billy was a big man, and scary when he was sober, but get him drunk and soon enough he'd be waxing rhapsodic about how tight he was with Ulysses, how he was helping him hunt monsters, all that manly crap." She snorted. "Only thing Billy ever went on the prowl for was the ladies. Caught most of 'em, too, except for the ones I snagged first."

I grinned at her. "You were a smooth operator in your youth, then?"

She cackled. "Like you wouldn't believe. Till I met Ling, at any rate. Then I got on the straight and narrow, quit hanging at Cliff's Pink and made myself respectable. Good thing, too – the bar didn't last long after Ulysses bought the farm."

"Bought what farm?" Mihaela asked in confusion.

"It's just a saying," I replied. "It means he died."

"Oh." A second later she asked, "Why didn't the bar last after that?"

"Money, I'm sure. Without Ulysses payin' to rent the backroom, Billy couldn't afford to keep the place. No surprise, given what a hole it was. And speaking of holes…" Phil stopped in front of an alley that we'd passed before, a narrow thing barely wide enough for two people to walk side by side. "It's down at the end here, on the left."

"Past the garbage?"

She peered down the alley. "Past the first pile of garbage, not quite as far as that second heap. Mind the rats. They were nasty back in the day, and I can't imagine they've gotten much nicer since then. Now." She thrust out a hand, and I dutifully handed over three twenty-dollar bills. Phil chortled and stuffed the money up the sleeve of her cardigan. "Not bad for five minutes' work," she said.

"Not bad at all. Thanks, Phil."

She left, and Mihaela turned to watch her go with an expression of concern. "Should one of us escort her back?" she asked quietly. "Just to make sure she gets there all right?"

"She was well prepared for trouble, Mihaela. I daresay Phil can take care of herself," I replied. The buildings that created this alley were so tall that the light appeared murky, an appearance not helped by the swarm of black flies buzzing around the piles of trash. Walking down it would be like entering an entirely new environment, one so pungent that you could practically taste the smell of it. *Delightful.*

Surprisingly, Mihaela took the lead, ignoring the filth and smell with the dogged determination of a woman with a goal. I followed her, pulling out my Glock just in case one of the rats decided to get fresh.

"Here," Mihaela called, stopping a few moments later in front of a door that had been partially boarded over. The door was set a foot deep in the middle of a scuffed brick entryway, and on the wall above it was the faded outline of a sign – painted right on the wall, so posh – that read "Cliff's Pink" in big block letters. "Here it is."

"Just as prepossessing as promised." My phone rang, and

I immediately pulled it out and snapped, "Lord, woman, what took you so long?"

"Oh, am I supposed to be at your beck and call? I don't think so," came the response from Misty Knight. I smiled despite myself.

"Out on the beat?" I asked playfully.

"I'm not a detective any more, which I think you know, Elsa. Can we get to the point of your call now?"

I frowned. "Who died and took away all your sense of fun and surprise?"

Misty sighed. "Look, it's been a long day and it's about to get longer. There's an infestation in the sewers–"

"Blimey, another one?" I demanded. "What, does New York City rent out its sewers to any villain who can pay? Do they give guided bloody tours? 'Best place to raise Brood down this way, best place to turn into an evil lair coming up on your right'?"

"It's not that bad." There was a pause. "OK, it's kind of that bad, especially this time around. Apparently, a scientist at Cornell–"

"Was it a *mad* scientist?" A few feet away I heard Mihaela huff and begin to tap her toe, but I ignored her.

Misty made an "eh" sound. "I mean, I'm sure he wouldn't call himself that–"

I scoffed. "They never do."

"Will you stop interrupting me?" Misty snapped. "The point is some guy was doing illegal genetic research on a bunch of different animals and got caught. He was fired from his job at Cornell, but he secreted some of the embryos away and went on to raise them in the sewers, whereupon they got out of control, ate him, and began a reign of terror under the streets. Seriously, with some of the things sticking their heads up out of manholes these days, it's enough to make you miss the rats."

Not bloody likely. "And how did you get on sewer duty?" I asked.

"I'm on a private contract for the city. They hired a bunch of us to handle different zones. They don't want to send regular exterminators down there. The first nip from an octo-puffer would put one of them down."

"I'm sorry, did you say 'octo-puffer'?"

Mihaela rattled the door, and I turned to glare at her and make a *ssshhhh* motion with my finger over my mouth. She glared right back, pointing at the door to Cliff's Pink. I rolled my eyes and looked away again.

"Yeah, the guy was researching chimerism and successfully created a whole bunch of freaky hybrids. The octo-puffer is the least weird of the whole shebang, trust me." There was a brief burst of gunfire, then she added, "It's still plenty weird, though. The thing is *huge* when it puffs up, but flexible like an octopus, and it can – OK, it's working up to another attack. Are you going to tell me what you want or not?"

"Well, I was originally calling to get help locating an old bar called Cliff's Pink in Harlem, but a friendly local octogenarian showed us the way here."

She latched on to the worst part of that statement fast. "'Us'? Who is 'us'?"

I sighed. "Myself and a client named Mihaela Zamfir, the target of a recent theft."

"Since when do you concern yourself with petty thieves?"

"Since they come armed with semi-automatic rifles and target people bearing bloodstone shards," I replied.

"Huh. Interesting." Misty sounded thoughtful. "But you've still got yours?"

I smiled sharply. "What do you think?"

"I think if you didn't have your shard, it would probably be because you were dead."

Aw, she knew me so well.

"Listen," Misty went on, "I know where Cliff's Pink is, and let's just say there's a good reason the place is deserted. It's supposed to be chock full of booby traps. Give me another hour to clean up here and then I'll meet you there, all right? It can't hurt to have backup going in–"

Whatever else she was going to say was cut off by the sudden screech of the door being forced open behind me. I whirled around and saw Mihaela vanishing through the doorway, her bag forgotten on the ground. "That minger," I growled. "Misty, I'm going to have to get back to you, I've got an AWOL civilian who's going to get herself blown up if she's lucky."

"And if she's not lucky?"

"Then I'll shoot her fool head off her shoulders myself."

"Don't go getting arrested for murder when I'm not in a position to… *Uh-oh–*"

Bang-bang-bang-bang-bang. A moment later, the line went dead.

TEN

I wasn't worried about Misty. She was the archetype of the no-nonsense badass and she had a Stark-made, multi-function bionic arm that gave her the physical chops to be a super hero. No octo-puffer would be taking her down today, but an unnoticed booby trap might certainly do Mihaela in if I didn't get after her fast. I shoved my phone into my pocket, grabbed my shotgun out of my weapons bag, then tossed a few moldering sacks of trash on top of our luggage to hide it from idle passersby. "Good enough," I muttered, then headed down the dark hallway with my shotgun in one hand, flashlight in the other.

"Mihaela, you daft mare!" I shouted down the way. "What do you think you're doing?"

"You were taking too long," she called back to me. "Come look at this!"

"Don't touch anything." I stepped carefully, keeping an

eye out for tripwires or pressure plates. Just because she'd made it to the end of the hall without triggering something didn't mean there was nothing there. A few seconds later I joined her at the actual entry to the bar, where thankfully she'd stopped to stare instead of pressing on.

"Look," she exclaimed, shining her flashlight all around. "It's like stepping into a time machine."

It was, in a way… if that time machine was set for a dirty, back-alley bar in the 1970s when beige and rust were considered the height of décor, the most popular beers were Coors and Miller Lite, and half the lighting came in the form of neon zigzags spelling various booze brand names out on the walls. There was a heavy layer of dust on every table and stool, and the air was so thick it tickled the back of my throat.

"Magnificent," I managed before sneezing so hard my hair hit the ceiling. "Look, this place is reputed to be booby trapped. Misty asked us to wait outside for her to show up before taking a look."

Her jaw firmed pugnaciously. "But we're already here," she pointed out in the kind of slow, overly reasonable voice that likely meant she was holding back numerous swear words. "I'm sure we can be careful enough to avoid any problems. Besides, do you want to wait however long it will take for your friend to get here to look around?"

That last point was the kicker. I was bored verging on stroppy, and I *was* rather good at detecting booby traps. "Fine, but don't touch anything," I told her. "And watch where you step. If you hear a click or see a light or–"

"*Durere bun*, you're as bad as my mother," Mihaela muttered as she took a step into the main room.

"And you're as foolish as our brother," I told her, easing past her with slow, measured steps. Nothing so far. I moved the flashlight in a slow, wavering arc in front of me, up and down as I went, up and down, looking for any spot where it caught the light differently – there. A tripwire. I knelt down and examined it for a moment, gauging where it led to and what sort of trap it might deploy. Gas was unlikely – not the style of a man who'd built his reputation on being big enough to haul troublemakers out with the trash. It was probably rigged to some sort of projectile, but from where…

"Ah." I had it. I shooed Mihaela back a few feet, checked one more time to make sure I had the trajectory right, then triggered the trap with a shove from the end of my shotgun.

Pwing! A second later a decent-sized crossbow bolt flew across the room, right at eye level. I watched it embed itself in the far wall – it got several inches deep into the brick. That was far too much tension for that wire to maintain for so long. "Good quality," I murmured, standing up straight and raising my light again. "Right, well, this will be pretty easy if they're all like that," I told Mihaela, whose eyes were wide in the dim light. "Very Indiana Jones."

"Who?"

"Indiana… Never mind, just keep looking. And don't trigger anything without bloody telling me first."

We methodically canvassed the rest of the front room, avoiding several more crossbow bolts, a spring trap that hurled the lovechild of a bouncy ball and a prickly pear cactus on a wild careen that I stopped with a gentle tap from my shotgun, and a device that abruptly dropped the big wooden beam crossing the ceiling down, smashing several tables to bits. "Good lord," I coughed, waving a hand in front of my face as a cloud of dust rose up. "Billy Brand was rather vociferously protective of his property, wasn't he?"

Mihaela wasn't coughing. Mihaela's eyes were riveted on the door behind the bar, her hands twitching with eagerness. "Then there must be something here to be protective of," she said. "We need to find out what."

"It could be nothing," I warned her. "Brand was a friend of Ulysses', which meant he was inevitably the paranoid type. This might have been his alarm system every single night, not just for special occasions."

"But we don't know that. We need to get into the back room. That is where he was rumored to keep our father's weapons, correct?"

"Something like that."

"And there are no more traps to trigger in here," she continued. "We have been very thorough. We need to go back there." She stepped forward, her hand reaching for the doorknob.

"Ah-ah-ah, ladies first," I said, hip-checking her hard enough to make her stumble before I grabbed the knob myself.

"I am a lady!" she said indignantly.

"On rare occasions, I suppose," I replied, holding up a hand to silence her umbrage. "Let's see what we have here."

It would be keeping in character for the door itself to be booby trapped. I turned the knob slowly, listening for any change in tone, feeling for any clicks or sticking points. Nothing. It moved smoothly, without a sound. I opened the door wide enough to see inside and looked for any kind of tripwire or attachment that could cause trouble. Nothing.

"Are you finished yet?"

"Are we there yet?" I replied in a whiny, childish voice, just for the pleasure of hearing her huff. "And I'd like to remind you that I'm taking all these bloody precautions for your benefit, all right? I'm not the one who's going to die if something shoots me through the heart or electrocutes me or crushes me – give me a bit of time to heal up and I'll be right as rain. *You* are the squishy one here, so unless you've suddenly developed a sense of caution and have decided to wait outside, I suggest you shut it."

She shut it. I finished my check, took a step back and to the side, and pushed the door open with the butt of the shotgun.

Nothing. Not a sound. Despite my thorough check, that was rather surprising. "Hmm."

"Now can we go in?" Mihaela didn't bother to wait for my assent, and simply stepped up and inside, her flashlight bouncing off the walls like light from a disco ball. How could she even see what she was illuminating when she flicked that thing around so fast?

"Anything interesting?" I drawled, stepping up behind her and looking around for more traps. I didn't see anything. Odd. I took a deep breath, then another, and realized another odd thing. The air in here was startlingly... *clean*. That was particularly strange considering there was a trapdoor in the floor that in all likelihood led down to the sewers. It was so like Ulysses to give himself an extra way out of wherever he happened to be.

"Where... where is everything?" Mihaela took another few steps into the room, still swinging her flashlight around like she was trying to see everything all at once. "This was his base, there should be weapons here, there should be *things*, pieces of equipment – I don't..."

I stepped up beside her and took my own slower, more fulsome look. The room was maybe eight by twelve feet, and apart from a scuffed wooden counter and a set of empty shelves in the corner, there was nothing there. Not weapons, not equipment, and definitely not a bloodstone shard.

"Can't say I'm surprised." Next to me, Mihaela quivered like a puppy in a thunderstorm, so full of emotion that she couldn't keep it all locked in. Now would probably be a good time for me to shut up. Of course, I rarely followed my own good advice. "It's not like we found anything at any of the last three places."

"But this one is different!" she insisted tremulously. "It

isn't built in the middle of nowhere, it's in one of the largest cities in the world! And all those traps, all that work – why would Billy do that if he wasn't guarding something?"

"I told you: paranoia. People who ran in the same circles as Ulysses Bloodstone didn't last long without a hearty sense of self-preservation, and that meant taking precautions that might seem ... excessive to the average person."

"But it isn't ... Wait." She took another step forward, something catching her eye. "What's that?"

I couldn't see what she was looking at, but my instincts told me it was bad news. This whole place was bad news. "Whatever it is, leave it alone. We need to get out of here."

"We just *got* here."

"Yes, but I don't think we're the only ones to have been here recently." It was too clean in here, compared to the front room. There wasn't enough dust, none of the sediment that should have settled to the floor after being so long neglected. The trapdoor in the middle of the room was worn, but the hinges at the side of it were suspiciously shiny. "We need to leave."

"In a moment." She reached for something small and black at the back of the lowest shelf. I didn't even know how she'd spotted it, but I didn't trust it.

"Mihaela, don't–"

She picked it up, and all of a sudden the room became so loud that I literally *saw* the sound, a blinding whiteness instantly blanketing my vision like I'd gotten a faceful of arterial spray. The noise came from all around us, brutally high-pitched sonic cannons set in the walls that I hadn't seen – that neither of us had seen. I should have. Blast it, I should have, but now wasn't the time for recriminations. Racked with a mind-searing headache, I reached for Mihaela, who'd doubled over with her hands covering her ears. *We have to get out of here.*

Too late, I realized that the sound was more than a weapon; it was a countdown. *Three... two... one...*

BOOM!

An explosion rocked the world around me, shattering the walls and cracking the ceiling right down the center. I ducked and covered just in time to take a heavy-duty crossbeam across my shoulders instead of the back of my neck, which was fortunate. It took for-bloody-ever to heal a broken neck, minutes that I certainly didn't have right now.

The weight of it drove me almost flat to the floor, but I managed to stay on my knees. This steel beam, big as it was, was probably the central one going over the room. If I held it up, then it might not crush Mihaela. If she wasn't crushed already.

More debris rained down around me, bricks and ancient insulation and broken bits of wiring. *Please don't let the whole wretched building come down on us.* That would take forever to dig out of, and I didn't have the time to deal with the fallout that would come from destroying an ancient apartment building in New York City.

At least the pestilential sound cannons had stopped, though. Gradually the patter and ting of more pieces of rubble falling into the room faded away, until I was fairly confident that nothing else was going to join the mess that was already covering me.

Pop. Pop. Crinkle. My back was trying to put itself together again, ribs wanting to return to their grooves along the spine, but the beam was simply too heavy for them to move into the right place. I needed to find a way to put it down, but first I needed to learn whether my sister was still alive.

"Mihaela?" My first attempt was barely audible, my lungs being rather squashed at the moment. I coughed and forced myself to inhale more deeply. "Mihaela! You there?"

"I'm… I'm here," she murmured after a few moments of unnerving silence. "I'm all right, I think, a bit bruised, but… not too bad."

"Lucky girl," I said, gritting my teeth against a groan. "Got your flashlight available?"

"It must be here somewhere… why?"

"Because I need to you find out whether you're in the path of this bloody big metal beam I'm currently holding up on my back before I try to move it."

"Oh… *oh!*" I heard her shuffling around in the wreckage, feeling for her light. "I'm sorry, I… Yes, I have it!" There was a *click*, and after another moment of fumbling she said, "Doamne Dumnezeu."

"Is that Romanian for 'oh ruddy world, I'm about to be squashed'?"

"Something like that. Yes, it's right there above me."

"Right." Good to know. "Can you get out from beneath it?"

I heard her shift and shuffle, moving herself from side to side as she tried to relocate. "No, there's too much around me. I can't push it out of the way because it just compresses against more debris."

This day just kept getting better and better. I couldn't see Mihaela because of the debris, so I'd have to take her word on the reality of her situation. "Right, I'll just try to... move this... over."

I straightened my arms and did my best to get my feet under me, but the beam was so big I didn't have any leverage on it. Instead of being able to tip it one way or the other and use that repositioning as an aid, it seemed to be intent on squashing me straight down, without any wiggle room lengthwise. Side to side was no better – the beam was quite wide, and the rest of the debris was quite thick. I could roll it a few inches in either direction, but once it took up that space it got stuck again and supporting it at a slant was even worse than holding it up flat-on.

"So, bad news," I managed to gasp after a few failed attempts to get the beam over. "There's no place for this to go other than straight down. You need to dig out from under it, quick."

There was silence for a long moment before Mihaela said, in a small voice, "Are you sure?"

Oh, unholy irritating existence, am I... "Yes, I'm quite sure," I gritted out. "Time to get a move on. There's a limit to how long I'll be able to keep this up, and if you're not out from under it by the time that limit comes, then you're pancake batter."

It was blunt, but nothing that wasn't true. A second later I heard her start scratching at the debris, vigorously enough that I swallowed my urge to shout at her to hurry up. I tried to steady myself to wait, but it was hard.

God, I hated enclosed spaces like this, being trapped in a tight spot with nowhere to go and nothing to do except wait for someone else to fix the problem while knowing that if I couldn't hold out, it wasn't just them who would be squashed into jam. I'd been nearly killed in lots of ways, but never by being smashed flat before. I wasn't at all sure that was the sort of thing I could recover from.

Aside from that, I was offended by this entire stupid situation. Other people didn't fix my problems, I fixed theirs! That was the way it was supposed to go, the way it had gone for practically my entire life. My memories might be a jumbled mess, but in all of them, real or false or whatever they were, I looked out for myself. It didn't pay to rely on someone else – it *never* paid to rely on someone else, other people would only disappoint you. I couldn't trust them, not enough to let them in, not really. Not my mother, not Adam, certainly none of my devil-may-care boyfriends. Teammates came and went, and the only person I could trust to do anything for me was… well, myself.

My phone began to ring. "Oh, hateful thing," I groaned. The phone was in my pocket and would require me to lift a hand to pull it out. If I lifted a hand off the ground right now, this beam might get the better of me. If it got the better of me, that would mean a fatal end for Mihaela at the very least.

Odds were, this phone call was coming from Misty right now. If she was calling to cancel on me... no, I needed to take this. "Are you out yet?" I asked Mihaela.

"Not yet," she said tersely. "Give me a few more minutes."

"No time for that." The call would go to voicemail soon. I had to get it now. "Don't worry," I said, then picked up my right hand and reached into my pocket.

"Why would I wo... *whoa!*" The beam shuddered precariously, pushing down like someone had just stacked a few more thousand pounds on top of it in the time it took me to jerk my phone out of my pocket. I accepted the call, then got my hand back under me and, swearing every inch of the way, lifted the beam back up to its starting position.

"Elsa, what is going on?" Misty barked. "Didn't I tell you to be careful of booby traps? The whole building looks compromised!"

"Then evacuate it and get your bloody arse in here to help me," I snarled. "Billy Brand's traps were nothing, but someone newer put high explosives in the back room. If I don't get help in the next few minutes Mihaela and I will be flattened."

I could practically hear her switch over to cop mode. "Evacuation is already in progress. I'm right outside the door in the alley. What's the best way for me to get to you?"

"That route is probably well and truly wrecked." There was another way into this back room, though. It was covered with debris, but Misty had a super-strong arm. If anyone could punch a way into here, it was her. "There's a sewer route that comes up right next to us, though."

Misty sighed. "Good thing I didn't bother stopping for a shower. I'll be there in five." She ended the call, and I began a countdown in my head. Five minutes. I could handle five more minutes of this, absolutely. I'd handled so much worse over the course of my career: bullets through every major organ including the brain, being stabbed and impaled a hundred different ways, excessive fire, egregious water, attempted cannibalism, zombies... Doing an Atlas impression for another few minutes was nothing.

It didn't feel like nothing at the moment, though. It felt like endless pressure putting cracks through every vertebra in my back, sending shivers of pain and weakness down my legs and arms. I hated feeling weak, hated it almost as much as I hated my father, and right now there was no escaping it. The tremors racking my limbs got worse and worse, nerves either flaring with pain or giving up and simply snapping. Tendons began to let go in my shoulders, and both of my kneecaps made a hard to hear but easy to feel *crunch* as they broke into a dozen pieces, crushed by my inescapable burden.

I might have been groaning. I might have been screaming for all I knew. I was trying desperately hard not to focus on me but to redirect to the world around me, anything to take me away from my own failing body. I heard the creaks and groans of the building above us, things shifting that had no business moving about. Mihaela was still clawing desperately at the debris surrounding her, trying to make a hole for her fragile body. Then she began to... sing.

I didn't know what she was saying, I didn't speak Romanian and she wasn't translating, but the tune was soft and soothing, the words spoken in a hushed, gentle tone. I could barely hear her over the noise of her banging about, trying to make room to slide over, but it was good to have something new to focus on. Misty was coming, and I could do this until then. Or at least until the song stopped.

The song didn't stop, though. It just lilted on and on until suddenly a crash sounded in the room from a few feet away. I lifted my shuddering head to see the edge of the trapdoor virtually explode, sending a new cloud of debris into the air. A moment later a gold-colored, metallic hand appeared over the edge of it, and a second after that Misty hoisted herself into the room, right in front of me. Even through my wavering vision, she looked just as I remembered – her hair formed a dark corona around her head, framing her lovely but stern face, and her red jumpsuit was still vivid despite the layer of slime and dust that was caked here and there.

"Damn, girl," she said, quiet for a moment as she looked at me before glancing around. "Where's the tourist?"

"Over here, and I'm *not* a tourist," Mihaela squawked indignantly.

"Please, you're doing the equivalent of a ridealong with a beat cop right now – you're a tourist." Misty plunged her super-strong arm into the rubble between us and Mihaela, and a moment later pulled my sister through. Mihaela was similarly dusty, but as unharmed as she'd said.

"Get… her… out of here," I managed between gasps for breath.

"Got it. One sewer special, coming right up." Before Mihaela could disagree, Misty grabbed her and lowered her, feet first, down through the trapdoor. "Don't step in the octo-puffer!" she called down, then looked back at me. "How do you wanna do this, Elsa?"

"Can you take the weight?" I asked, not truly looking for a yes but hopeful all the same.

"Nah, not without better leverage," came the expected answer. Misty's bionic arm was super-strong, but the rest of her body wasn't. "You think there's enough in the way to give you a few seconds before it comes down?"

"I… have no… bloody… clue…"

"Let me make sure of it." She leaned over and heaved various bits and pieces of building into a row on either side of me. "All right. You're gonna hit the floor, the beam will hit the blocks, and I'll pull you into the sewer before they give out."

I chuckled. Blood dripped out along with my saliva. "That's… your… plan? Tr'ble…"

"It's not like you've got a better option coming at you right now," Misty pointed out. "You're about to give, girl.

On three, OK? One." She moved herself to the edge of the trapdoor. "Two." She held out her arms, ready to catch me as I fell. "Three!"

I dropped, and the beam dropped with me. Not *all* the way, though, not quite. First it impacted on the thick wood and heavy bricks and chunk of concrete that Misty had dug up from somewhere, and those were indeed just enough to hold it up long enough for her to pull ninety-five percent of my body through.

The last five percent, my right ankle and foot, were smashed on the way through the trapdoor, but I barely felt it with all the adrenaline coursing through my body. A second later Misty laid me flat on my back on the slimy bricks beneath us, the sewer lit up by a combination of flashlight and lantern. The surface beneath me felt oddly soft, but I was too preoccupied with my body's efforts to rebuild itself to care why at the moment.

The pain was so hideous that I didn't have the words to describe it, not in a way that would make sense to anyone without a healing factor. It was as though every broken bone in my body was like a jelly donut that had been squished flat. Those parts all needed to refill, and the jelly had to come from *somewhere*. That source was partly magical, thanks to the bloodstone shard, but it also used every last scrap of me that it could get away with to help things along.

Five minutes after Misty had put me down, my broken bones were healed, I was thirsty enough to drain an entire bar, and so bloody hungry I could barely think straight.

"Here." Misty handed me a protein bar as I sat up, panting as all of my ribs finally slid back into place. I tore into it, ravenous, and downed the whole thing in three enormous bites. She handed me another without blinking, then turned to look at Mihaela. "You hungry too? I've got more."

"I'm fine, thank you," Mihaela said, looking at me as though I were some sort of odd zoo animal she was puzzled by. She was filthy, completely coated with a layer of brick and plasterboard dust, and was sitting back on her hands like she couldn't quite believe we were out of there.

"More," I managed, and Misty handed over another two before the gnawing ache in my stomach finally began to recede. "Water?"

"Yes, but only this once," she chided me as she handed over a water bottle. "I'm not your momma."

I drained the water in one long go, then smacked my lips and breathed a sigh of relief. "Too bad," I said with a grin. "I can think of plenty of people who could use your style of tough love."

She rolled her eyes. "I know too many people like that already, Elsa. Don't send me your scraps."

"So." I glanced overhead as the last rumbles and tumbles finally came to a stop. "Did the building collapse? Am I going to have to become a fugitive from the law?"

"I think we'd know by now if the building collapsed all the way. No street in this city is good enough to keep all *that* from smashing us," she replied. "And I don't think we have to bring you into it. Authorities have known for a long time that Cliff's Pink was down here and needed to be taken care of by professionals. They try to stick that on you, you could chalk it up to gross mismanagement on their part, so… you're probably in the clear."

"Lovely." I never enjoyed getting into legal battles if I could help it. They were so much more boring than regular battles.

"That said, what was that?" She pointed up toward the trapdoor. "You're the last person I'd have thought would go setting off a bunch of old explosives like some sort of rookie."

Oh, the misconceptions, they burned. "Firstly, those were not *old* explosives," I said. "The old traps were easy both to find and disarm, and none of them were especially explosive. The explosives were placed by someone far more recently, someone who I suspect bypassed the bar and came straight up through that trapdoor."

"Huh. Explains why the hinges opened so smoothly," Misty allowed. "Still, that doesn't explain you setting them off. Didn't you check for–"

"That was my fault." Mihaela coughed self-consciously into her hand. "I, ah… I was perhaps not as careful as I should have been. I saw something on a shelf and I picked it up without stopping to check what it was."

Misty looked at her with an incredibly unimpressed expression. "And what was it?"

"Some sort of remote detonator. I grabbed it, heard a

click, and then…" She waggled her hands beside her head. "Noise. Painful noise, and then the explosions."

"Hm." Misty looked at me, and I could tell she was thinking the same thing.

"Yeah, the noisemakers were rather rude, but we probably wouldn't have survived without them sounding a countdown," I said.

She frowned. "Weird."

"Quite," I agreed.

Mihaela glanced between us, clearly not following. "What do you mean?"

"Why bother with the sonic blasts?" Misty said. "Why not just blow the place up and kill you both quickly? No warning, just *BAM* and then, well… jam."

"I'd have survived it," I said waspishly. If I told myself that enough times, then perhaps it would even be true.

"Maybe. Still would have sucked. But with the noise coming at you first, you were already on alert."

I nodded. "There was a *literal* countdown in there, among all the clamor."

"There you have it. Somebody is toying with you. They want you to survive."

That was the same conclusion I had come to, and I liked it even less than a straight-up murder attempt. I was *not* put on this earth to give tacky would-be assassins chuckles. "How comforting," I snarked. "Yes, there's nothing like a good old near-death experience to get the blood pumping. I always like to thank my enemies for those clarion moments."

"Don't front, you do, girl."

Well… "Maybe."

Misty scoffed. "No 'maybe' about it."

"Excuse me," Mihaela interrupted loudly. She wiped at the dust coating her left cheek, grimaced as she realized her hand was covered in slime, and glared at me. "So you're saying we were beaten to the strike again. Someone got here before us, took whatever might have been left of Ulysses' cache, and left traps for us. *Again.*"

"It's 'beaten to the punch' and yes, that's precisely what I'm saying," I replied.

Her scowl was very nearly lethal. "This is ridiculous."

"Yes," I said, as patiently as I could manage under the circumstances. "That's what I've been trying to tell you."

"No! It is not our goal which is ridiculous, it is the fact that we are too late *every time!*" She punched one hand into the other as she shouted the last part. "There must be a way to find these places faster."

I shrugged. "Not unless you've got a time machine to let you see Ulysses build the bloody bases."

"That is *not* what I meant!" Mihaela shouted.

Misty held up her hand. "Ladies," she said, her voice hard. "It's been great and all, freeing you from certain death, but I can't sit around here all evening and listen to you fight. I've still got a job to do."

"Lord, you haven't finished off that octo-puffer *yet*?" I marveled. "Is your age finally catching up with you?"

She pointed a finger at me. "First off, I will happily smack you into the sludge, don't think I won't. Second, I *did* finish the octo-puffer. What do you think you're lying on?"

Ah, that explained the squishy, soft layer beneath us, then.

"But it wasn't the last one of these critters out there, not by a long shot, and I get paid by the head." Misty stood up and brushed off her jumpsuit. "So if you're feeling better, then I need to get back to work." She cocked a hip. "Unless you're feeling up to a hunt, that is."

Was *I* feeling up to a monster hunt, after nearly being pulverized by thousands of pounds of building, contemplating not only my own death but the death of the woman who'd dragged me into this whole mess in the first place? Was *I* feeling up to a monster hunt, after losing my favorite guns and crushing my fabulous boots so badly I'd have to break the heels off just to walk in a straight line? Was *I*, Elsa Bloodstone, feeling up to a monster hunt?

Did the sun rise in the east, barring alien and/or supernatural forces messing with it?

I smiled my prettiest, most shark-like smile. "Darling, I thought you'd never ask."

ELEVEN

"I need to get some gear from the alley up there, but after that I'm all yours," I continued, then turned to look at Mihaela. "Don't feel constrained to join us. You can go and get a hotel and wait for me to–"

"Absolutely not." Her voice was swift and sure. "For all I know, you will get crushed by another building and leave me with no leads to follow."

"I beg your pardon, but this building falling on us was entirely *your* fault," I pointed out.

"No," she said, "it was the fault of whoever put the explosives there in the first place."

She had something with that, not that I was going to let her know I agreed with her about anything.

"And I am sorry for my part in it," she added, "but right now you are my only chance at recovering my bloodstone shard. I can't risk you getting hurt." *Or leaving me behind,* the unspoken words went, but I read them as clear as day off her face, dusty as it was.

"Well, I guess you might not be completely useless," Misty said, not exactly putting a shine on it – but then, that had never been her way. "Even if you are a tourist."

"I wanted to be an *actual* tourist," Mihaela said, a little mournfully. "Now I will never be able to come here without thinking 'Boom, bang, crash!' It's going to ruin this place for me."

"Not if you go hear the New York Philharmonic play the *1812 Overture*," I suggested.

She swatted me on the arm, which was utterly uncalled for. I was just trying to be nice! I refrained from swatting her back – I was apparently more mature than a woman in her sixties – and reached down to my shoes, snapping off both heels before I had a chance to regret it. "I'm going to have to go shopping before I leave this bloody town," I muttered. Actually... "Give me a moment to place a call home and get my backup guns," I said to Misty.

She heaved a sigh. "Fine, but hurry it up. I've probably already lost out on the snake-bear because I detoured to save your ass."

"Yes, yes, keep flogging that dead horse until it turns into a zombie and tries to eat your face off."

"Get my bag too," Mihaela called out as I headed down the tunnel to the nearest manhole.

"Not your maid," I called back.

I ended up getting it for her, though, because I was

such a sucker. I arranged for Adam to overnight me a bag containing a few things I might be needing in the upcoming days, as well as some things I'd *definitely* be needing, like another pair of my custom boots. Then I grabbed my second-favorite shotgun out of my weapons bag and enough ammunition to take down an octo-puffer, a snake-bear, and whatever other deranged hybrids that villainous scientist had released into the wild. I gave Mihaela an adorable pair of pistols, handed over her bag, and we followed Misty north through the sewers, taking guidance from the radio attached to her belt that was calling out tips.

"–lion at the intersection of Odell and Powell, I repeat, reports of a bee-lion buzzing beneath the intersection at Odell and Powell."

"A bee-lion?" *Good grief.* "What on earth is the point of that sort of mix? One is a pollinator, the other a predator. What would they eat? How would they reconcile all those conflicting instincts?"

"Having gone up against some of these already, I think I can safely say that the guy who designed these things wasn't thinking much beyond 'big, fast, aggressive'," Misty replied. We were only a few blocks away from the location of the reported chimera, and I could now hear the buzzing myself. "Here's the play, ladies: shoot the stupid thing if you can, and don't get in my way."

"Lovely plan," I said. "So succinct, so clear. Allow me to make an addendum." I hoisted my shotgun and stalked past her. "Don't get in *my* way."

If there was one good thing I could point to about New York City, it was that they'd really stepped up their infrastructure game. Blimey, the place got rebuilt so frequently they were pretty much forced to update it on a regular basis, and the sewers were no exception. They were surprisingly spacious, with walkways on either side to keep travelers out of the filth in the center. The walls were concrete, not crumbling brick or piles of bones, or piles of bones shoved *into* a bunch of crumbling bricks, like some of the places I'd been. There were even reinforced ladders leading in and out of every manhole, making it shockingly easy to get from place to place.

Of course, all these amenities were why the baddies liked the sewers as well, and allowed the mad scientist's animal experiments far more room to maneuver than would have been ideal. Still, the bee-lion wasn't all that bad, as long as you stayed away from the stinger. Once I perforated its wings so that it had to land, Misty ran in and hit it with a concussive blast straight to the face. The bee-lion dropped like a rock, and she finished the job a few seconds later.

"Up for another?" Misty asked once she was done radioing our success in.

"Please, this was just a warm-up," I replied. "Bring it on."

I wasn't often given to regretting my choice in words – I had too much respect for my own judgment for that – but in this case, I had come on perhaps a bit strong. The next animal was one that was far better adapted to a watery environment, and had more teeth in its long, dangerous jaws than I'd ever seen in a monster in my life.

"Who," I yelled between blasts with the shotgun, which hardly seemed to phase the beast, "in the blooming universe would cross a crocodile with a great white shark and then make it *five times larger than either of them*? Is the bloke who did this still alive? Because if he is, I've got a pair of steel-toed boots looking for a good time in his midsection."

"Oh, he's dead," Misty shouted back, trying to hit the shark-odile in a weak spot with her bionic arm's concussive blast. Unfortunately, it didn't seem to *have* weak spots, and its ability to mostly submerge itself between attacks meant the water bled off a lot of our firearms' utility. "Thought he'd had these things trained to listen to him and him alone. I'm not sure which one took him out, but there wasn't enough left of the guy to fill a bottlecap once it was done with him." She unleashed a beam of cryogenic energy, only to have the creature shrug off the freeze like it was nothing and turn its gaping jaws on her, snapping them shut just a few inches from her face.

Mihaela distracted the beast with a barrage of bullets from her pistols, giving me time to slam an incendiary round into my shotgun.

"Ah-ah-ah!" I fired straight into the shark-odile's mouth. The round flared like the dragon's breath it was named for, not causing much damage but doing an admirable job of getting the creature's attention. "No no, darling, pay attention to Elsa!" It listened to me, or close enough that Misty could shimmy out from the danger zone and move beyond range. I got another shot off before it submerged again, sending a wave of filthy water over my decidedly compromised boots.

"Where is it?" Mihaela shouted from a few meters back.

"It's gone deep," I called back. "Why are these things so bloody deep?" I added, glancing toward Misty.

"It's supposed to help keep the sewers from overflowing during hurricanes," she explained. "More room for the water to go down, less pressure for it to fill up."

"Well, that's nice but it's something of a nuisance at a time like this, isn't it?" I waved at the sludge not two feet away from me. "I mean, there was a time when a person who was a fool but not entirely suicidal could jump right in here and only expect it to go up to her waist! Now if someone were to jump in, the water would close right over her–"

Like a demon leaping straight up out of hell, the enormous wedge-shaped head of the shark-odile erupted from the depths, driving straight at me. I had no time to fire my weapon. All I could do was fling every limb out in a desperate act of bracing as the creature's jaws completely surrounded me. It tried to snap downwards, but I endured the innumerable incisions its razor-sharp teeth cut into the flesh of my hands and feet as I strained against the pressure.

For the second time in less than an hour, I was on the verge of being crushed to death, only this time I would also be chewed up, swallowed down, and, for extra indignity, eventually shat out somewhere. If the prospect of being squashed to death was mortifying, this was a hundred times worse, and far harder to see a way out of.

To think I'd been pining for this sort of confrontation in Glasgow not three bloody days ago. I could slap myself for tempting fate that way. That is, if I had a hand to spare, which I most decidedly didn't under the circumstances.

"*Elsa!*" I saw Mihaela through the gap in the monster's jaws, watched her leap forward out of the shadows. With no heed to her weapons, she ran right over to the shark-odile and laid both her hands flat on the very end of its snout. "*Nu!*"

To my intense shock, the pressure relaxed. It didn't die off altogether, but it certainly didn't get any worse. The creature seemed to go into something of a trance, every writhing muscle in its body slowly losing tension. I heard Misty shout something, felt the muted *thud* toward the back of the shark-odile's head that probably meant she was standing on it, but I couldn't focus on that right now. All I could do was hold this thing's jaws apart with every ounce of strength I had and watch my sister charm it into a state of oblivion.

She caught my eye through the massive serrated teeth at the edge of its jaw. "You will be all right," she promised me, and in that moment, I absolutely believed her.

Bam-bam-bam-bam-bam! A series of muted impacts right at the base of the monster's skull made the pressure relax even further, and the shark-odile gave an enormous, putrid groan, then slowly began to sink into the sewer. I pushed hard, oblivious to the extra cuts, until its mouth opened wide enough for me to get out. Mihaela extended her hand and I took it, leaping back onto the walkway just before the beast slipped entirely into the muck.

"Holy... flaming... hellfire," I managed after a moment. "First time in... a long time... I've nearly been eaten."

"Are you all right?" Mihaela's hands fluttered like shy butterflies a few inches away from my body. "Your *hands*, Elsa..."

"Ah, right." I lifted my shredded hands up and took a peek. "They're fine, already healing." My feet were doing the same, although the boots were mostly just a band of leather around the top of my calf at this point.

"Heavens, woman," Misty swore as she came over to us, her expression the proper shade of angry to convey a certain amount of worry as well. "There's no need to turn yourself into fish food to get the job done, you hear me? If you'd made me go into that water to fetch you, I would have whupped you myself once I had you out of there."

"Darling," I cooed, doing my best to recover my aplomb, "it's so sweet to know that you care."

"Uh-huh." She watched the last of the shark-odile's gray knobby tail disappear beneath the water. "Well. Here's what we're gonna do. We're going to call this kill in and let the city come retrieve it, because I am *done* with this for today, and then we're going to get cleaned up and eat my local pizza joint out of food. Sound good?"

"Sounds brilliant," I said, then turned to Mihaela. "All right, you. Care to explain how you did that?"

"Did what?"

"Hypnotized that monster into not biting down any harder. I was strong enough to keep holding its mouth open, but I probably would have lost a finger or two before long, and if it had gone under the water…" It didn't bear thinking about that part. "So how did you do it? I have to know."

She shrugged. "It was simple. The hybrid was part crocodile, part shark, yes? Haven't you ever watched those videos of sharks surfacing beside boats, and seen the people put their hands on their snouts and calm them down? I thought it was worth a try."

"But what if the nose part had been more crocodile than shark?" Misty asked. "What if it hadn't worked?"

Mihaela hefted her pistols. "Then I probably would have gone back to using my guns."

Good answer. "Well." I cleared my throat. "I, um. I suppose I should… thank you."

"I agree," Mihaela said, then waited for a moment. "Oh, was that it?"

What, that wasn't good enough? "Nnnn…no?" I tried again. "Thank you for hypnotizing the shark-odile and keeping it from crushing me and/or plunging me into fetid water." I turned and grinned at Misty. "Lord, listen to my life. I should write a book."

"No one would ever believe it," Misty shot back. "C'mon, let's go."

After a brief shouting match over the phone, in which

Misty detailed to whomever she was speaking with exactly *where* the monster's corpse was and that no, she *wouldn't* be dragging it out of the sewer, they weren't paying her enough for that, we headed for her apartment. A cab would have been nice, but no self-respecting cabbie or rideshare driver would have let us into their car looking like we did, and Misty's place wasn't far. It was nice, on the second floor right above the pizza parlor we were going to be getting dinner from.

Being cleaned up was nicer and sitting down in a booth and eating my weight in pizza was the nicest part of all. Apparently, Misty was enough of a regular that she merited a reserved spot at the back of the joint, comparatively private, which was good since I was utterly done with interacting with people for the day. Misty was the perfect company for the comedown after a rather decent fight. I appreciated that she was more interested in relaxing with good food and decent beer than she was in hashing out every last detail of the altercation, trying to glean what could have been done better out of something that was already finished.

Mihaela, the same as last night, ate next to nothing and excused herself back up to Misty's apartment after a few minutes. While she was with us, she kept her head down, her face practically blanketed with her thick dark hair, and only responded to my questions with monosyllables. After she left, I turned to Misty. "She took some of the good painkillers, right?"

"I gave them to her," Misty replied. "Whether she took them or not, I don't know." She sat back in the booth and kicked her feet up into the seat Mihaela had just vacated. "What's her deal?"

I swallowed a bite of double cheese, double pepperoni and wiped the edge of my mouth on a paper napkin. "What do you mean?"

"Why is she riding shotgun with you on this thing? And don't give me a song and dance about how she's just here as an observer," Misty added. "Those were not the actions of a mere observer down in the sewers, those were the actions of someone heavily invested in keeping your ass safe."

"Well, she is my half-sister," I said after a moment of consideration. "That might be factoring into her decisions a bit."

"Really? You take her for the warm and fuzzy, bonds of sisterhood type?"

Ha. "No."

"What was it, then?"

"Well…" I wasn't sure how much I wanted to share this, but I didn't want to keep it to myself either. Misty was as close to a neutral party as I was likely to find. "I mentioned we're on the lookout for a bloodstone shard, yes? Either one our father left behind or, barring that, clues that will lead us to whoever took Mihaela's."

"You mentioned something like that in one of your messages, yeah." Misty laughed and shook her head. "Sounds like a fool's errand, you ask me."

"Oh, I agree. I'm more in it for the adventure at this point. Plus, it doesn't do to let mercenaries waltz around thinking I'm a decent mark. But Mihaela's been absolutely bent on recovering hers. That's the main reason that bloody bar collapsed. She couldn't be bothered to take enough precautions. She's laser-focused on retrieving the one she was given by our father as a young woman, although any shard is better than none." I took a sip of my beer, grimaced and set the glass down again. It was all right, for an American brand, but a cup of tea really would have hit the spot. "I think she might be addicted to their power."

Misty looked sidelong at me. "You think she's in withdrawal right now?"

"Jitters, high anxiety, refusing food and company? I certainly think it's possible. I should also point out, if she *is* addicted to wearing a shard, that there is *one* bloodstone shard quite close at hand." I gestured to my neck.

Misty considered it for a moment, then chuckled again. "There's no way she could take that thing from you. You might not be as good as me–"

"Oh, you *wanker*–"

"But you know what you're doing. You move like a cat and fight like a wolverine, and you do it all in heels and toting more guns than most people can even name. You're a stone cold badass, Elsa Bloodstone." She raised her glass in my direction. "Here's to our mutual aid pact."

"Long may it hold." We drank, and I tried to put the matter out of my mind. Misty was right – Mihaela couldn't hope to take my bloodstone shard away. She was in her sixties, for crying out loud, and likely to be incredibly sore for the next few days. I might have to send her back to Boston by herself to recover while I went on in search of… wherever the next bloody base was. And that would be fine with me.

I thought again about holding up that beam with my back and focusing on Mihaela's song, and how incredibly hard it had been to hold that monster's jaws open before Mihaela had hypnotized it.

Sure. She can go. That would be… just fine.

Just… bloody… fine.

Curse it.

TWELVE

The following morning, I lay awake on the couch and listened to Misty pound half a pot of coffee as she talked to someone on the phone, someone who seemed rather insistent that she put in an appearance at their place today. She seemed peeved about it. "Why do you need *me* there to talk to them? You're the lawyer, they're your client – done."

There was a long pause, then – "You of all people ought to remember I'm not a cop any more, for the love of… No, I don't miss it, I have plenty going on! I took down a legit *shark-odile* yesterday, that's what I've got going on."

"With help," I called out, hoping the person on the other end could hear me. "She did it with help from a sixty year-old woman who's watched a lot of Discovery Channel specials."

The person on the other end of the call was laughing now, the sound faint but clear through the phone's tiny speaker.

Misty poked her head around the corner of the kitchen and pointed a finger at me. "That's enough out of the woman who did nothing beyond play bait."

I batted my eyelashes at her. "But I did it so well, pet."

"Yeah, those don't work on me. And if you think… no, I'm not talking to you, I'm talking to Elsa. No, you can't talk to her! Fine! I'll be there in half an hour." She ended the call and shoved the phone in her pocket, muttering about "nosy lawyers who don't know when to quit."

I swung my feet over the edge of the couch and stood up. I was wearing one of Misty's old basketball jerseys and a pair of men's boxers as nightwear, my own having gotten hopelessly damp in the sewers. They were taking up most of the machines in the building's laundry room right now. "I take it you're off, then."

"Yeah, 'fraid so. If I don't go to him, he'll come here, and the *last* thing I need is for the two of you to meet Matthew Murdock."

"Why? Afraid we'll hit it off?"

She snorted a laugh. "No, I know you won't hit it off. Did you miss the part where the guy is a lawyer?"

"I love lawyers," I said, slightly petulant. "I greatly admire the work they do."

"And the charges they get you out of."

"Those too," I agreed. "Then again, Barnabus is something special." And not just because he was a vampire, although it certainly helped to have a lawyer who was available at *all* hours.

"Yeah, well." She slung a leather jacket over one shoulder and looked at me. "If you take off before I get back, just leave the clothes and bedding in the laundry basket. Help yourself to whatever you can find in the fridge." Misty smiled suddenly, small but genuine. "It's good seeing you, Elsa."

"It's good to be seen," I replied. "Thanks for all the fun. We *must* do it again sometime."

"Maybe without the blown-up buildings," Misty said, then turned and left the apartment. I let the quiet click of the closing door settle in the air before getting up and making myself a cup of tea. There was coffee left, but – ugh, no, not if I could help it. Perhaps Mihaela would want it.

Speaking of… I checked the clock on the microwave as the water started to boil. Nine-forty. It was quite late, all things considered, but we'd been in Mombasa just yesterday morning. Mihaela probably had a terrible case of jet lag. Who knew when she'd gotten to sleep, snuggled comfortably in Misty's guest room like the thieving wench she was, while I got the couch. If she was still asleep, I should probably let her get on with it.

On the other hand, she was the one who wanted to stick to an especially hectic schedule, not me. If I'd wanted to sleep in, I had no doubt she'd have been banging her bloody fist against the bedroom door hours ago. Not to mention, yesterday had been even worse, physically speaking, than the night before when she'd fallen through a roof. This time, the roof had fallen on *her*. Right, that tore it. I needed to check up on her.

I poured an extra cup of tea and carried it over to the guest room, then knocked twice. "Mihaela? You up yet?"

Silence. I knocked again. "Mihaela. Don't think I won't break down the door if I have to." Misty would be mad, but she'd be mad while I was likely hundreds of miles away, so it could be a lot worse. "*Mihaela!*" If something had happened to her in the night, if she was unconscious, if she was... she was...

"I'm here." She sounded subdued, depressed. Oh lord, was she having some sort of emotional breakdown? Was I going to have to handle *feelings* this morning? I didn't want to handle feelings.

I didn't want her to stay holed up in Misty's apartment for the rest of the day either, though. "I'm coming in." I opened the door, and found the room shrouded in darkness. There was a window, but Mihaela had hung the comforter up in front of it, blocking most of the light. The door to the bathroom was cracked open, and a little light from the vanity filtered through, but that was it.

Mihaela sat on the bed, completely dressed – she even had her shoes on. Her hair was still loose but had been tucked back behind her ears. I could finally see her face – enough of it, at least, given that the light was so dim. The moment I laid eyes on her, I knew what was going on. And here I was, with only my Bowie knife on me.

Stop it. No need to jump ahead to the bloody part. I set the cup of tea down on the dresser, then sat at the end of the bed, a few feet down from Mihaela. I turned to look at her and said, "So, care to tell me how long you've been a vampire for?"

She laughed mirthlessly. "I'm surprised you're bothering to ask. Shouldn't you be cutting my head off about now?"

Well, that was just uncalled for. "Look, I know we got off to a rather rocky start, but I think I've demonstrated rather amply over the past few days that while I do quite enjoy my work, I don't always kill first and ask questions later. I've met plenty of excellent people who also happen to be monsters – blimey, I've dated some of them. I live with one of them. And there are far worse things out there than are dreamt of even in my philosophy, so how about you drop the defensiveness and answer my question?"

Mihaela nodded stiffly. "I'm sorry. I've gotten so used to hiding this part of me that to have it revealed now, when I can do nothing about it, is… very disconcerting. Painful, honestly. But you deserve to know the truth." She glanced up at me, her eyes unnaturally bright in the darkness. "I was born at the end of the nineteenth century, in a small Romanian village. I was born human, with nothing exceptional about me other than my parentage. It was a scandal, of course, but what I told you before, about my mother remarrying, that was all true. I had a very normal childhood."

"Normal for a girl living in the late eighteen hundreds, that is," I murmured.

I could imagine it – a small village full of people who knew too much about each other, a family full of love that was nevertheless hard to handle sometimes, a little strange for the girl who had come from another man. I could imagine the cold of the winter, the sicknesses that might have spread through the town on a regular basis. I could imagine a predator looking at such a place with pure avarice, knowing it was ripe for harvest.

"Who turned you?" I asked. "When?"

Mihaela laced her fingers together. "I was nineteen. On the verge of being married, actually. Oh, my mother fought long and hard for that marriage," she said with a broken laugh. "I was irrevocably tainted in the eyes of the village, of course, but my stepfather was well off, and very supportive of me. They arranged it all, and I was open to it – it was what girls did back then. I was excited to begin a new life as a wife, the mistress of my own home. We had just welcomed my fiancé and his family to our house for the wedding preparations when they first attacked."

I waited while she brought a hand to her face, rubbing the edges of her eyes even though they were dry. Vampires didn't cry – they didn't have the water to spare for that. Especially not when they were starved, like I was betting Mihaela was at this point.

"I think they were Nosferatu," she said after a moment. "I know we weren't their usual prey, but we'd had an early snow that season, and the roads had been impassable for weeks. We'd thought it was lucky that the rest of the wedding party had made it to our house, rather than having to turn back halfway. There were... three of them. Two of them were young, vicious, but quick with their kills. They strode through the village like evil gods, pulling people from their homes and draining them right there in the streets. The third one, though...

"He was different. Older, more measured. He was the one who came to our house first. He rounded us up like sheep in the kitchen and looked each of us over. When he saw me..." She shrugged. "He immediately knew I was different. He grabbed me and bit me, drank right from my neck. Not enough to kill me, just enough to... to taste." Her mouth twisted with memory. "My fiancé, Piotr, tried to stop him. The vampire killed him without even looking at him, hit him so hard that his spine snapped. After that, it was chaos."

I knew just the sort of chaos a vampire, or worse yet, a group of them, could cause in a crowded household. "A slaughter," I said.

"In every way. I'd say we were sheep, but to these vampires we were less than sheep. Sheep are valuable, creatures to be tended to and cared for as well as shorn and killed for meat. But my family?" She looked at me again, hatred in every remaining line on her now-youthful face. "They were like ants to these brutes. The other two must have been attracted by the screaming, because they joined in after a minute. They couldn't have been hungry at that point; they had already feasted on the rest of the village. They killed my family for the simple joy of killing them. Everyone, all my younger siblings, my stepfather. My mother."

Breath shuddered out of Mihaela. "My mother was the last, before they turned their attention solely to me. The whole time the two younger ones were gnawing at her, the eldest just held her head and spoke to her softly, making her look at me. He told her what a wonderful thing she'd done by creating me, that I was so much more delicious they would save me for dessert. And my mother, my good mother who loved me so much, her last act was to look at me and apologize. She said she was sorry for bringing me into this terrible world." There was a sudden ripping sound as the sheets under Mihaela's nails were shredded into ribbons.

Best I hurried this confession along if I wanted any of Misty's belongings to survive it. Besides, it didn't do to let your mind dwell on the dark moments for too long. They could swallow you whole if you let them. "How long did they keep you?"

"Three days," Mihaela said quietly. "In my own house. The storm was so bad, not even they wanted to travel in it, so they kept me there in my own house surrounded by the dead. They wanted to turn me. They said I was delicious, new, and that if they turned me, they could feast on me forever."

Sick no-good gits. "I take it this is when Ulysses showed up?"

She nodded. "Just before dawn on the fourth day. I still don't know if he was in the area, or if he had been tracking these vampires, or perhaps if... if he had heard I was to be married and had come for the wedding."

I could practically guarantee the obsessive man hadn't been there for the wedding, but from the wistful light in Mihaela's face the thought of it was a treasured moment for her, and it wasn't my place to lay waste to it. I held my peace and waited for her to go on.

"He knocked on the door. Actually knocked. I was surprised to hear it. I think we all were. There was no one left in town alive, so we all knew it had to be a traveler seeking shelter. One of the young ones went to kill him – it was nearly light out, time to retreat to the cellar – and as soon as the door opened…" She smiled, bright and wide. I couldn't quite see her fangs from this angle, but I knew they were there.

"Father blew the vampire's head right off. I don't know what sort of ammunition he was using, but it was shockingly effective. The other young one tried to take him down next, and Father grabbed him in midair, then slammed him against the floor so hard he broke half the boards. He used one of those boards to stake the vampire through the heart.

"The elder had figured out faster than his companions who had come to the door. He held me tightly, his hands clenching my head. He told Father to leave, that he would finish me off otherwise. And Father…" She laughed. "Father said that he had already finished me off, because he had turned me. And he charged, and the vampire broke my neck, and then our father killed him."

I blinked. "Wait, the vampire…"

She nodded calmly. "Broke my neck, yes."

Sweet mother in bloody heaven. And here I thought being thrown into a pit full of monsters armed with a pocketknife was bad. "Yet you survived it."

"As Ulysses knew I would," Mihaela confirmed. "He knew I was no longer human. I could survive a simple neck break. If the elder had torn my head clean off my shoulders it might have been a different story, but that would have taken time and effort he didn't have. And so, our father saved me, and he staked the bodies of the other three in the sun so that they would never be able to recover. Then he began to teach me."

Oh, did he now? "Teach you what, exactly? How to be a vampire?"

Mihaela looked at me with wide eyes. "What? No! Why would you even think that?"

"Well…" I waved a hand at her. "You're clearly still around a hundred years or so after you got turned, which means the vampire part stuck. No last-minute reversals, no hidden fixes. You're a vampire, so did he teach you to live like a vampire?"

She shook her head. "No, no, you misunderstand. This was when he gave me a bloodstone shard." Her eyes lit upon my neck, staring avidly at my adornment. "He told me he could not make me human again, but he could give me the semblance of humanity. He broke off a piece of his bloodstone for me, just for me, and set it in a gold bracelet. He said it would control my cravings and make it possible for me to appear to age, that I would be able to walk in the sun and eat food like a normal person. It didn't do anything to diminish my strength or agility, but that is what he spent weeks thereafter working on with me." She was speaking so quickly now that her words were almost unintelligible.

"He taught me how to feign weakness, how to move with control, how to grab another person without bruising them. He taught me how to be human again, Elsa, how to be myself again." She closed her eyes briefly. "I can never thank him enough for that. After those weeks, when he said he had to go, I knew I couldn't follow him, but I was no longer mired in despair. Do you see? He gave me a reason to go on living, and the means to do so! The shard restrained the vampire parts of me so well I forgot they were there."

"Until it was taken from you," I pointed out, and her smile became a frown.

"Yes, until that. I should have fought harder, but the truth is that I forgot I *could* fight harder." She raked a hand through her hair, her jaw tightening. "And now I've been without it for nearly five days, longer than when I was with those vampire *pigs* in the beginning, and I can't… I don't… I don't know what to do without it, Elsa. I can't be a vampire. I don't want to be one. I never want to be like those demons who killed my family. All I want is to live like the human I used to be." She looked at me with wide, haunted eyes. "Is that so much to ask?"

"Yes," I said bluntly. "It is. Because you're not a human

any more, and frankly it's irresponsible for you to walk about the world as a vampire without knowing how to handle yourself as one."

Mihaela flinched back, her earnest expression shuttering, but I didn't care. It was time for some hard truths. "You're a vampire who used a magical device to keep you from fully manifesting, and now for the first time in a hundred years you're trying to get by without your talisman. This makes you a danger to yourself and to everyone around you. Well," I added with a smirk, "not to me, but I'm a special case. Are you too far gone to take sunlight any more?"

"I don't know," she said coldly. "Why?"

"Because I want another cup of tea, and I don't care to drink it somewhere that reminds me of a cave." I grabbed her still-steaming cup off the dresser and took a sip, then turned and walked out of the bedroom. "Are you coming?" I called over my shoulder.

She rose to her feet but stopped before she got to the open door. "But... isn't it..."

"Dangerous? Yes, it is, but we don't know *how* dangerous it is because you don't know anything about your own body. So, let's establish some basic facts and then go from there." She stared at me, and I finally added, "Look, I'm not trying to get you killed, all right? If it burns you that badly, I'll be the first to shove your arse back in that bedroom, but we need to know one way or another."

"Fine," she snapped, visibly steeling herself before stepping forward. She winced, but I didn't see any burns developing on her few sections of exposed skin, not even a tinge of color, yet.

"So far, so good," I said. "Right, let's sit down and figure out what you need to make your way in the world without taking damage. We've got a few more hours before the heliophobia sets in hard, I think, and I know Misty's got contacts here who can get us access to things like special UV-blocking creams and–"

"I think there is a simpler solution available to us," Mihaela broke in.

"There is," I agreed. "It's sending you back to Boston to squat in the mansion while I get things done, but I know you'd cause a ruckus for Adam if I tried that. I'm trying to be generous instead."

She shot me a look of pure irritation; her eyebrows drawn together like angry caterpillars. "No, not that. Obviously, I'm speaking of you lending me your bloodstone shard."

I couldn't stop myself. I began to laugh. I laughed so hard I had to set the tea down on the table beside my Bowie knife or risk spilling it. "Are you mental?" I finally managed to gasp. "Let you put on my shard? What good would that do?"

"It might allow me to stave off the final stages of transformation," Mihaela said, her tone gone from annoyed to entreating. "My shard helped me maintain my humanity, keeping the vampirism from taking me over. If I transform completely, I don't know that my shard will be able to take me back to what I was any longer. Please, just… just lend it to me, for a moment, to see if it makes a difference. I'm not asking to keep it, of course not, I just—"

"No." I cut off her pleas with a firm head shake. "It's untenable. First off, even assuming my shard worked for you, you'd have to keep wearing it in order to maintain your current state, and I've got need of it myself, especially given that we've headed into a trap or fight or both at every base we've visited so far. We still have two to go, and I'm not going to walk in underprepared. Secondly, being a vampire is part of your reality whether you like it or not. Even if you regain your shard and it helps you return to what you were before, it would be the height of irresponsibility for me to allow you to go about life without knowing how to handle yourself in every incarnation. Your avoidance is a weakness, Mihaela, a weakness that could easily be exploited by another thief or an unethical magic practitioner."

She shook her head all through the second half of my statement, and now she slammed her hand down on the kitchen table so hard I could hear the legs creak. "You talk about the future as though I'm not suffering in the present," she snapped at me. "Are you so much of a sadist that you can see me in pain and remain dispassionate?" Her eyes glittered mercilessly. "Or is it that you're afraid? I thought you were supposed to be a mighty monster hunter, Elsa Bloodstone. What could I possibly do to you in the few seconds it would take to try on your shard?"

I shrugged my shoulders and sipped up the last of my tea and then sheathed my Bowie in its spot on my waist. "I don't know what you could do given that amount of time, and I don't care to learn, either. You can't have my shard. That's final." I got up from the table and headed for the sink to put the empty mug away.

There was a sudden clatter, and a second later Mihaela's unnaturally strong hands closed about my neck from behind, jerking me backward as she tried to rip the bloodstone choker off. I instinctually kicked into a flip above her, swinging one arm up and past my head to clear her hold on me even as I grabbed my Bowie knife with the other hand. I checked myself at the last second. Tempting as it was in the moment, I didn't want to murder my half-sister, much less do it in Misty Knight's apartment. She'd never get the bloody security deposit back.

I landed on top of the kitchen table in a crouch, the blade held out in front of me. "Stop and think about this, Mihaela," I warned, but I could already see it was too late for warnings. She was lost to her rage, overwhelmed by an intense thirst for blood and feeling the capabilities of her fancy new vampire body for the first time. Her pupils were huge, her fangs completely visible, and, as I watched, the skin on the side of her face closest to the kitchen window began to turn red.

Oh, no. The heliophobia was setting in faster than I expected. I needed to get her into the dark of the bedroom, pronto. I lifted my hands in what I hoped was a reassuring manner. "All right, let's just–"

Mihaela leap-tackled me off the table, through the

kitchen door, and onto the living room carpet. Her teeth snapped dangerously close to my face, and her hands grasped my wrists in a punishingly tight grip. *So much for being reassuring.*

So much for being on the ground, too. I kneed Mihaela in the arse hard enough to send her into a sprawling roll over the top of my head, then sprang to my feet. "Look, you can–"

The next thing I knew there was a brass floor lamp with a beautiful stained glass shade swinging at my head. It was an art deco reproduction, or at least I hoped it was a reproduction, because otherwise a lot of money had just been broken against my face. Glass scattered all over the floor, cutting into my feet as I staggered a step to the right.

Just stab her already! I still had my knife, it would be so easy to take her down… but in the full light of day, she was already taking wounds by standing there. Add in a few cuts from the silver part of my blade and I might compound the damage so much it would take her a long time to recover, if she ever did. Baby vampires were shockingly easy to kill – they were too strong to know what to do with themselves, so fast they overshot every target, and so hungry they couldn't control themselves in the face of food. My sister, despite being over a hundred years old, was in her own way a baby right now. More than that, she was my sister. I hadn't asked for her and I didn't know what to do with her, but I knew I didn't want her dead. My training might say "kill her" but my mind was saying "save her" , and I chose to override my instincts in a way she wasn't capable of right now.

Mihaela stared at me with pure malevolence, hissing as she swung the long brass floor lamp at me again. This time I ducked, and when it came at me again, I grabbed it and wrenched it out of Mihaela's grasp, making the metal twist alarmingly. She charged after it, driving me onto the couch as she clawed at my face with too-sharp nails. I braced one arm on her shoulder, grabbed her wrist with my other hand, and surged to my feet, turning and throwing her down onto the couch.

I threw her possibly a little too hard. That or Misty was cheapening out on her furnishings, because the couch practically exploded in a shower of splinters and springs, sending detritus all over the room as we hit the floor. Mihaela struggled and, grabbing me tight, rolled us over so that I was on the bottom this time.

Even with her vampiric enhancements, I was stronger than Mihaela. The couch had amply proven that. Blast it, I didn't even need strength to have five different ways of getting her off me in less than two seconds, all of them the product of superior skill and an expert understanding of leverage. The issue at hand was bringing her back to herself. I might be able to knock her out if I hit her just right, but the longer it took, the longer she'd be fighting back, exposed to the sunlight streaming in through every window in Misty's living room. Even now, the top of her head was beginning to smoke, but she didn't even seem to notice as she strained hungrily toward my throat.

Stop thinking and do something! Right, fine then, I'd do something – by doing nothing. I dropped all my resistance, relaxed myself completely, and tilted my head to the side. It was all the invitation Mihaela needed to sink her sharp new teeth into my neck. She bit down, and I winced – this part was never fun – and waited for one second. Two. Three…

"*Phauggghhh!*" Mihaela reared back off me, clawing at her bright red lips and spitting out droplets of my blood. Enough had already gone down her throat to sicken her, though, and she bent over, clutched her stomach, and moaned pitifully.

"Serves you right," I told her, only a trifle spiteful. I jumped to my feet and gathered Mihaela off the floor, levering her over my shoulder. She made a suspicious sound, and a moment later something wet splashed down my back.

"Oh, for… mind where you're chundering!"

I stalked into the bathroom, dropped her to her knees in front of the toilet, then stripped off Misty's jersey. Sure enough, there was a red streak down the back of it. "Bloody hell," I muttered, plugging the sink, turning the water on cold, and tossing the jersey in there to soak.

I glanced down at my pitiful sister. Mihaela was at least vomiting into the bowl now, but she was lost to her misery – all the fight had gone out of her. "You're an idiot," I told her, then glanced at my neck in the bathroom mirror. Apart from a few residual drops of blood on the skin, no one would have known I'd been bitten by a vampire a moment ago. I used a washcloth to rinse the droplets off, cleaned the residual vomitous ooze off my back as well, then headed into the living room to grab a new shirt out of my duffel bag.

Oh dear. It looked like... well, like a crazed vampire had carelessly swung a heavy duty, five-foot tall brass lamp around out here before breaking it into pieces and destroying a couch. Glass, blood, and chunks of said couch were spread all over the room. There were two holes in the walls, and a dent in the ceiling. Lord, we were lucky we hadn't taken out Misty's flatscreen.

The doorbell rang. "Oh, for the love of..." It was probably an irate neighbor ready to shout us into oblivion, or perhaps the landlord, or – wait, no. I grabbed my phone out of the rubble and checked my messages. Ah, Adam had tried to let me know, then. I walked over to the door and opened it.

A young man in a Yankees ballcap stood in the hallway with a heavily secured suitcase on the ground next to him. "Delivery for Elsa Bloodstone," he said in a perfectly flat voice.

"Fabulous." I reached for the bag, but he held out a hand to stop me. "I *beg* your pardon," I said coldly, straightening up and staring down at him. Even without my shoes on, I had a good two inches on the man. More powerful people than this had quailed at my stare, but he didn't even blink.

"I need some identification, please."

Interesting that he didn't say he needed to *see* some identification. I went with my standby phrase for proving my identity to Adam. "Right then, how about this? 'Hand over my bag with a smile and I won't throw you into a pond populated with mutated mud skippers and watch as they use your head as a springboard.'"

He did crack a smile this time. "Yeah, you've got to be Elsa Bloodstone."

"One of a kind," I purred as I took the bag. It was quite heavy – good, I'd gone through most of my hardware already. "Wait here a moment." I pulled it inside and went to get him a tip, then paused. I brought my wallet back to the door. "Are you a local?"

He nodded. "Boricua boy from the Bronx, here."

"And you handle these sorts of special deliveries on a regular basis?"

He smiled wider. "I know all kinds of people."

"Good. I need four pints of O-negative blood within the next half hour. Do you think you can handle that?"

He tried to glance over my shoulder, but I drew the door in close to my body. "No, no, no peeking," I chided him. "I'll give you a hundred dollars per pint if you hit my time frame."

"I can do it."

"Good lad." I gave him a fifty for bringing my bag. "And I want it responsibly sourced," I added. "No setting up a quick blood drive in the alley behind this place with a few donors from God knows where."

He held up his hands. "I wouldn't do that."

"Good. See you in thirty minutes, then." I closed the door, turned around, and surveyed the mess in front of me. Mihaela, starved as she'd been before biting me, likely wouldn't be recovering from my blood before the new supply arrived. That gave me time to figure out what to do about this bloody mess.

There was no help for it. I was going to have to clean. "Cast it all into the fiery pits," I muttered, then went to find the vacuum.

My foray into mundanity was blessedly brief. Forty-five minutes later the living room was somewhat barren but pristine, a new couch was on its way, and an exact replica of the Tiffany lamp had been ordered. I'd also gone through the bag that Adam had sent and been pleased. The double-barreled shotgun was one of my old favorites, I had a delightful boost to the kind of ammunition at my disposal, I was in stylish but arse-kicking boots again, and he'd also sent the… specialty item. I was still reluctant to use it, but at this point I wanted to have the option. Time was against us, and this might be the thing that tipped the odds in our favor at last.

Speaking of "us"… I also had four fresh pints of blood sitting on the kitchen table courtesy of my courier, just waiting to be consumed. Mihaela had stopped retching a while ago. I grabbed one of the blood bags and walked into the guest room.

Mihaela still sat on the bathroom floor, looking absolutely ghastly, but when she glanced up at me her eyes were sane. Hopeless, but sane.

"I–"

"Nope." I cut her off before she could say something I didn't want to hear, which at this point was basically everything. "First things first." I dangled the blood bag in front of her. "Drink this, then we'll figure out the next step."

She made a face of pure disgust. "I don't want that."

"Funny, you wanted plenty of it not so long ago," I said.

Her disgust gave way to misery. "Elsa, I'm so–"

I shook my head. "Stop. Drink this first, then we talk."

Anger and frustration made Mihaela's red-rimmed eyes seem to glitter. "I don't want it!"

"You do, though." I could see the need in every line of her body, in the way she subtly arched forward even as her head tried to hold her back. "You do want it, and there's no shame in that. It's a part of you now. There's only shame if you try to deny it and cause a load of problems because of that denial, which – I've got to say, we've already gone down that road and it didn't turn out well for you *or* Misty's apartment. Let's not try again, hmm?" I wiggled the bag. "There's a cap at the top, just twist it off and drink."

Her mouth twisted with disgust, but she finally grabbed the bag. As soon as it was in her hands, instinct took over. She didn't even bother with the cap, just lifted a corner of it to her lips and bit straight through the plastic. Blood gushed into her mouth and Mihaela swallowed every drop, ravenous just like I'd known she'd be.

"There's more in the kitchen," I said as she polished the last of it off, licking her lips. "Knock on the door when you've put yourself together and I'll bring it in to you." She wouldn't be able to handle the light in the rest of the apartment now, but I could work around that until my next order arrived.

I had time to make some lunch for myself before Mihaela knocked. I'd heard the shower go on – hopefully she felt better now. I warmed up a bag of blood and poured it into a teapot, which I'd be washing thoroughly before Misty got home, grabbed an empty cup and headed for the guest room. Mihaela opened it just as I arrived.

The windows were still covered, but now the overhead light was on. She'd pulled her hair back from her face, which was strikingly beautiful, if austere. As I watched, the last few threads of gray turned as black as the rest of her mane. All of her burns were healed.

"You look much improved," I congratulated her, entering the room and tapping the door shut with my hip before setting the teapot, cup, and saucer down on top of the dresser. "But still a little hungry."

"I think I've had enough for now," she replied, as aloof and proud as ever.

"Oh really?" I tilted the teapot, and a dark red stream of blood poured into the cup. The sharp, metallic scent of it filled the room, and as I watched Mihaela's tongue darted out and touched her lips. "I think you need a bit more."

"I- I'm sure I don't, I can–"

"I'm not going to be nice if you attack me again," I said, not bothering to beat around the bush. "Especially when the fix is so bloody, pardon the pun, simple. Drink it."

"*Fine.*" She snatched the cup out of my hand but lifted it to her mouth as daintily as any English matron. She sipped, then drained the cup in one long swallow. I refilled it, and this time she was able to go more slowly.

"So." I sat down on the edge of the bed and extracted a tube from my pocket, then tossed it to her. She caught it and looked it over, but there was no label, no writing of any kind. "That's sunblock. Vampire-strength. It's both topical and soaks into the skin, so if you apply it thick enough and leave it for long enough it should be good for most of a day. It's still not as good as covering up completely, though. I've got an outfit in my bag that will work for that. A helmet would be nice, but that'll make you stick out in the wrong places, so we'll go with goggle-style sunglasses and say you're a die-hard fan of steampunk. We should–"

"Elsa." Her soft voice stopped mine in a moment. "Are you sure this is what you want?"

"You'll have to be a bit more specific, pet."

"This whole… looking after me thing." She stood as tall and steady as an oak, but there was fragility in her eyes. "I lied to you. I attacked you. I bit you. I don't understand why you're not sending me back to Boston, or perhaps to Romania."

I frowned. "I thought we covered this. Did we not cover it? You wouldn't stay–"

"I would, if you sent me now." She looked down at the cup in her hands, shamefaced. "I thought I was so much better than what my body was trying to become. I thought

I could control it. Even when it got worse, I still assumed that I would be able to… to cover for myself. But I was wrong." She laughed caustically. "So wrong. And now I don't know how to trust myself. I certainly don't know how to ask you to trust me."

Oh, dear. Now wasn't the time for her to be getting the willies. It wasn't impossible that her bloodstone shard could still help her beat back the full range of vampirism's effects, even this far along in her transformation, if we got it back in the next few days. If she left now, though, that chance would be effectively blown. Even if I found her shard, the delay in returning it would be too great. Then she would blame me, and blame herself, and the blame game would get so repetitive and intense that eventually she might simply choose to end it all. I was willing to be party to plenty of not-so-savory things, but devastating my half-sister's mental health wasn't one of those.

Such a softie.

Yeah, a bit. "Trust between us from here on out is going to be solely a matter of preparation," I said. "If you use that sunscreen, if you stay covered up, if you drink blood when I give it to you and don't go trying to bite any more necks or wrists or other easily accessible body parts, we'll be just fine. I want your help on this. Hell, you kept me from being eaten by a mutant shark-odile not twelve hours ago, I think you've amply proven your utility."

Mihaela frowned, but there was a glimmer of hope in her face. "But everything I just did to you…"

"Was the result of starvation and stupidity, not necessarily in that order," I agreed. "Not the act of a monster, though, if you don't let it become one."

"I… I would like to avoid that." She glanced at my neck, but without a hint of greed this time. "Why did your blood hurt so much?"

"Ah, lucky me, I happen to have blood that's toxic to vampires!" I said brightly. "Not sure if I was born with it or if wearing the bloodstone makes it so, but either way I'm not complaining. Now." I stood up. "I've been in touch with Adam and Barnabus, and they haven't been able to narrow the location of the next base down any closer than 'Antarctica, somewhere outside the Savage Land,' so I think we need to talk to an informant."

"Who do you have in mind?"

I smiled. "Barnabus was able to help with that, too. We're going to talk to a woman named Samantha Eden."

THIRTEEN

I made some calls, retrieved our laundry and packed our bags, helped Mihaela ensure that her sunscreen was thick enough to protect her, then got us a flight to Paris. Samantha had been willing to talk to us, but she didn't feel comfortable giving out specifics over the phone.

"No disrespect intended, but if you think I'm going to talk about Ulysses Bloodstone where any old government can tap in and hear me, you're crazy," she'd said frankly. "Especially under these rather murky circumstances. I've had to fend off attacks before thanks to my association with him, and I'm not eager to start all that up again in my seventies."

"I'm sure you're more than formidable," I said.

"Oh, I am," she agreed with a chuckle, "but it's a lot of fuss and bother, and my arthritis has been acting up lately. You know how to find me, then?"

"I do." Thanks to Charles, who was as expedient as ever in his investigations.

"Perfect. Try to be discreet when you arrive, all right?"

Discretion was asking a bit much, considering who she was talking to, but I'd do everything I could to make sure we weren't being tailed. As much as was reasonable, at any rate. Time, after all, was of the essence.

I glanced at my bag. Maybe I should use the... but no, we could be in Paris on the nearest Stark jet – a fortunate happenstance, as there was a scientific conference in Paris that one of their vice presidents of Research and Development was attending – in a little over five hours. That was fast enough.

It had better be.

I froze the remaining blood bags solid and brought them along in a special cooler for Mihaela. If past experience proved me right, she'd be fine for several days, but I didn't want us to get caught out again. She seemed... controlled but subdued as we left Misty's apartment.

"Are you sure she's going to be all right with the damage we did to her home?" Mihaela asked hesitantly as we got in a cab to the airport.

I waved a hand dismissively. "I'm sure she will. After all, I'm replacing all of it, and I contacted several handymen on her behalf who can fix the dents. It should be just fine."

It was not, in fact, "just fine", a point that Misty made rather vociferously when she got home and found us gone, her apartment in a very different state from how she left it, and an explanatory letter on the kitchen table. "– were you thinking? You said you had it under control!"

"And now I do," I replied. "Huzzah for all of us! Mihaela had her journey of self-discovery in a safe and supportive environment, and–"

"Safe and supportive my ass, you broke half my furniture!"

"Oh dear, what was that last part?" I said, holding the phone farther away from my face so I sounded fainter. "We're heading out over the Atlantic, I'm afraid you're breaking up! So sorry, we'll talk again soon, ta!"

"Elsa Bloodstone, if you think this is over–"

I ended the call before she could finish threatening me, smiling down at my phone for a moment before turning it off and tucking it away.

"I'm sorry," Mihaela said miserably from beside me. The Stark Industries VP, a woman with an admirable poker face, was sitting across us reading the paperwork spread out in front of her like she hadn't even heard any of that noisy conversation. I knew she would be discreet, but decided to keep the conversation fairly vague, just in case.

"Oh, don't be. She wouldn't know what to do with herself if she didn't have something to whine at me over, and her last couch was shockingly lumpy. I could scarcely fall asleep on it, and I can fall asleep standing on one foot if I have to." I shrugged. "Misty knew the risks associated with letting us into her home, and she accepted them when she accepted us. I compensated her for the damages and then some. The next time we meet she'll probably try to shoot me a couple of times, and I'll try to shoot her back, and we'll yell at each other for a while and then it'll be over."

"You have odd friends."

Before this, I wouldn't have called Misty a "friend" , more like an acquaintance-at-arms, but upon reflection it seemed that Mihaela was probably right. If we hadn't been friends, Misty would be airborne right now coming to try and kick my arse. "Odd but good, I think."

"Very good," she agreed.

The sun was setting by the time we reached Paris, but it wasn't called the City of Lights for nothing. Mihaela gaped at the view from the window as we came in for a landing at Charles de Gaulle. "I've never seen the Louvre like that before," she murmured, staring at the illuminated pyramid that lay like a golden topaz on the velvet background of the city, along with thousands of other glittering gem-like lights.

"You've been here before, then?" I asked. I was all too aware of what might happen if we didn't get the bloodstone back to Mihaela. That was our first priority. Still, seeing her awe of the city was almost… adorable.

"Several times, but all long ago." She glanced uneasily at the other woman, who was packing up her briefcase. "Very long ago."

"Ah." It was too bad we didn't have any time for sightseeing. Paris was one of my favorite places to while away the hours between hunts, many of which had happened in the catacombs that spread across the underbelly of the city. "Well, there's always next time."

Mihaela smiled. "You're an unceasing optimist."

"On the contrary, I'm a realist. I'm also quite good at what I do, though, so it doesn't pay to go around exuding doom and gloom when in all likelihood I'll be killing things that go bump in the night for years to come."

The VP, who had moved toward the door, suddenly came over and held out her hand. "I'd just like to thank you two for being the best in-flight entertainment I've had in years," she said with a half-smile.

I grinned and shook. "You're quite welcome."

By the time we exited the airport, grabbed a cab to the city, and got out onto the cobbled streets of Paris, it was finally close to the time the locals deigned to begin considering dinner, and quite crowded. That helped us to blend in, as did the fact that, well, we were in *Paris*. An outfit like mine stood out in a place like Glasgow or Boston, but in a fashion-forward city like this not even my high heels were the most outré thing out there.

I had the cabbie drop us off outside the Opéra Garnier, in a part of Paris famous for its nightlife. Samantha lived close by in an apartment between here and the Gare du Nord, and, despite all our luggage, on a night like tonight I preferred to walk. Paris was too beautiful for anything else.

It was a busy evening on the streets, with music flowing out from restaurants and clubs and beautiful people drinking, smoking, and talking together as they clustered here and there. We attracted attention as we walked – of course we did, we were both objectively gorgeous – but most eyes ended up on Mihaela.

I couldn't say I was surprised. Even in her fairly conservative clothes, she was stunning, and she strode down the streets of Paris like she owned them, skillfully deflecting any attention that tried to go beyond a simple look with a brush-off or, in one persistent case, a pointed glare. The gentleman got the picture immediately and scuttled back to his friends to lick his wounds. It made me laugh, to see him put in his place so effectively.

"Oooh, well done you," I teased as we picked up the pace again, this time blessedly, *pointedly* alone. "You got him to go away without a hint of bloodshed, nice."

"What on earth was that attitude?" she asked me.

"What attitude?"

"That one! That 'Oh I am here paying attention to you, let me talk to you and take up your time and ignore your wishes' attitude."

Interesting. Did she really not know about… "It's how a lot of rude people try to get dates," I said. "Haven't you ever had to deal with that sort of unwanted attention?"

"No! When would I have?" she demanded. "I was engaged to be married at nineteen, for heaven's sake! And after that there were the wars, and then the communists, and I looked older and older… no!"

"Oh. Dear." She was going to have a rough reintroduction to her youth, then. "There's so much you have to learn about being a single and stunning woman in the modern era." I thought for a moment. "Also, social media is the devil and I suggest you avoid it for as long as possible."

"I know that much," she said with a huff. "I was a professor of biology in a major university, after all. The number of phones I confiscated because someone couldn't stop texting..." She *tsked*.

I grinned and bumped her gently with my hip. "That's the spirit, you delightful old curmudgeon."

"And do not forget it." Mihaela rolled her eyes, but there was a hint of a smile on her face.

We reached Samantha's place a few moments later, a beautiful old brick building with wrought iron balconies extending from all three stories. I pushed the buzzer at the door, and a moment later her smooth, elegant voice said, "I see you, come on up." The door clicked, and we walked inside and headed for the elevator.

Samantha Eden, famous muckraking journalist of the Seventies and Eighties, lived in a small but lovely apartment on the top floor. She greeted us at the door, her white hair falling in soft waves down to her shoulders, a smile on her spectacled face. I could easily see the young woman she'd been when she'd known our father, see it in the arch of her eyebrows and the curl of her smile. Now that I looked at her face to face, I knew she was the one in the picture we'd found back on Bloodstone Isle. From the way Mihaela abruptly stiffened, she'd recognized Samantha too.

She wore a light pink blouse and carried a cane in her left hand. "My goodness," she said, looking between the two of us for a moment and adjusting her glasses. "The resemblance is uncanny, isn't it?"

I smiled at her. "My family specializes in uncanny."

She chuckled. "It does, it really does. Lord knows I experienced enough of that when I was hanging around with your father. Come in, come in!" She waved us inside. "Can I offer either of you something to drink? A coffee, some water, some wine…" She peered more closely at Mihaela. "Perhaps something more specialized?" she hazarded.

"Is it so obvious?" Mihaela burst out.

"Not at all," Samantha soothed. "I promise, it's not. You'd have to know what to look for, and I… happen to know what to look for, that's all." She shrugged. "After everything that happened with Ulysses, I made it my business to know as much about the world below the one I had grown up in as I could. I got used to picking people with a paranormal air out of the crowd, and it didn't take a lot of investigation to confirm in most cases. The point is, dear," she looked at Mihaela, "that if something other than wine appeals to you, you should feel free, as long as you don't go biting one of my neighbors."

"I'm fine for now, thank you," Mihaela said, a bit stiffly, but at least she was making an effort.

"I'd love a spot of tea," I said, and Samantha nodded and headed for the kitchen.

Five minutes later we were ensconced on the balcony, Samantha wrapped in a shawl and sipping on chamomile while I indulged in a hearty Earl Grey and Mihaela stood around looking awkward.

"So." Samantha looked between us. "You want to know where your father's bases are."

"We've already visited most of them," I said, wanting to make it clear that we weren't totally useless on our own. "There's the ones in Antarctica and Moscow left to check, and neither of those locations are kind to random people wandering around."

"No, they wouldn't be," she agreed. "While I never visited either of them in person myself, I can help you find them."

"How?" Mihaela asked, not exactly hostile but with a definite edge in her voice. "How do you know these things when no one else seems to? Even my sister's people don't know the location of these bases, not even the man that our father entrusted his home in Boston to."

Samantha smirked. "I know what I know because there was a brief period of time when Ulysses was infatuated with me, and gave me access to all the archives on Bloodstone Isle as a result. I did quite a lot of research during my time there."

Mihaela's mouth dropped open. "You… were on the island?"

"Oh yes. All by myself, too." She chuckled. "I accidentally activated the base's defenses just as your father was approaching once, almost shot him down. Obviously, I managed to salvage the situation, but wouldn't that have been a hoot?"

"Why?" Mihaela demanded. "Why would that have been funny, shooting down the man who gave you such liberties in his home?"

"Oh, my." Samantha sighed. "There are so many reasons. First and foremost, it would have been his own fault for not telling me how to make anything work before leaving me there by myself. I suppose he just expected me to sit pretty and admire the view until he got back. Lucky for him I was pretty handy with technology, not that he knew or cared about my proficiencies."

I raised my eyebrows. "No?"

Samantha chuckled. "No, oh no. He was more interested in my proficiency to charm rather than my ability with a weapon." She glanced out over the street. "Just like most men during those times. All of us had to get used to it, but some of us were able to turn it to our advantage."

Mihaela crossed her arms. "You used him?"

Our hostess smirked. "Oh, hardly. We both enjoyed the rush of investigation, of discovery. The fact that we didn't really trust each other because we had our own ends in mind was secondary."

"Still, that wasn't kind of you."

"Kind women rarely get ahead in the world," Samantha pointed out. "They let others pass, they wait their turn, and eventually they fall so far behind that they can't catch up."

I raised my teacup in a toast. "Well said."

"Thank you." We clinked the gold-rimmed ceramic edges together and took another drink.

"Why bother with him, if you disliked him so much?" Mihaela asked, obviously still affronted on our father's behalf.

"Because he knew things, particularly about the story I was pursuing at the time, and I wanted to know them too." She looked down into her cup. "Also, my ex-boyfriend had been working as his assistant for a while, and I wanted to see how he was doing." She shrugged ruefully, for a moment looking every minute of her age. "He ended up dead, right before Ulysses died himself. It was a rather depressing time in my life, all told. Almost everything I gleaned from your father's archives never saw the light of day. What I did put out there I made fairly generic, to avoid becoming the target of his 'fans'. And he had some rabid ones back in the day, let me tell you."

She glanced at the bloodstone shard sitting in the hollow of my throat. "There are people out there who will do terrible things to have the kind of power Ulysses wielded, the sort of people who don't understand the concept of consequences. I had my differences with the man, but I always respected the fact that he set limits on his own reach. I didn't want to invite the kind of trouble that doing an exposé on him would bring into my life, so I did my best to disassociate myself from your father completely after he died."

"Well, Mihaela and I can certainly both vouch that those

people still exist and are still utter prats, but we have no interest in leading them to you," I assured her. "They've beaten us to the punch every time," which indicated a level of preparedness that was making me more and more uncomfortable, "but given how challenging it's been to find information on these final bases, I figure talking to you is our best shot to get ahead of them for once."

"To what end?" she asked.

"It's personal," Mihaela interjected. "Private."

"If you say so." Samantha pulled herself to her feet, steadying her grip on the cane. She sighed. "It's a useful thing, but I hate needing it. I was shot in the leg during my last investigation," she said with a frown. "I don't recover as fast as I used to. Come on, dears. I've got the map inside."

The "map", it turned out, was a cleverly disguised painting on her wall. If you didn't know you were looking at countries, at continents, it would just appear to be a modernist, multi-media work of art, with numbers scattered across swirling lines in complementary colors. I complimented her on it, and she inclined her head.

"I painted it myself," she said, her tone modest but her eyes bright with pride. "Everything hanging on the walls in here is related in some way to one of my unfinished investigations. Ulysses doesn't exactly fit the bill, but then I always assumed this knowledge would come in useful someday, and look." She waved a hand at the two of us. "Now it has. So." She pointed a finger at the map. "You've covered Boston, New York City, Mombasa, and

Bloodstone Isle, correct? *Bloodstone Isle*," she added with a derisive snort. "It used to be called Largos, but that egoistic barbarian went and named it after himself."

"That egoistic barbarian kept a picture of you in his home there," Mihaela snapped at her, evidently fed up. "I wish he had known how poorly you thought of him at the time. Perhaps he wouldn't have wasted the paper."

Samantha stared at Mihaela with a gimlet expression. "You know very little about him, don't you?" she said after a moment.

Mihaela narrowed her eyes. "I know that he was the bravest—"

"No," Samantha interrupted, "I'm not talking about him being a hero, a monster hunter, a near-immortal. I'm talking about the man beneath all those trappings. And he *was* a man, despite his thousands of years of life and everything he'd done over the course of them. Almost no one ever saw that, though. I did, I saw him for who he was and I called him out on it, and you know what? He loved me for it." She tugged at a lock of her white hair. "Not for my golden 'do, not for my pretty face, not for the way I filled out my bellbottoms. He loved me because I saw him for who he really was, and that was rare enough to be considered precious even though it wasn't complimentary.

"I didn't love him back, but you'd better believe I appreciated what he did for me, and for my career. He gave me a boost in a time when women journalists had to fight hard to be taken seriously, and to do anything other than treat him with the honesty he deserves would be an affront to his memory. Now." She banged the end of her cane on the floor. "May we get on with this?"

"Let's, please," I said, intrigued with the byplay between the ladies but feeling more and more the pressure of time. I couldn't help but notice that although Mihaela was in a state of high aggravation, she was barely flushed. She ought to be beet red with anger, but the only sign on her skin was a nearly invisible flush at the top of her cheeks. Whether she realized it herself or not, her window back to humanity was narrowing faster and faster.

Samantha was already facing the map. "Now, as far as I was able to glean, Ulysses' Antarctic base is just outside the Savage Land, which, as you ladies surely know, is located at the base of the Palmer Peninsula. One of the peaks penning that refuge in is called Mount Coman, and that's where Ulysses put his base. From what I understand, it's a mere half an hour's walk from the eastern edge of the Savage Land, so I don't anticipate you having to do a lot of climbing. As for finding it, though?" She shrugged. "I don't know if he marked it in any special way, to make it easier to locate. I suspect not, in fact, because apart from Boston and Bloodstone Isle, he preferred to keep these bases discreet.

"As for the Moscow base, I believe that it's in a building on the edge of Golosov Ravine, right across Andropova Avenue." She touched a green swath of paint that was meaningless to me, but obviously meant something to her. "Golosov was his favorite place to go monster hunting in

Moscow. From what I understand, there's an unpredictable rift of some kind in there that allows for time travel, and all sorts of interesting beasts have come through over the years." She smiled slightly. "Anyhow, there's a hidden tunnel at the end of the ravine that leads through to the building he used. That's probably the easiest and most covert way to get in."

"Fantastic." And it was, truly it was, but of the two remaining targets, Moscow was likely the easier one to reach. Therefore, we should get the tough one out of the way now. It would be smart to tackle Antarctica while Mihaela was still on an even keel, neither desperate for blood nor for the bloodstone. Except... "Well, hell."

Both women looked at me. "What?" Mihaela asked. "What's wrong?"

"I can't think of a good way to get to Antarctica."

"You've had no problem getting rides on Stark Industries planes so far," she pointed out.

"Yes, as long as they were already headed in the right direction. There's no reason for SI to be doing a conference in the wilds of Antarctica, as far as I know."

"There's always the genie," Samantha suggested with a mischievous smile.

Ugh! I scowled at her. Honestly, the lamp wasn't the sort of thing you brought up out of nowhere. Beyond the importance of keeping mum about it in general – because there was always someone who would come after you for the lamp so they could try their luck with wishes, the fools – it never, ever worked the way I hoped it would. "I said good ways."

She wasn't wrong, though. I'd already gone to the trouble of requesting the lamp from Adam – it was nestled in a custom carrying case at the bottom of my bag.

Mihaela looked between us suspiciously. "What genie?" she asked. "What are you talking about?"

"I'm talking about a means of getting us anywhere in the world instantaneously," I replied, crossing my arms. Perhaps I was feeling a little defensive about the whole thing, given that we were on the clock, but I had good reason to be wary.

Sure enough, her eyes went wide with shock, then narrow with anger. "You mean the story with the lamp is real? And you could have sent us across the world like that–" she snapped her fingers "– in no time at all, and you chose not to? Are you hoping that we will fail? Did you intend for this curse to consume me?" Her hands tightened into fists, her words blurring as her fangs became more prominent.

"Do calm yourself," I told her coldly, "or I will put you down, tie you up, and sit on you while the grownups are talking."

"There are issues with using the genie," Samantha said, a peace offering on my behalf that she didn't have to make. I appreciated it, though. "It will send you as close to where you specify as possible, while also sending you to the nearest source of trouble. It can't help it."

"Popped me straight into the middle of a nest of vampires

once." It had been my first time using it, too – that had taken the shine off magical artifacts fast. "Back when I was starting to get the hang of things. Since then, I've landed up to my neck in a marsh full of ghouls, fallen fifteen feet out of a tree where the Beast of Bladenboro was resting for the night, and nearly got my face sucked off by an Andean monster that looks like a cow hide."

The last one seemed comical, but there was something intensely disturbing about landing flat on your back in a shallow stream in the middle of nowhere, only to immediately be pounced upon by a floating skin with a bony spine and stalk-like, alien eyes. If the creek had been a little deeper, it might have drowned me beneath its bulk. I shuddered. Slice my head off, disembowel me, jerk my heart right out of my chest cavity – right, fine, part of the job. But bloody drowning? It was so undignified. Any idiot could drown – heavens, idiots drowned every day. Drowning deaths were nearly always accidental, not the result of a proper fight. I'd be damned before I succumbed to something like that.

"In this case though," I said after a moment, "I don't think we have a choice. It's going to have to be the damn genie." I pulled out my phone to check some time zones and paused. "Did you know there are twelve different time zones in Antarctica? All right, it's eight here, which means… well, there should still be some semblance of daylight down there." I reached for my non-weapons bag and shifted things around until I came to the lamp's hard case. I also moved my cold-weather gear up to the top – I'd be needing it soon.

I opened the case and pulled out the lamp. It was a small thing, a bit tarnished around the edge of the lid. I'd have to polish it up. I might not like the way the thing worked, but that was no excuse for letting my equipment fall into disrepair. I opened up the lid. "Hello in there."

"Hello, Elsa," the genie said, so quiet I could barely hear it. "It's been a long time."

Not long enough. "Yes, well, you do have a way of keeping me on my toes whenever I ask you to work, don't you? In fact, I think I actually lost a toe that last time."

"It grew back," the genie pointed out. "And honestly, can you blame me for trying to find a way to alleviate the boredom of my situation? It's not like I *chose* to be in here."

"It's not like I choose to keep you in here," I replied, "but you shouldn't have made a bet with Ulysses if you couldn't handle the consequences of losing. Now, I need a ride for two to Antarctica – a very specific spot in Antarctica," I added as the lamp began to glow. "Simmer down, let me explain." I glanced at Samantha. "You have the coordinates?"

"Mm-hmm." She adjusted her glasses and moved closer to the painting. "Whenever you're ready."

"We're heading for one of my father's old bases," I said to the genie. "And it's not just me, I've got a passenger, so it's quite important that you get us as close to the base as possible. No side trips, no journeys into the unknown, and no monsters. Got it?"

"Your wishes, as ever, are crystal clear," the genie replied. "Budge up together with your friend, all right? It'll make it easier on me."

"Get your bag," I told Mihaela, and she snatched it up and brought it over, standing so close that our arms touched. I rucked up similarly and fought down the frisson of nerves I felt every time I used the bloody lamp. It would be all right. Even if it sent us into danger – and of course it was going to try – the Savage Land was mostly pacified these days. Sure, there was the occasional rogue mutant or evil scientist gadding about, but I could handle those. Probably. "Be ready to move fast when we arrive," I murmured to Mihaela, who looked startled.

"Is the Savage Land really such a dangerous place compared to what we've already been through?" she asked.

I nodded definitively. "Oh, yes. Absolutely."

Her mouth tightened.

"What, have we finally found a prospect that scares you more than not getting your bloodstone back?" I teased. "You've handled all the monsters we've encountered surprisingly well so far."

"I haven't had a choice, have I?" she replied. "Don't worry, I won't break."

Not yet, at any rate. This expedition of ours would be a lot for any monster hunter, much less a novice like Mihaela, but I would take her word for now. I turned back to our host.

"Right, Samantha, thanks for everything," I said. "Try not

to get shot on your next assignment – amateur move, dear."

She rolled her eyes. "I'll try to remember that. All right, ladies, here are your coordinates." She read a string of numbers off to me, latitude and longitude, and I repeated them. The lamp glowed brighter and brighter, until all I could see around me was its reddish-tinged light. I felt the familiar whoosh of magical transportation, and a moment later my feet touched down on solid ground again.

Actually, not solid at all. Kind of muddy, and–

A massive, shadowy figure appeared above us, blocking out all the light. A second later the ground rumbled, and literally shook me so hard I bumped a few inches into the air.

A second after that, something tried to squash us flat.

FOURTEEN

I reacted before I even identified the danger, grabbing Mihaela by the arm and jerking her back with me as an enormous saurian foot lowered itself right on top of where we'd just been standing. *"Bloody mother–"* My rant at the genie ended as I realized that Mihaela hadn't quite gotten clear of the dinosaur's stomp. Even as the foot lifted off, she was clutching at the bottom half of her left leg, which ...

Yeah, being in mud and not on hard-packed soil had helped, but I'd be damned if every bone in there wasn't broken. "Curse it," I muttered, getting to my feet in a hurry and moving to pick her up. "We have to–"

"Elsa, behind you!"

I dropped Mihaela and swung my shotgun around in one smooth motion, just in time to shoot an enormous, clearly carnivorous dinosaur right in the front teeth. It roared and reared back, but I could already see that my regular shells weren't going to do much against it. I switched out for a round of triple-doom shells, each filled with a slug, buckshot, *and* birdshot, and let loose with those next. They made ripples and bloody marks in the creature's hide, but mostly seemed to serve the purpose of infuriating it.

"Right, that's not good," I muttered, reaching into my bag and ripping out the big blade I kept inside the hard shell along the back. Forget using my Bowie knife. To a dinosaur this size – lord, was it some variety of Tyrannosaurus rex? – that would feel like nothing more than a splinter. Even my respectable, four-foot five-inch longsword might not penetrate deep enough to do the kind of damage I'd need to for us to survive this. And there was no way Mihaela was going to *drink* one of these things to death.

The T-rex – whatever, I was going with it – loomed over me like a giant, its jaws partially gaping as it inhaled, trying to figure me out by my scent. I'd irritated it, hurt it just enough to make it a bit cautious, but I couldn't count on that keeping it back for long. I had to lead it away from Mihaela. "All right, you enormous pain in my arse," I shouted even as I began to step to the right, away from where my sister lay helpless in the mud. "Let's not muck about, right? You want dinner?" I waved at it with my sword. "I'm right here! Come and get me!"

The dinosaur seemed to consider it, its eyes focused on me, following me avidly as I stepped through the churned-up sludge beneath my feet. I kept eye contact as best I could, hoping I wouldn't slip. I had fabulous reflexes, but no one could be perfectly on point all the time. It took a step toward me, then another. I drew in a steady breath, ready to jump over its maw and onto the back of its neck the moment it came close enough. One good stab at the base of the skull and I could–

It stopped, its nostrils flaring. Drool slithered off its long, sharp teeth, and a second later it turned away from me and back toward Mihaela, who had managed to get herself into a sitting position.

"No! Bad dinosaur!" I shouted, leaping after it and slashing at its hind legs. No good – the blade, relentlessly sharp though it was, didn't even penetrate. I'd have to use physics to get my point across.

It was less than five feet from Mihaela now, who to her credit had her gun out and firing, although she was in too much pain to properly target the eyes. The dinosaur roared, making the air around us seem to echo with its power and ferocity, then lunged forward.

No, you don't! I leapt high into the air and, using every ounce of strength I could muster, jammed my sword straight down through the end of the T-rex's tail, not stopping until the crossbar of my hilt had practically stapled the last wriggling foot of flesh against the ground.

There. I straightened and watched with satisfaction as the dinosaur roared in pain, straining against its new limit and finding itself wanting. *Lovely.* I'd pinned that blade into the earth deeper than Merlin had stuck Excalibur into a stone.

Mihaela was already shoving herself backward, even using her damaged leg to help her. I was glad to see she was doing better – had to love that vampiric rejuvenation. That would make the *rest* of this fight a lot easier.

The dinosaur roared again and began to turn to face me. I loaded a few Dragon's Breath rounds into my shotgun and prepared for a long and tiresome bout of "exhaust the big beastie until it can't fight any longer and then do everything in your power to slit its throat" when suddenly, a whole new world of trouble opened up to my eyes.

Another T-rex charged out from behind a massive, flattened tree – a decidedly tropical tree – and roared its own terrifying cry. If I'd *ever* doubted we were in the Savage Land, with its perilous time bubble filled with ferocity, the balmy temperature and the dinosaurs had definitely set me straight there. The new dinosaur charged us, far enough away to get up some real speed, its jaws open to catch and consume me.

No thanks, I'd had more than enough of that with the shark-odile. I jumped onto the back of the other T-rex, firing one round of Dragon's Breath at the incoming beastie before ducking another set of snapping jaws, turning, and firing the second round at the first T-rex's face. Both of the dinosaurs reared back, unaccustomed to flame, and I jumped down again and ran over to my sister, who'd finally reached the questionable safety of yet another fallen tree. Good lord, what had been going on here? Some sort of earthquake? That was all I could think of that might knock over a tree three times bigger than one of these bloody carnivores.

"How's the leg?" I asked, pushing a filthy hank of hair out of my face. Muddy, again. I couldn't seem to avoid the stuff, even in Antarctica.

"Healing, but…" She winced. "Not quickly enough, I'm afraid."

"Nonsense," I said bracingly. "We just have to get some blood into you, and you'll be right as rain."

"I'm afraid my blood bags might be compromised at this point," Mihaela said, gesturing toward the dinosaurs, where… Oh. Yes, she had a point, by the way they were clawing our belongings into the dirt as they fought to free the pinned dino.

"I hope they crush that bloody lamp," I muttered. "I hope that blighter of a genie feels every last pound of pressure, too. Think it knew it was sending us into a pack of T-rexes?"

"Giganotosaurus, actually."

I paused in reloading and stared at her. "I beg your pardon?"

"Those are Giganotosaurus. Pack hunters, bigger than Tyrannosaurus rex."

"Well, you little paleontologist, you."

Huh. I learned something new every day. I might have said more, except just then the Giganto-whatsit I'd pinned managed to rip its tail free, sending the sword spinning off into the jungle ten meters to the right of us. The massive predators, now done with their brief preoccupation, turned all their attention back to where it had been before – squarely on us. Instead of immediately running in, though, they snorted and butted at each other, perhaps working their nerve back up after I gave the one a few stings. Whatever – I'd take any delay I could get.

"Get up, we need to get you into a tree," I said, looking at those around us for some decent low-hanging branches. There was no way I could run with her, not far or fast enough to outlast two bloody dinosaurs who stood twenty feet tall and were twice as long. I barely came up to one of their kneecaps.

"You should run," Mihaela said.

"No good, we can't move fast enough to–"

"No, I mean, you should run." Her jaw was locked down so hard if she'd clenched it any more she might have broken one of her pointy new teeth. "Leave me here."

I would have laughed if it hadn't been so idiotic. "Right, yeah, leave you, sure," I said, getting my arms under her and hoisting her into a fireman's carry. She muffled a scream of pain as her leg was jostled, but I didn't much care.

"Elsa! Just go, make it easy on yourself."

"Shut your face." I jumped onto the lowest branch of a tree that extended up about a hundred feet.

"Elsa, really–"

"I said *shut–*" another jump "*– your–*" I needed to use my hand to help with this next one, ten feet straight up at twice my bodyweight was a stretch even for me "*–bloody* face, Mihaela!" One more jump and a swing and we were a good thirty feet up in the tree, high enough that we had some breathing room as the Giganotosauruses tried to figure out their next line of attack.

Boom! The entire tree rocked as one of the enormous lizards slammed the side of their head into the base of the trunk.

Perhaps I'd only grabbed us a few more seconds to see doom coming. That said, I wasn't about to quit. "You stay here," I said sternly, wrapping her hands around the branch. "If you even think of jumping, I will truss you up like a prize pig, blindfold you, gag you, and drag you to the next base, do you understand me? You're not expendable!"

"I was trying to be practical!" Mihaela snapped as the tree rocked again, farther this time. I reached out and grabbed her arm to stabilize myself. A crunching, crashing sound began to build somewhere in the distance, hard to place. The sound of our tree trunk giving up?

"There's no point in sacrificing yourself to save me when there's nothing much left to save," Mihaela finished.

How dare she? Oooh, she was going to regret those words once I got us out of this.

If you get us out of this.

Shut up, brain.

"I can handle it, just let me think for a moment," I snapped. I needed the sword back – the shotgun had been next to useless and I didn't have much better.

Well, actually…

I pulled one of the fragmentation grenades off the

bottom half of my bandolier and tossed it down behind the Giganotosaurus, putting their bodies between it and the tree. I hadn't had much of a chance to use these yet, beyond messing with the monstrosity on Bloodstone Isle, and now was as good a time as any. One comforting *bang* later and …

BOOM! The tree wavered as one of them hit it even harder than before. Oh dear, that had riled the beasties, but not in the way I'd hoped. I hadn't expected the grenade to kill one of them with a throw like that, but making them think twice would have been nice. Instead, it had only made them angry.

I had two left, though. I could still pull this off without resorting to chopping the stinking things to bits with the sword I should have sharpened more. "Right, I'm going down."

"Elsa!"

"What did I tell you?" I slammed her reaching hand back down onto the trunk hard enough to make her finger bones creak. "Hold onto this bloody branch and don't let go until I say you can." I gauged the distance to the broadest yet-unmolested branch beneath me, then dropped down to it. I landed like a cat, perfectly balanced – then almost fell off as another head smack made the tree begin to list to the side. That crunching, cracking sound grew louder. It seemed too loud to be a single tree, but I couldn't see anything else around to account for the noise.

"No time to waste," I muttered to myself, pulling one of

the grenades off and gauging my throw. It would have to go straight down the Giganotosaurus's throat to have any effect, that much I was sure of. I could do that, though. I had a decent angle, and that one in particular was looking up like all it needed was an excuse to roar and show off for its mate…

One bright yellow eye found me, and sure enough, the dinosaur dropped its jaw and roared. "Cheers," I said, and gently lobbed the live grenade straight into its mouth.

Or rather, it would have gone right into its mouth if the ground hadn't chosen that particular moment to shake, the cracking sound so loud it was deafening. The grenade fell to the earth, where the dinosaur stepped right on top of it. A moment later there was a dull thud from beneath its foot, and it snarled with even more rage.

"Oh, come on!" I only had one left. Even if this next one worked, I'd still have one giant carnivore to deal with. Perhaps they were cannibals – that would be nice, if the body of one was sufficient distraction for the other to leave us alone.

"Elsa!"

"Don't make me come back up there!" I warned Mihaela as I grabbed my last grenade.

"No, you don't understand – look at what's coming!"

Coming? I lifted my head just in time to see a massively long neck appear over the trees just ahead of us. It was dark, like someone had taken a swatch from a midnight purple sky and turned every star into a pebbly bump. I couldn't see the creature's head – that was somewhere lower down – but I did see the effect it had on the Giganotosauruses menacing us. They turned as a single unit to face the new threat. A moment later there was a tremendous *POW*, and with one sweep of an enormous tail, the newcomer knocked both of the massive predators off their hind feet. One of them flew so far, I couldn't even see where it ended up, while the other was trapped beneath a tree that went down with it.

I would have laughed, except the tree Mihaela and I were perched in got the tail end, pardon the pun, of the same whack. The trunk, already weakened by attacks from the Giganotosaurus, finally hit the point of no return. The bottom of the trunk wavered, then split, and with a resounding crack the whole tree began to fall over.

"Hang on tight!" I called up to Mihaela, who didn't bother responding – smart woman. She needed to focus on not being a screw-up for the ten bloody seconds it took this tree to go down. If she ended up getting crushed again, so help me…

The bushy canopy fell against its neighbor, where it stuck for a moment, allowing me the time I needed to jump down to the ground. I leapt aside as the tree rolled, then finally thudded the final fifty feet down. Mihaela was somewhere tangled in the branches, but I didn't dare look for her. I was still within stomping range of the enormous newcomer, whose head I could make out now.

If you lined three busses up in a row, you still might not make a dinosaur quite this large. It was immense, bigger than any living thing I'd ever seen in person before, and I'd seen dragons. Fin Fang Foom had nothing on this marvel of nature. Its flat teeth told me that it was a herbivore, but its sheer size made it the biggest threat in the near vicinity. My sword was just a few feet away. I picked it up, mostly just as a way to make myself feel more prepared in the face of such a titan, and waited. If it noticed me, if it dubbed me a threat and felt like stomping on me... there was little I could do apart from try to dodge.

The dinosaur lowered its tremendous head, scanning the ground for threats with eyes as big as my torso. I didn't move, but it saw me anyway – did it notice my hair? Could a dinosaur even differentiate between colors that way? It saw me at any rate, and leaned in close, so close I could smell its musty breath. It smelled a bit like a cow, honestly. A whole herd of cows.

I held perfectly still, doing my best to have all the interest and animation of a beetle, something well beneath the notice of a beast like this. It huffed a wash of hot, malty breath over me, tilted its head to look more closely, and...

"Raaaaaaawr!"

The dinosaur reared back, the calm moment between us broken as the Giganotosaurus it had trapped beneath the tree announced its rage, still scrambling to escape from its wooden prison. It was doing a decent job of it, too, and might become a real problem in a few moments unless–

Crunch. The bigger dinosaur stomped down on the tree trunk, crushing it into the muddy ground. The

Giganotosaurus stopped moving. A few moments later, after sniffing about to ensure it was looking at a job thoroughly done, the dinosaur moved on, every footstep sending a rumble underfoot. I watched it go, then checked around for the other Giganotosaurus, just in case. Nothing. There was no movement except for the occasional insect, all of whom were bigger than I was comfortable with, and the breeze through the leaves.

"Elsa? Are you all right?"

And there was Mihaela. A surge of relief washed through me, and I closed my eyes for a moment to savor it before putting my soft feelings into the padlocked trunk buried at the bottom of my psyche where they belonged. Then I shouldered the sword, stomped over to where she was fighting free of a mass of leaves and broken branches, and gave in to my urge to yell at her.

"In the bloody name of… What do you think you're playing at back there, trying to be a martyr?"

Mihaela blinked. She had a long scrape down one side of her face, courtesy of the fall, I supposed. It was healing, but slowly. Her leg looked improved, at least. "I … I only meant that you shouldn't have to lose your life just to try and save mine, especially in a hopeless situation."

"Hopeless situation? *Hopeless*?" Fury rose up in me like a squall, washing away every hint of tenderness that might have remained in my stupid head. "What, hopeless like the one we were just in? The one that ended with us safe and sound while the creatures that attacked us were taken out of the picture by a third party? That situation?"

"Elsa, please, I just–"

"No, this is not something that you're going to make better by explaining, so don't try," I shouted at her. "You don't know what a 'hopeless' situation even is! You've lived safe and sound and helpless and *liking* it that way for most of your life, so don't tell me you know better than me because of your age or experience or *whatever* it is you're about to haul out of your bloody gob to justify that trash."

I pointed a finger at her. "I am not here to be party to your death, do you understand me? Not by dinosaur or by mercenary or even by your own boneheaded decision-making, so do me a favor and stop thinking you know anything. All right? Stop thinking you can't handle what's coming, or that you know what terror is, or that you've got any clue of what's best for either of us, *especially* you, because it's remarkably clear to me that you don't!"

In fact… "Let's remember that the only reason I'm here is to help you get your shard back. I've got mine, I'm not in trouble, *you* are. So don't tempt me to do what would be in my best interest anyway, all right?"

Mihaela nodded stiffly. "I'm sorry. Clearly I let my emotions get the better of me."

"Too bloody true," I agreed.

"And I'm not as experienced in matters of fighting as you, I can see that," she continued.

"Such insight, coming so nearly on time!"

"Will you shut up?" she snapped. "I'm trying to apologize

nicely here, and you're just throwing it back in my face."

Ah, there was the fire I was looking for. "Yes, that's what I do," I said to her with more kindness than she merited. "So, enough of all that nonsense. How's the leg?"

Mihaela stood up, but grimaced. "Still broken, but I think I can get about with a crutch."

"Good. You look for a likely branch, I'll go inspect what's left of our supplies." I was under no illusions that any of our belongings had gotten out of this mess unscathed. It took me a moment to even catch sight of the bags, buried under the churned-up ground as they were. I walked over and... Oh. Oh dear. They'd been stomped on by not one, but two different types of dinosaur, with the effect of basically squashing the bags flat. Our only saving grace might be that the ground was muddy enough to absorb some of the creatures' weight.

"Let's see what's survived," I muttered, and tore into the already tattered one on top of the pile.

Right, my clothing was basically a loss, which was too bad since I'd packed with a mind to help me tolerate the cold. Eh, I'd just have to suck it up. The extra shotgun ammo had also broken into pieces, but my three handguns and their associated ammunition had all survived, so bully for me. Mihaela's blood store was indeed squashed into jelly, although her sunscreen had survived. The lamp was, as I'd expected, flattened. I picked it up and brushed off the worst of the chunks of mud. "You did this to yourself," I told the genie.

"Screw you!" echoed a tinny voice from inside the mushed lamp. "You need to start taking better care of your belongings, Bloodstone! This is no way to treat a priceless magical artifact!"

"Maybe you'd have been treated better if you didn't drop us into the middle of a dinosaur war," I replied. "Frankly, I think you had this coming to you."

"Oh, get stuffed, you…" It continued to curse even as the dents slowly popped out, the brass of the lamp smoothing bit by bit until it was just as pristine as it had been before our arrival.

Well, it wasn't like I'd been counting on cooperation from the cretin of a genie anyway. It was user beware every single time. I wrapped the lamp in a pair of Mihaela's granny panties, stuffed it into the least-damaged bag along with my remaining ammunition, Bowie knife, and her sunscreen, and walked back to where I'd left Mihaela, who…

Who was standing tall on her own two feet, no crutch necessary, wiping her lips with the back of her hand as she walked away from the corpse of the Giganotosaurus. "Oh really?" I asked archly, nodding toward the beast.

To her credit, she didn't look at all embarrassed. "It was rather gamey," she said, "but very robust. I feel much better."

"Good on you." That was one of the nice things about working with a newly turned vampire – she hadn't had a chance to develop eating preferences. The number of prissy bloodsuckers who disdained to have anything to do with a meal that wasn't from a particular bloodline or carried the flavor of a certain type of magic, *honestly*. If I hadn't killed some of those blokes, they'd likely have died of hunger. Few vampires cared to lower themselves to eat from animals, and it hadn't even occurred to me to offer that to Mihaela… but she'd figured it out on her own.

I smiled at her and handed over her sunscreen. "Put on a fresh coat, we're getting out of here." We needed to get to the edge of the Savage Land and climb out, then hightail it for the base. We were losing too much light as it was.

"All right." She slathered on the sunscreen, taking special care around her mouth and nose, then pulled her dark goggles down over her eyes. She looked like the heroine on every gritty steampunk novel I'd ever seen from the neck up. It clashed terribly with her businesswoman's attire and sensible shoes, but at least she was protected from the sun. "Lead on."

FIFTEEN

Getting to the edge of the Savage Land wasn't hard.

Climbing out was bloody difficult, though. It was nothing but crumbling sedimentary rock and unstable vines for nearly a quarter mile straight up, and I wasn't exactly wearing the right shoes for an extended climb. Not to mention I had to rope up to Mihaela to help keep her from falling, which ended up being necessary several times. It was fortunate she had some of a growing vampire's strength now, because otherwise I don't think we could have made it out of there before the next morning. After the crap we'd just gone through to get down here in good time, that sort of delay was intolerable.

The moment we pulled ourselves up over the rim of the basin, the cold struck me like a sledgehammer. It wasn't snowing, but the wind was so fierce that it didn't make a difference, because snow was flying through the air hard enough to blind us anyway. I shivered and blew on my hands. I could heal simple things like frostbite no problem, but in weather like this I'd be healing nonstop, which meant I'd be very uncomfortable for however long we were out in this mess.

"Let's get a move on!" I shouted over the howl of the wind. The sunlight was vanishing fast. We'd be in total darkness soon, which would be safer for Mihaela but worse for me. I could still make out the looming bulge of Mount Coman in the distance, though. Somewhere at the bottom of that was our father's base, so that was where we needed to be.

I took a few steps, wary of plunging waist-deep into the snow, but it was cold enough that not even my stiletto heels could punch through the icy crust without extra effort. Good – I didn't have time to fashion a set of snowshoes, although I'd blasted well have a specialized pair made if I was going to make a habit of venturing into the frozen places in the world. Which... I shivered and pulled my long coat more tightly around myself as I moved forward. I rather hoped I wouldn't have to come back any time soon.

At a dead run, we could have crossed the distance in fifteen minutes. As it was, we managed a jog that was occasionally stalled by a fall or misstep, so it was thirty minutes later when we got close enough to the mountain to start looking for any sign of the base. By God, if he'd buried it twenty feet deep and put shielding over the front of it to keep me out, I was going to scream bloody murder. But...

no. Was that a red light? A red, flashing light? What was going on over there?

Mihaela figured it out before I did. "A helicopter," she exclaimed, pointing at the base of Mount Coman. She was right. I could see its blades picking up speed as it prepared to take off.

There was only one reason for a helicopter to be out in the literal middle of nowhere in the middle of a storm like this, and it had nothing to do with science and everything to do with the blighter who was beating us to every single base. I didn't hesitate, just pulled my closest firearm and started shooting. Mihaela followed my lead, homing in on the rotor from the look of the flying sparks. *Good girl.*

"Run!" I screamed at Mihaela as I took off for the chopper. They weren't going to get away this time.

I could tell the moment we were spotted. A stream of holes from rapid gunfire erupted in the ice in front of us, a fast, steady spray that meant they had at least one machine gun. I jumped over the incoming rounds and off to the side, angling my landing so that I slid across the ice on my hip and kept my guns in play. One distant shadow went down, and the gunfire briefly stopped before picking up again – ah, I'd hit paydirt that time. I paused long enough to reload, then got to my feet and kept firing, concentrating on the bodies, not the helicopter. I didn't have the ammo to take that out until I got up close.

Fifty meters.

Thirty. A bullet carved a path across my right hip, but

thanks to the cold I barely felt it. Ha, so all this frost and snow *was* good for something. It was enough to make me laugh.

Twenty meters. Another man went down.

Fifteen.

Ten. I was so close–

"Elsa!" That was Mihaela's voice, barely audible over the wind. "Elsa, help!"

She needed me. I was seconds away from bringing this crew down, but Mihaela wouldn't be calling for help unless she needed it. And after I'd just gotten through scolding her about not sacrificing herself, I couldn't leave her to struggle or die in the cold.

"Blast," I hissed, and pulled my sword off my back. Even as I began to retreat back to where I heard her voice, I hurled my sword as hard as I could at the helicopter, trying to penetrate the driver's side cabin or the fuel tank. No luck – the blade went in, but it didn't cut anything vital. A moment later the mercenaries had loaded themselves and their casualties back into the vehicle and taken off into the air. We exchanged a few more petulant bullets as I backtracked, and then they were gone and I was looking around desperately for Mihaela, trying to see her through the blowing snow.

"Where are you?" I called out.

"Here… I'm – be careful, it's loose!" she added as the ground suddenly cracked beneath my feet. Heaven help me, there shouldn't be this kind of instability in the permafrost during the winter. Next thing we knew all the penguins would float away on the world's last icebergs, thanks to bloody global warming.

I carefully made my way over to Mihaela's voice and saw... nothing. Just a dark spot in the ice that was decidedly not her head. "Where are you?" I repeated.

"Down here!"

The dark spot turned out to be a narrow crevasse, into which Mihaela had apparently fallen and subsequently gotten stuck. It was lucky she had, or she could have dropped for hundreds of feet, but, as it was, she was wedged pretty tight about six or seven feet down. She didn't have the leverage to use vampiric strength to her advantage down here, and if she pushed too hard on the ice that was holding her in place... freefall again.

"Right." Well, there was going to be no elegant way to do this but do it I would. I straddled the crevasse, one foot on either side, then lowered myself down into it, digging in the metal toes of my boots to hold me in place. "Reach up, then," I said as soon as she was within grabbing distance. She extended a shaking hand, and two good pulls later I had her unstuck – which was good, because the ice was starting to crack again. "Climb up, up, up!"

She used me as a ladder to get out, then pulled me out by one leg behind her. Together we ran for it as the tiny crevasse suddenly became a rather large one.

I managed to find our bag and fling it into the base ahead of us, which was wide open thanks to those black-garbed goons, and we ran inside and slammed the door shut against the wind. Thankfully, the crevasse had stopped forming a few meters back, so at least we weren't about to plunge into the ground. Still, it was bitterly cold in here, although there was at least a bit of light from a big, hefty flashlight one of the mercenaries had dropped. I picked it up and shined it around the space.

Not prepossessing, I had to admit. It was circular inside, built in the shape of a half-dome, but inefficiently packed. The plain metal shelves against the walls were straight and didn't conform to the space at all. Ulysses must have done this one up in a hurry. The shelves themselves had been ransacked, with various boxes and bags strewn all over the place. I saw an oversized parka peeking out of one of them and put it on, feeling ten times better as my body heat was finally radiated back at me.

"Well," I said, "I'm not holding out much hope for anything good after those blokes beat us here, but we should look through it all anyway. Then we've got to think about how to get to our next stop. I know the temptation to use the genie is strong, but considering where it left us last time, it might be worth taking a more sedate method of travel to Moscow…" I turned and finally noticed that Mihaela was not only completely silent, she was also slumped against the door. She noticed me watching and managed a ghastly smile.

"I'm all right, just… a little bit shot, I think."

"Good lord, why didn't you say something instead of

letting me prattle on?" I demanded, walking over to her and setting our bag down, then easing her on top of it. "Let's see, then."

"A little bit shot" turned out to be five bullets, four of which had passed right through her abdomen and one of which was lodged in her shoulder. Or as my professor sister put it, "in the infraspinatus muscle just below the acromion! Do you not know simple human anatomy?"

Nerd. I knew monster anatomy well enough to take out a score of different pests with my eyes closed, but get one little muscle name wrong and I was due a lecture.

I managed to pry it out – her body was already trying to pass it, which helped a lot – but it wasn't pretty, and it certainly wasn't painless. Mihaela took the impromptu operation as well as anyone could, but she needed some time to heal. Even full of dinosaur blood, she'd endured an awful lot of grievous injuries over the past few hours.

"We'll rest a while before we carry on," I said, and I didn't think I was imagining it when she looked relieved. I left her there against the door and went on searching through the rubble.

There were some ancient MREs, which, come to think of it, were supposed to be good for years and I was starving, so I tried one. It tasted dubious, but my stomach didn't immediately reject it, and I'd been burning a lot of calories lately. I ate it, then ate three more, then found a canteen and drank the water in that too, although it tasted strongly of metal. I didn't find a bloodstone shard, though, or anything dropped by our attackers that would help with identifying them. All in all, a rather disappointing haul. The corpse out front *might* be able to tell us more, but I wasn't walking out into that storm again to check.

Once I'd picked through everything twice over, I sat down next to Mihaela with a sigh. She hesitated for a moment, then reached out and patted me on the shoulder. "Thank you for rescuing me," she said with a wry sort of grimace. "Again. I'm afraid I haven't been pulling my weight on this trip."

"I think you've done all right," I said, because while what she was saying was true, I wasn't about to kick her while she was down. And goodness, she'd almost been *all* the way down, given how things with that crevasse had been trending. "Thank God you're a vampire, though. Otherwise I'd have lost you back in Mombasa, and then Adam would have been disappointed in me, and Barnabus would have given me that look that I can't stand, and it wouldn't have been a good time."

"And also, I'd be deceased," she said, but there was some humor there.

"Yeah, but it would be too late for you to mind. Whereas Adam and Barnabus might just live forever and would hold that sort of thing over my head for at least that long."

She laughed, which was the point, then got pensive. Thoughtful. "You really don't mind it?" she asked.

"Mind what?"

"That I'm a vampire. It doesn't give you any pause?" she said.

I shook my head. "Not in the slightest, no."

"I know you mean that, but it's also hard to reconcile with all your…" She gestured at me.

It was my turn to laugh. "Oh, I know. I put on a good show, and to be fair, this is me, ninety-nine percent of the time. I love my work, I *love* it, and I would never give it up, but it pays to be discerning. Besides, some vampires are quite tolerable. Charles, of course… and Blade is practically friendly, if you meet him on a good night." There were also a huge number of hideous, vengeful disaster-vampires out there who were just begging to be killed, and I was working my way through their ranks in due course.

She nodded. "That's good to hear."

"Glad you think so." I hesitated, knowing that what I was about to say wouldn't be welcome, but I decided I needed to put it out there anyway. "You know you don't really need the bloodstone to get by, right? You can continue the way you've started and live a happy, fulfilling life as a vampire. You could–"

"No." She shook her head firmly. "I want it back. It's my only chance of living a normal life, and apart from that, it's mine. I won't let it rest in the hands of someone who would spend so many lives trying to stop us. Who knows what they will do with such a powerful artifact?"

Well, certainly, there was that murderous psychopath to consider, but… to my surprise, I found that at this moment I was more concerned with my half-sister's health and happiness than the baddie on the other end of our caper. I wanted her to understand that being a vampire didn't have to mean ending up like the scum who had turned her. I wanted her to find some sort of peace with who she was, and who she might well stay.

Mihaela held up a hand as soon as I opened my mouth. "No. Please, don't. Whatever you're going to say, I just… My mind is made up."

All right, then. So much for trying to be comforting. I stared balefully at our bag and the few items left in it. The most basic of guns and ammunition, plus my single grenade, plus a nit of a genie in a lamp that part of me desperately wanted to throw down the crevasse outside. I didn't want to use it again to get to Moscow. Good God, who knew what would happen to us if we let that thing drop us off in Golosov Ravine. We'd probably fall straight into a rift in the space-time continuum and end up in a bizarre alternate dimension where monsters were plentiful and guns were nonexistent. What a nightmare. I didn't mind killing them by hand, but lord, it was such messy work, and I'd already ruined two pairs of boots and my good coat on this dismal venture.

Right, no using the genie. What were our options for getting out of here, then? We wouldn't be catching a lift with any visiting mercenaries, that was for sure. Too bad I hadn't managed to take more of them out. We could have taken their helicopter and flown ourselves to a more hospitable clime. There were bases out on the peninsula north of here that were associated with actual countries instead of individual curs like Ulysses, but they were all too far away to hike to, especially in a storm. I could call in some lesser favors and get another aircraft of some kind to come in and pick us up, but that would take time that we didn't have.

We were racing against a clock that we couldn't see, to get to these bases before our unnamed enemy could, and find what they were looking for. The fact that they'd been here when we arrived told me several things: one, that it was likely there really was something valuable in one of these bases that their employer wanted, and two, that we weren't so far behind them any more. Still, the odds of them making it to the Moscow base ahead of us were fairly good. After all, that base was in the middle of a city, not on an entirely separate continent in the grip of subzero temperatures.

On the other hand, as far as I knew, Samantha was the only one who knew where either of these last two bases were, and I didn't think she'd been intimidated into giving information up before we saw her. After we left? Who knew, but hopefully she was still unassailed. So, if there was a chance we could get to the Moscow base before our enemy did, and possibly find the thing they were looking for, whether it was a shard or a weapon or something else Ulysses had socked away for decades, then wasn't it worth it?

I sighed heavily. Yes, it bloody well was, but that didn't mean I had to like what I was going to have to do.

"What's wrong?" Mihaela asked, one hand pressed to

her still-healing shoulder.

"How're the wounds coming along?" I asked evasively.

"Um..." She checked a few of the bullet holes. "Pretty well. Another few minutes and I should be back on my feet."

"Lovely." Yes, absolutely delightful, I was pleased she was going to be well but blast it, I was about to burn one of the biggest favors I'd ever been owed to get us to Moscow, and that stung. Not that Strange wouldn't be happy to discharge the debt, but I preferred more black in my ledger to red. "As soon as you're ready, let me know and I'll get us a ride out of here."

"Elsa..." Mihaela looked at the bag with a pained expression. "Please, there must be another way out of here than journey by genie."

I had to smile. "What, you don't fancy another dinosaur fight?"

"I would be quite happy to never see another dinosaur, living or dead, for the rest of my life."

"I completely understand the sentiment, and no, we won't be relying on that ninny to get us out of here." I sighed again. "I'll be calling on Doctor Stephen Strange."

Mihaela blinked, her eyes going wide. "You mean... the Sorcerer Supreme?"

"What a bloody load of trash that title is," I snapped. "There are plenty of excellent sorcerers out there, and most of them aren't nearly as dodgy as Doctor Strange. The ego on that man, honestly."

"Yes," Mihaela said, her voice so heavy with sarcasm I was surprised the words could even float through the air, "because you are so uncomfortable with big egos."

"Hahaha, aha, ha." Yes, I knew I had a big ego. That was part of what made working with other people who had them so irritating – there was always more friction than fun. Even with someone as relatively accommodating as Misty, I could only put up with so much before smiles turned to snarls. How any superpowered team lasted more than a week with some of the people they put on the roster, I truly didn't know. "At any rate, he owes me a favor for helping save him from a doppelganger back in the day. It was a very embarrassing incident for him, one I know he's eager to put all trace of in the past, so he'll probably be more than happy to give us a lift to Moscow via portal."

"How is he going to know we need him?" Mihaela asked. "Do you have a special magical signal?"

"Not exactly. It's more a matter of putting the right words with the right intent," I replied. "Are you ready to go?"

"Yes!" She staggered gamely to her feet, eager to see the magic work. Ugh, a groupie. I tossed her the bag, considered the enormous parka I was wearing, and decided to keep it on. We were heading to Russia, after all, who knew what the temperature would be.

"All right." I blew out a breath, then concentrated as I'd been told to and said, "Doctor Strange, it's Elsa Bloodstone. Time to repay that favor you owe me."

At first, nothing happened. Then, more nothing

happened. After a few minutes solid of nothingness, I heard Mihaela shift on her feet – probably trying to work up the nerve to ask me if I was completely mental.

Oh, for God's sake. "Anytime now!" I snapped, and–

There it was. The portal began as a tiny dot of golden light right in front of me, no bigger than a pinpoint, before expanding into a swirling, sparking oval big enough for two to walk through. "Elsa Bloodstone," the voice on the other side said pleasantly. "I didn't think this day would ever come."

"Yeah, yeah, save your gloating." I held out a hand to Mihaela. "Ready?"

"Ready," she said, and I led her through the portal and out of our father's penultimate base without a backward glance.

SIXTEEN

It was nearly midnight in Moscow when we arrived. Although it was cool verging on cold, the air felt like a hot summer afternoon to me after coming from Antarctica. I could feel my joints loosen with relief, even though we had just been deposited in a rather forebodinglooking ravine, with high grassy walls that left Mihaela and me standing in a sea of shadows at the bottom of it.

"Golosov Ravine, as promised." The glowing golden portal we'd come through began to close. "I would say it's been fun, but…"

"Yeah, yeah," I said, waving a hand at the man standing two feet and approximately five thousand miles behind us. "Thanks for the ride, and don't let the portal hit you on the way out."

There was a rich chuckle before the portal closed, leaving us in darkness. I turned on the flashlight I'd nicked back in the Antarctic base and swung it around. "Hmm." Everything the light touched was lush and glistening like it had just rained, from the tall green grass along the sides of the ravine to the thin-limbed trees jostling each other for space alongside us at the bottom of it. There was a gravel trail beneath our feet, and I could hear the sound of a burbling creek running close by. Quite lovely – Golosov Ravine appeared to be the Platonic form of a piece of nature while still bound by city walls.

Of course, you should never judge a place by its appearance.

"He could have been more precise about where he was leaving us down here," Mihaela said, sounding a bit put out.

"Strange has never gotten hung up on niceties," I replied, still looking around. The back of my neck was crawling, which only happened when I was being watched. Something was creeping around in the darkness out there. "He tries to come off as a gentleman, but you know what they say – once a narcissistic egoist, always a narcissistic egoist."

Mihaela blinked in surprise. "Do you really not like him?"

"I don't dislike him," I said, keeping my voice even as I focused on my senses, homing in on whatever was out there watching. If it was a person, they were about to get a rude surprise. If it was a monster, well … they were about to get an even ruder surprise. "Strange has his uses, and of course he's a terribly talented man. Otherwise, he wouldn't get the title 'Sorcerer Supreme' no matter how big his ego is, but he's been known to assume things about his own strength that leave him vulnerable. Whereas I–" I smiled at Mihaela, who could no doubt see it with her vampire vision "– try not to make assumptions that can get me kidnapped or killed. Speaking of…"

In one smooth motion, I pulled my gun, whirled around, and leapt in the direction of the heavy breathing I'd detected. It wasn't a terribly grand jump, just ten feet or so, but the creature I landed on top of certainly seemed surprised as it grunted and flailed slow, long-clawed hands at me. I nearly impaled myself on an antler evading the bloody thing's grasp as it grunted with frustration.

Tall, moss-like, deep voice… leshy, most likely.

I locked my legs around its neck and spun, using my momentum to whip the monster to the ground – no, it wasn't *my* trick originally, but I knew a good thing when I saw it. Then I landed soft as a cat on my battered soles, knelt down, and pressed the muzzle of my gun to the leshy's skeletal, antler-topped head. It stopped struggling immediately. *Good. This one knows civilization.*

"What, no pack of wolves for backup? No clan of bears?" I asked mockingly. I might not know much about leshy lore, but I knew they didn't usually work alone. Then again, it was probably hard to provide for a predatory entourage in Moscow, even if you did live in a verdant place like this. "You were going to take on two unknown travelers in the ravine by yourself? Isn't that a little risky?"

The leshy growled at me, then said something guttural in Russian, which wasn't my best language. Fortunately, Mihaela stepped in. "He says, yes, that there's no way to get wolves or bears into a place like this," she said, then hesitated.

Ah, there's more. I was pretty sure that wasn't everything he'd said. "And?"

"And he called you something rather rude," she said a bit reluctantly.

That was the word I recognized. Naturally I had a better handle on Russian swear words than pleasantries. "Well, we're off to a cracking good start here, you're honest." I smiled brightly, then stomped down hard on the arm he was slowly raising beside me. "No, no, don't try to get up. It's not going to work and will only serve to annoy me. Now. Did you know we were coming?"

The leshy carefully shook its head and said something else.

"He says that this is a popular spot for teenagers who want to make mischief," Mihaela put in. "They go after the sacred stones of Kolomenskoe with spray paint. He stops them."

"Sacred stones of what now?" I asked. Were we about to get whammied with some sort of mineral magic in addition to the potential for time travel?

"Kolomenskoe." She spoke to the leshy again, who rumbled something back. "Of course, apparently they're large pieces of sandstone here in the ravine, originally dedicated to Veles. A Slavic god of the underworld," she added, undoubtedly taking in my confused expression.

"Oh." I eased up the pressure I was keeping on his arm. "Well, restoration is a worthy cause. The archbishop of Glasgow would like you."

The leshy spoke again, in an even lower, more grinding voice.

"He says that sometimes…" Mihaela's voice faltered for a moment "Sometimes the youths come down here because they're in pain and they want to be away from people, or because they've had enough and want to… end it. He watches over them either way and tries to stop them from shooting or drowning themselves. He doesn't keep them, though. It brings too many people like… well, like you."

Oh, huh. That was rather nice, actually. I knew that leshies were more like fairies than evil monsters in a lot of Russian lore, with a reputation for taking in children who had been cursed by their own families, but this was my first time meeting one in the flesh, so to speak.

"Well, I don't want to cause him trouble or take time away from that benevolent task." I moved off the leshy and back a few steps. It pressed slowly into a sitting position, staring at us with ancient, glowing eyes. "Right, we'll be off in a jiffy. If you would be so kind as to point us in the direction of Andropova Avenue first, please."

The leshy didn't say anything. It stared at us, unblinking, as still as a statue.

"Andropova Avenue?" I repeated, then tried again in

Russian. It still just stared. "Oh, come on, I know I'm bad at this, but my accent isn't *that* horrible." I started to raise my gun again, but Mihaela put a restraining hand on my arm.

"Please," she said. "Let me do the talking."

"I can beat it out of him," I protested.

"I'm sure you can," she said soothingly, "but let me at least try before we resort to more violence. All right?"

I knew I was being handled and hated it, but also… well, I didn't mind saving my energy for the main event, so to speak. "Fine." I lowered my arm, and even holstered my gun in a show of good faith. It wasn't like I couldn't draw it again faster than the leshy could blink, if he ever did.

Mihaela took a step forward and said something that sounded very calm and peaceful, similar to the tone she'd taken with me a few times when she was trying to be soothing. The leshy listened in silence, and when Mihaela stopped, he raised a long, gnarled arm and pointed behind us, due west.

Very good. I assumed the direction of the street came from the distant, ambient sound of traffic, but it was always nice when the person you were with wasn't trying to play you. "Thanks for the tip," I said.

The leshy pushed to his feet. He loomed over even me from that height, a good foot taller and much wider. He rumbled something directly to Mihaela, then turned and plodded down the gravel path a ways before… goodness, just about disappearing into thin air. Now *that* was a neat trick. Some sort of inherent camouflage ability? I looked to see if any new trees or bushes had sprung up, but there weren't any. Hmm, maybe he was using some sort of portal to–

"Elsa." Mihaela sounded quiet but insistent. "He said that we were fools to think the trap we were heading into was anything of *his*. He doesn't like it at all. He's already rescued two kids from it."

"Ah." That refocused my thoughts rather unhappily on the problem at hand. "Other people have likely accessed the door at the end of the canyon, then."

"If the leshy bothered to notice them? Yes."

"And we're walking into a trap that's been laid for us for lord knows how long," I said. Whoever our opponent was, they seemed to suffer from an overdeveloped sensibility of what it meant to "play with your food", even if I was forced to admit they were clever. At this point, who knew how long this trap had been set up for us?

Mihaela nodded in reply to my statement. "Yes."

"And you're still willing to risk it in order to get your bloodstone shard back," I said, knowing the answer was going to be yes.

"Yes, but–"

"Ah-ah, no buts, we're past that sort of nonsense now." I crossed my arms and looked down the path thoughtfully. "The way I see it, we don't have a choice at this point but to press on."

"But you do," Mihaela insisted. "I assure you, I–"

"No, I don't think I do." In fact, the more I thought about

it, the more I was positive that, in fact, I didn't have a choice in the matter. If I didn't walk into the trap now, then it would only necessitate another one being set for me later, one that might affect my family, or my home, or both. And there would certainly be another reckoning for Mihaela, even if she gave up her chance at the shard now, which I was sure she wouldn't. She still saw this as her last shot at her old life, the life she loved, given to her by the man she idealized. She wouldn't give up now. But even if I walked away and somehow convinced Mihaela to come with me, we were only setting ourselves up for trouble down the road.

We'd been presented with a series of obstacles, one after another, at every base we visited. We'd short-circuited the last one by getting there as the mercenaries were leaving, but I had no doubt that if we'd given them more time, they'd have left a deadly present behind for us to find. Someone was playing games with us, but we might be a bit ahead of them right now. Not totally ahead of them, obviously, since our opponent seemed to have inside information on the locations of these bases, but better than we would've been if we'd traveled from Antarctica to here in a more traditional fashion. The question was, were we far enough ahead for it to make a difference?

There was only one way to find out, and frankly I was tired of being toyed with. Whoever we were dealing with was a masterful planner, but also a physical coward. Mihaela was in a good spot right now, I still had a decent amount of ammunition and the advantages my own bloodstone shard gave me... No, now was the time to press on, not fall back.

"I think it's time we wrapped this up," I said, then glanced at Mihaela. Her shoulders seemed to slump in relief. "There's no point in trying to outrun whoever this is. We've come all this way, and now we've got to see it through."

Mihaela hesitated for a moment, then reached out and laid a hand briefly on my shoulder. My, my, the second time she'd voluntarily touched me since we'd started this adventure. "Thank you."

I grinned at her. "Thank me if we survive this. And whatever else happens..."

"I know," she said, neatly circumventing me having to say anything emotional, which I greatly appreciated. "Lead the way."

I did so, striding down the path with my back straight and my head held high, every bit of confidence I felt and quite a lot that I didn't feel evident in my posture. If we were being watched, I wanted to be seen as in control, as dominant. Yes, this might be a trap, but it was my choice to walk into it. Besides, I'd sprung quite a few traps of my own in the past. I knew what to look for and was confident that I could handle the worst of it before it got the better of us.

At the end of the path was what looked like a solid rock wall, covered with more of that lush Golosov greenery. "We need to find the entry," I said, leaning in against it and tapping my fist here and there. Solid, solid, solid all the way through. Perhaps the entrance was in a different place?

"Here," Mihaela said, and stomped her foot hard on the ground. *Clang!* "Ah, a trapdoor."

Another bloody trapdoor. Let's hope this one didn't lead into a sewer tunnel as well. I dug through the sod until I found a handle – with about a week's worth of growth covering it, interesting – then lifted. It rose without a creak. Well maintained, then, certainly not Ulysses' original installation. "Right," I said and shone the flashlight inside. Nothing. "Here we go, then." I turned to hand the flashlight to Mihaela to hold, knocking some dirt into the tunnel as I did so. All of a sudden, a burnt smell arose from the air a few inches down.

"Hmm, what have we here?" I tested with another sprinkling of dirt, this time watching as it hit, and sure enough there was a brief flash of fire as the soil impacted on something I couldn't see a little way into the tunnel. "Laser. Interesting."

"What are we going to do about it?" Mihaela asked.

"Hmm." There were all sorts of things one could do to manage a laser, but since I didn't know where the power supply was and lacked a lot of my regular tools… "Let's see if we can't find the leshy again."

She frowned. "He's not going to want to go in there either, Elsa."

"No, but perhaps he might be willing to give us a hand when it comes to rerouting the stream over there." I didn't know much about a leshy's powers, but given his status as a nature spirit, I wouldn't be surprised if he could move a trickle like that a couple of meters. "We can drown the laser. I doubt they bothered to invest in the kind that's effective underwater, and for all we know this one is only initiated a few dozen feet away."

"The tunnel is longer than that," Mihaela rightly pointed out – it had to be if it went from here to the other side of Andropova Avenue.

"Yes, but our mastermind's plan, not to mention their budget, might not extend that far." I stood up and brushed off my knees. "Let me see if I can rustle the old guy up."

"Why don't you let me try again?" Mihaela said, laying a hand on my arm. "After all, I'm the one on speaking terms with him."

And she was the one who hadn't recently held a gun to his head. I pointed a finger at her. "Excellent idea."

Mihaela nodded, then turned to face the creek in the center of the ravine. She called out to the leshy like she was speaking a prayer, like she was participating in a ritual as ancient as nature itself. Was this something she had learned from our father, or something that had come from her long-dead mother? Had her village of good Christians still practiced older forms of worship on the sly, a sidelong nod to the gods of old?

She sounded hypnotic, and just like a siren, the leshy wasn't able to resist her lure. A minute after she'd begun her entreaty, the creature appeared out of the mist like a ghost and muttered a few words.

"He will listen to your proposition," she said.

I blinked out of my stupor. "Ah, lovely. Here's what I'm thinking…"

Once I explained to Mihaela what I wanted and she passed the plan on to the leshy, it nodded and stepped down into the creek. The water only came up about a foot around its feet, but as it bent over and dipped its long, branch-like fingers into the water, that changed.

The stream slowly but steadily began to rise, and in five minutes' time it flooded up and over its own banks. It didn't run about willy-nilly, though – the leshy directed it straight into the entrance to the tunnel. A moment later there was a sharp *hiss*, abruptly cut off. That might have been enough, but I waited until the leshy himself finally straightened up, with the air of someone who knows they've done a good job.

"All finished then?" I asked. To my pleasure, it nodded directly at me.

I glanced into the entrance to the tunnel. The water was high, almost to the top of it, but even as I watched it began to ebb and flow away through cracks in the concrete structure. "Oh, beautifully done," I congratulated the leshy. "We're quite in your debt."

He shook his shaggy head and rumbled something.

"He says he will consider the debt fulfilled if we get rid of whatever is on the other side," Mihaela translated. "He says he hears… Oh dear."

"What?"

"He says he hears screaming coming from there

sometimes," she said somberly. "Also a few explosions. More over the past few days."

Screaming and explosions... delightful. "We can handle that," I said with all the confidence I could muster. "He can count on us."

He said something else, and Mihaela laughed. "What?" I demanded.

"It's an old Russian saying," she chuckled. "Something like 'When you rush, you make people laugh.' It means–"

"Yes, yes, don't be overconfident, I've got that part, thank you very much." Good grief, where was the faith? "We can handle it from here." I believed myself, too, but given what had already happened to us there were a few smart precautions we could take to protect ourselves in a small, enclosed space. I reached for the bag, which we'd pretty much emptied at this point, and searched for my – aha! Toiletries kit, right where I'd left it. It was thoroughly smashed, but that didn't matter given what I was taking out of it.

Mihaela blinked when I handed the items to her. "What, really?"

"Yes, really." I was already putting mine in place. They weren't a perfect solution to issues we might have if our enemy set off a flashbang grenade in the tunnel, for example, but if they kept our eardrums from being burst, I was all for them.

She shrugged and followed suit. "I just didn't think you'd need things like this to help you sleep at night."

"You've obviously never tried to fall asleep next to Wolverine," I replied wryly. "Touchy gent at the best of times. It saves both time and blood to ignore his ability to saw logs like a lumberjack."

Her eyebrows went so high up they nearly hit her hairline. "I'm sorry, *Wolverine*? Honestly?"

I sniffed. "There's no call to be so judgmental. Right." I adjusted the ear plugs further, then nodded. "Let's get going, then." The water looked to be only as high as my ankles now. I dropped another handful of dirt inside. When there was no reaction, I slowly followed it, shining the flashlight around. No sudden, burning pains, no shifts beneath my feet or other evidence of pressure plates. It was good enough for a start.

SEVENTEEN

I gave the bloodstone at the base of my neck a pat, the power of it echoing comfortingly through my body, then stepped forward. Mihaela dropped in a moment later, murmuring something behind her to the leshy. A moment after that, the hatch closed again, leaving us in darkness except for the flashlight.

"Keep your senses sharp," I murmured. I took one slow step, then another. Water sloshed gently around my feet for the first thirty seconds, but then it was almost completely drained after that. The laser didn't come back on, so it seemed we'd done permanent damage to it.

I walked, and Mihaela followed, stepping directly in my footsteps. No rushing in this time for either of us – we'd learned that lesson. I held my backup Sig Sauer in my right hand, Bowie knife in my left in case anything aggressive made an appearance. There was nothing, though. I was surprised – one laser trap and nothing else? It was so quiet as to be oppressive, although after a few hundred feet I could feel the faint rumble of traffic overhead. We were passing beneath the road. Soon we'd be on the other side, and there, I assumed, we'd find whoever our enemy was. Perhaps we'd surprise them. Probably we wouldn't. But given the myriad ways we'd been tested so far, I doubted we'd get to the other side just to take a bullet to the head.

I mean, that was what *I* would do, but I was absolutely no fun when it came to killing, or so several friendly sociopaths of my acquaintance had told me. I was good for quips, but bad when it came to savoring the warm glow of terror in my victims. With those people, I never bothered to explain the difference between "target" and "victim" because for them, it was the same thing.

And now we were headed up into the lair of someone who was probably quite like that. Well, at least I knew what to expect.

Instead of a trapdoor on the other end of the tunnel, we found a set of concrete stairs leading up, no door blocking the top of them. The building they let out into was dark. I turned off the flashlight and glared up at it.

"Well?" Mihaela asked quietly. "What do you think?"

"I think this is all rather–" Suddenly a *hiss* caught my attention, which meant it had to be pretty loud, given my current state. Starting back where we'd begun, gas was now being pumped into the tunnel. I couldn't see it billowing out, but I could hear it coming, new canisters firing every few feet, filling up the space and coming our way fast. Very likely it was incapacitating, probably even for vampires.

"Up," I said, shooing Mihaela for the stairs. "The game has begun, and this is the opening maneuver, so we've got to get with the program. Up, up, up!"

"But it looks like they want us to go up!"

The gas was almost here – I couldn't smell it, but I could feel my nose starting to tingle, sense my upper respiratory system beginning to give my healing abilities a workout. Powerful stuff.

"And we knew we'd have to do it, so get!" I shoved her ahead of me and vaulted up the stairs. The moment we cleared the last step, a metal plate fell straight down from the ceiling – *CLANG!* It missed us by inches, landing squarely on the exit we'd just come out of and sealing off the gas. Mihaela was caught up in coughing, but I was already scanning the darkness for clues. No visible lights, but the space was big, I could tell that much. The echo of the plate's fall reverberated through the large room or warehouse, broken up here and there by obstacles, free-standing walls or strange things like that. I couldn't hear anyone else moving around, but–

Light! All of a sudden, the space was flooded with light, and then sound. It was a sensory assault, just like our enemy had done back at Cliff's Pink. A dazzling array of floodlights washed over us, followed by circus lights springing up in all directions, attached to cutouts that

I couldn't identify yet, it was all so bright and new. The lights were accompanied by the loudest calliope music I'd ever been subjected to in my entire life. It was shrill, strident, horrifying. It defied more detailed classification because it was firmly established in a category of "intensely annoying" that only someone like Deadpool could match. We should have been writhing in agony, making ourselves into hapless targets as we folded up against the floor, trying to protect our senses from the cacophony.

Instead, I pressed my earplugs in more deeply, glanced at Mihaela to make sure she was handling the noise and brightness all right, and ran for the nearest cutout, in the shape of an amorphous black ooze that bubbled with eyes and teeth. How charmingly familiar. Every eye was a lightbulb, glaring in their intensity even through my squinted eyes. I located the power cord at the bottom of the morbid decoration and cut through it with my Bowie knife, severing our closest source of irritation.

"Oooh, what's this?" a voice asked over a loudspeaker. The rest of the noise continued, but this new question was layered on top of it, louder than everything else so we could make it out. "Have Elsa Bloodstone and Mihaela Zamfir actually come into a situation prepared, for once? What are those you've got there… ah. Ear plugs, it looks like." The voice, high but masculine, laughed. "I see my games have already left their mark on you!"

Mihaela tapped my shoulder, then pointed to the right. Yes, I could see them – three black-suited mercenaries were creeping up on us, or trying to, at least. With those guns, they could have shot us from much farther away, but I could only imagine what their directives were at this point. Did they get bonuses for making us bleed? A bigger payout if they killed one of us up close?

Well, no one was going to be making any money off my suffering tonight. I spun and fired three shots – *bam bam bam!* One for each head. The mercs went down in a sprawl, like marionettes who'd been abandoned by their puppeteer.

Thus began one of the most brutal firefights I'd ever been party to. There were people everywhere, it seemed – behind more cutouts, in blinds against the walls, even hanging from the ceiling. As soon as the first shots were fired, target practice was a go, and in this case, Mihaela and I were the targets.

"Carve someone out of their cover and take it!" I shouted at her. She had her own gun, but not as many bullets as I did, and she was still recovering from her recent wounds. "I'll handle the floor show!" She nodded, and I swung into action.

It wasn't every day that I dug deep into the full benefits of the bloodstone shard. Yes, it gave me incredible strength and speed, it improved my focus and endurance, sharpened my senses, and made me nearly impossible to kill without someone holding me down and cutting my head off. Fantastic abilities all around, yes, but no more than any superpowered individual might have. But I wasn't just any superpowered individual. I was Elsa Bloodstone, and whether I'd actually done it or not, my mind thought I'd been training for battle all my life.

The bloodstone shard did more than keep me sharp. It kept my skills at a lethal level all the time, so that I could respond to any threat with deadly violence. Many heroes had the ability to take a breather when it came to their hyperawareness – I didn't. The shard didn't allow for it. There was never an ebb to the power in my veins, never a time when my muscles couldn't tense in a microsecond, especially if I was ready for the attack.

And oh, but I was certainly ready for attack right now.

The room echoed with gunshots, with people shouting, with the hum and buzz of electricity powering all these annoying lights. It should have been hard to home in on a particular sound, but the vastness of the space only improved my timing. I focused on the *crack* of an incoming salvo, someone just beginning to fire, and kicked off the ground into a flip that took me right over two other shooters' attempts to get me.

Bang. I got the new shooter through the base of the neck, where the armor was the weakest, then ended my flip with a spin that sent my Bowie flying in one direction and a bullet in the other. *Bang-thwock!* Bullet to the head, knife straight through the chest – the armor was vastly better against projectiles than edged weapons.

I had six bullets left. Time to get another firearm. I arced toward one of the fallen, sliding in sideways on the floor so I could use his body as a barrier and pluck up his gun at the same time. Too late I realized that it was a smart weapon, one I couldn't fire without the corresponding bit of jewelry on my person. Blast it all. Fine, I would improvise, then.

I put the gun back into the dead man's hand, found the closest crop of shooters, and used his digit to squeeze the trigger for me. My accuracy was low, but I just needed a few lucky shots to get those gents out of the way before moving on to the next cluster. The extended magazine blared, the bullets found their targets, and soon the air was filled with moans.

Right. On we go, then.

It wasn't that I was immune to damage, even when I was making mincemeat of my opponents. Two bullets grazed me, and several more perforated my long coat. That was the whole point of the coat, though. It didn't just look fabulous, it changed my silhouette, blurring the lines of my body's vulnerabilities. I could handle a shot to the calf, a wound to the gut. They resolved so quickly I barely had time to bleed, and no one even came close to hitting me in the head. My long ponytail was practically a shield, when it came to messing up lines of sight.

Bang. Bang. I heard the particular tenor of Mihaela's gun firing – lovely, she'd found shelter then. I felt oddly touched listening to her shoot at our enemies, being proper backup despite how exhausted she was, and still a baby vampire to boot. I rolled out from behind my body-shield and shot straight up at a gent hanging from a harness with a P90 in his hot little hands. One more down, and it sounded like... seven, perhaps? Seven to go.

"You *are* good at this," the voice over the loudspeaker said admiringly.

Who, *who* was that? There was something so familiar about them, but the voice itself didn't match up with any enemy I could recall.

"So much better than I was led to believe, given what I've seen of your family before now. I should have known if I wanted a really good game, I should stick with the experienced one. Elsa, I commend you." A dull grind sounded on the other side of the warehouse, like an enormous gate or door was being lifted. Something roared. "I think it's time you put those monster-hunting skills on display for the rest of us!"

I tensed, waiting for something hideous to come around the corner. I didn't have to wait long. A moment later, there trotted out into the open...

A chihuahua? What? It looked about as ferocious as a turtledove. It even had on a pink rhinestone collar. What kind of bloody prank was this?

"Oh," the voice mused. "Did I mention it's absorbed Hulk-like levels of gamma radiation and hates loud noises? Because it has, and it does."

A moment later the music was on again, louder than ever. The chihuahua howled... and grew. A second later its brown coat had turned greenish-gray, its body was the size of a dire wolf, and judging from the bullets that struck it from the mercenaries still up and kicking in here, gunfire wasn't going to make a difference.

The Hulk-uahua howled again and ran toward the nearest group trying to give it trouble, ripping at their feeble shelter and tearing it apart in an instant. It snapped and barked and honestly wasn't that effective a killer, but it didn't need to be particularly effective when it was one step below indestructible.

I had a plan, but it didn't include attacking the dog-thing. Instead, I ran to where I'd triangulated Mihaela's hiding place. She looked stunned. "What is that?" she yelled at me.

"It's a nasty bit of radioactive engineering, but it's not the dog's fault," I shouted back. "Give me your earplugs!"

"What?" She clutched her ears and winced.

"I know, but this is important if we want to make it to the next round!"

"*Fine.*" She took them out and handed them to me, and I removed my own as well. The Hulk-uahua was just finishing with the last two mercenaries, still howling like crazy from the noise. At least, I hoped it was from the noise. I also hoped that pup didn't get any bigger. I was pushing my plan's feasibility as it was.

I put my guns away, as it was clear they weren't going to be any help, and headed for the dog. It must have sensed me coming – I don't know how it could have heard anything over all that terrible music – and turned to face me with a growl. "It's all right," I said soothingly, holding my hands out in as inoffensive a posture as I could manage. "I know you're a good puppy, aren't you? Yes, you are. You just don't want to be in all this bloody awful noise. Who could blame you for that? Not me."

The Hulk-uahua snarled viciously but didn't attack.

"I had a puppy like you for a while," I went on. "His name was Jeff. Technically he was a Land Shark, but he was just the cutest little guy I'd ever seen." And I'd promised to take care of him, and then he'd been teleported away before I could make good on my promise. I still thought about that sometimes. "He was a good boy too. Aren't you a good boy? Yes, yes you are."

Four meters. Three. Two.

"Yes, darling, that's right, you're a good boy and I'm going to make all this horrible cacophony stop. Yes I am." I was close – close enough to lunge if I needed to, but given how quickly this pup could move, I didn't think that was my best bet. "Yes, that's right, that's a good boy."

I didn't hold out my hand to sniff – that would be asking for trouble. I did try giving the Hulk-uahua a scratch on the very top of his head as I sidled around to his left side. He didn't attempt to bite my arm off, so that was a win. "Good boy... good, so good, yes..." A second later, I stuck my hand down his massive ear canal and stuffed two earplugs into it.

I think they stuck, but I didn't know for sure, because the abrupt movement made the nearly pacified dog go wild again. It howled and spun in a circle, clawing at its ear for a moment before turning on me. "It's OK," I tried. "Let me just–" But the dog wasn't having any of my nonsense any more. It lunged at me, and I barely leapt out of the way in time to avoid its snapping teeth.

I couldn't turn on it and attack it in an attempt to put the earplugs in on the other side. That would scuttle any chance of it ever trusting me, which might make it keep attacking even if I succeeded. I needed to give it time to calm down, which right now meant working on my evasive maneuvers.

I jumped on top of a cutout of the popobawa – just about the last thing I ever wanted to see again, thanks so much, you wazzock – to get me off the floor where it might be harder for the Hulk-uahua to reach me. No such luck. It was just as good at jumping as it was at ripping people apart, and it seemed to be distressingly good at ripping people apart. It jumped, and I barely ducked in time. I leapt for the next cutout, a taller one – a dinosaur?

When in the name of all that was unholy had our ridiculous captor found the time to make that? It was astonishing, the sheer amount of work our captor had gone to just to leave traps behind in each of the locations we'd run down. And to have created an entire funhouse of ridicule and danger here in Moscow, in such short time? What sort of villain were we dealing with?

I'd only find out if I survived the Hulk-uahua. I ran up the dinosaur's long tail, over its back, and climbed up to its head so I could make a play for the ceiling.

"Ah-ah-ah," the voice on the loudspeaker chided me. "No, no, you naughty girl, no attempting to escape. You can't get out up there anyway, but just to make sure you know it's a bad idea–"

A low, snapping hum added to the sensory torture that was this warehouse.

"Now it's electrified! I think a hundred amps is enough to put even you down for a while, and as your body tries to recover from the inevitable heart attack and massive burns, the doggy will have ample time to tear you to shreds. You can try anyway, if you want. I'd kind of like to see that."

And I'd like to see this bloke get frisky with an industrial-grade cheese grater, but that would have to wait until I could pacify the pup, who was nowhere near pacified at the moment. It tried to jump onto the dinosaur's back, but was too heavy for the plywood to take – it fell right through. I took advantage of the brief reprieve to rip the dino's pointy head off and tap it like a frisbee. "Hey, doggie!" I called out. "Fetch!" I sent it winging across the warehouse. The dog watched it for a moment – there was some definite interest there – before refocusing on me. Right. It was a start. Now all I needed to do was–

"Elsa!" Mihaela had come out of hiding, giving the dog a wide berth but holding out her hands. I could see what she intended, and honestly it wasn't a bad idea, as long as she didn't balk at the finish line.

She'd better not. I threw her the earplugs, then slid down the dino's neck and leapt onto the spindly roof of a mock-up of my own mansion, complete with a stiff-necked Adam painted in garish green, holding a tea tray. The dog snarled and crashed through the bottom of it, making the entire structure shudder. Blast! I threw the nearest things I could rip off across the room – several mock shutters, a corner of the roof, and eventually the top half of Adam himself. The dog got more interested every time, its chasing instinct engaged by the moving targets.

Finally, it went after one, and that was when Mihaela caught it, just as it turned and began to lope after Adam's bottom half. She stuffed the ear plugs into the Hulk-uahua's other ear so smoothly I barely saw her do it, nothing like my rather more ham-fisted attempt, and the dog didn't even stop to growl at her before it began to shrink. A few seconds later it was chihuahua-sized again, and looking much friendlier now that it had escaped the shrillness of the calliope.

"Oh, well that's just not fair at all," the loudspeaker voice said, sounding a little petulant. "That's practically cheating."

The chihuahua trotted over to the nearest cutout, a recreation of the bar in Cliff's Pink, pissed on the edge of it, then went over to the wall and settled in for a nap on the remains of… someone. Someones, perhaps. It was hard to be specific from this far away, and gruesome besides.

I looked up and turned a circle, spreading my arms out wide. "Are you ready to press pause on this ridiculousness?" I asked. "I'd rather like to meet the man who's made so much trouble for me over the past few days."

"Hmm. I suppose that, seeing as you've passed all the preliminary tests, it's time for you to… meet your maker, in a way. Or rather, your *un*maker." The music faded, the flashing lights dimmed, and a projection suddenly appeared on the far wall. The man in the image grinned widely. "Hello, Bloodstones."

EIGHTEEN

Oh. No. He. Didn't. Son of a –

"Arcade," I snarled. "Bloody hell, I thought you were dead."

"Turns out that clones have lots of uses," he replied, twirling his cane twice before setting it down and leaning against it. What an affected louse. He looked just as Cullen had described him, and like the pictures I'd seen – red hair styled in a man's version of a bouffant, white suit with a green bowtie, and a matching green vest beneath it. The soles of his shoes were thick, and he seemed to glimmer in the light. Some sort of force field?

That was a question for another day. The question right now was, "Where is Mihaela's bloodstone shard?"

"Look at you two girls, first name basis and everything," Arcade said, ignoring everything else with the self-assurance of a narcissistic villain. I'd met so many at this point, spotting them was like looking up and seeing that the sky was blue. "I considered the idea that both of you might become allies, but I didn't think you'd go and become friends. Bonds of sisterhood coming out to play, then?"

"Not at all," Mihaela snapped, her glare sharp and her teeth even sharper. "But what cannot be avoided must be endured. Where is my bracelet?"

Arcade gasped, pressing a hand to his chest. "She just called you something to be endured! Doesn't that hurt your feelings, Elsa?"

"If you had any idea how many exes have said the exact same thing to me after we've been forced to work together post-breakup, you wouldn't be surprised," I said dryly. "Let's skip the meandering evil genius speech and get to the point, shall we? I mean, you've heard one villain monologue about their brilliant plan, you've heard them all. Blah blah revenge, blah blah Bloodstones, blah Cullen blah power blah immortality, wah wah wah. Reckon that about sums up what you were going to say anyway, right?"

The smile was gone from Arcade's face. "I'd be more careful about mocking me if I were you," he announced.

"Why? What are you going to do, throw the actual Hulk at us if I don't?"

"No, not at all. What a waste of a Hulk that would be." He sighed. "I wish I could have set this game up for you ladies on Bloodstone Isle. It would have been so appropriate for you to die on your father's monument to himself. I'm a big fan of your dad's, by the way. Naming a whole island after yourself? That's some colonial-level chutzpah. But it was just a bit too crowded there, what with the malignant, magic-eating ooze and all." He shrugged, his grin coming back full force. "This spot has made quite a nice runner-up, though. Have you heard the legends about Golosov Ravine?"

I affected an air of utter boredom, checking my nails. Two were freshly broken – what a nuisance. "Which one? The monsters, the religious iconography, or the time travel?"

"Oh, the time travel ones, of course. Those are my favorite," Arcade confided smarmily. "And it turns out, there's more than a grain of truth to them! There really are portals in Golosov Ravine that activate on occasion, creating wormholes that can suck people from the past into the present and vice versa. It wasn't too hard to harness one of those energy signatures and expand it to surround this warehouse. As of two minutes ago?" He twirled one finger in a circle. "This building is half a second off from its surroundings."

Mihaela shrugged. "Half a second doesn't seem so bad."

"You wouldn't think so, no," Arcade mused, stroking his chin. "Not until you consider the difference half a second can make to your body if, say, you were trying to step through a door to the outside world. Oh, you'd make it... mostly. But at the very least, none of your arteries and veins would be in quite the right place any more. Or your heart... or your brain." He laughed and twirled his cane again. "I think that even the relentless Elsa Bloodstone would have trouble healing a nonexistent heart, although to me that metaphor seems pretty spot-on already."

Well, hell. If he was telling the truth, then we were in trouble. I wasn't willing to give him that much credit yet, but sometimes it paid to humor sociopaths. "Then I suppose we're your captive audience."

"Well phrased, well phrased," he agreed. "And oh, you've been such fun to watch. The tenacity! The way you just go, go, go and never stop, Elsa, truly, it's inspiring. If your insipid little brother was half the fighter you are, he would have won the Murderworld game I let him play in, hands down."

Rotter. "Let's leave Cullen out of this."

"I almost didn't, you know." Arcade looked pensive, one hand stroking his chin. "I almost pulled him into this too, just to see how you'd react, but, honestly, I've had my fun with him. He's… boring, at this point. Too easy to break. Whereas you? You don't have the same sort of weak spots, Elsa. I could have killed everyone you love, shot your mother in front of you, burned Adam and everything you own to the ground, and you would have shoved away that pain and come after me with everything you had. And plenty of things you stole, I assume." He shrugged. "I'm ambitious, but I'm not suicidal."

"So, what's your plan, then?" I asked. "Now that you have us here, now that we've passed your tests and provided you with all the entertainment you could ever want."

"Oh, but the list never ends." He grinned viciously. "There's always more out there to covet, Elsa, and I'm an expert at getting the things I want. Every defeat I've ever suffered has only served to make me stronger, better at planning, better at staying alive. I'm so good at it now, I wonder if there's anything or anyone out there that could actually take me down."

Oh, my lord, was he serious? "I daresay there is. Why don't you find it and have a go? Test the old reflexes and see how you fare."

"Not. Suicidal." He looked at me in mock concern. "Honestly, Elsa, are you all right? You seem to have memory problems."

"And you have a problem with being a bloody spanner."

"Elsa," Mihaela whispered warningly. Arcade heard it anyway.

"Yes, Elsa," he cooed, "don't poke the power holding you captive, you might not like what happens next."

"I'm not going to like it anyway." I waved my hand to encompass the entire room. "There's nothing about this situation that makes me think anything I say or do will suddenly give you a sense of mercy. You sent all your men in here knowing they would die. You sent that poor dog in here hoping it would die while maybe getting in a fatal blow on one of us before the end, but still. There is nothing I can do to make you change your mind about the path you've already decided on. You've been following us every step of the way – my God, you did this place up like a hallucinogenic highlights reel from our journey here, not a single step missed."

Although, not everything we'd gone through was on display here. His intel wasn't perfect. Hmm... "I'm not going to waste my time and energy tossing virgins into an erupting volcano. You want to make life terrible for us, you can, but don't expect me to beg you for favors along the way."

Arcade made a funny face. "I didn't think virgins were your style."

"I didn't think non-sequiturs were yours, yet here we are." Beside me, Mihaela heaved a sigh. It was a sound of deep regret, of fatigue and sadness and irritation all at once. I glanced at her, but she was staring straight at Arcade.

"I want my bloodstone shard back," she said, her accent thicker than I'd heard it before. "I want my life back. I don't want to be stuck in this place with that woman for any longer than I have to." The look she shot me was venomous. Overly venomous.

Oof, that was... rather unexpectedly painful to hear. I stiffened my spine against the sudden urge to hug myself. Not that I didn't know I could be difficult, but I thought we'd come to an understanding. How could she treat me like an enemy now, when we needed each other the most? That wasn't like the Mihaela I'd grown to know. It seemed so uncharacteristic, so... oh.

Oh. Perhaps she was laying the groundwork for us to have a potential advantage.

I let my defensive hug happen and took a step away from Mihaela as she went on, "Please, whatever you have planned, just... tell me I have a chance."

"Oh, there's always a chance, Mihaela Zamfir." Arcade held up his left wrist and shot the cuffs of his jacket. The bulk that I'd mistaken for a watch was a gold bracelet, practically a cuff with how thick it was, plain and undecorated except for the glittering bloodstone shard in the center. That was certainly my father's work – jewelry that was more utilitarian than decorative, but you'd nearly be able to deflect a bullet or brain a zombie with the bulk of it.

"For example," he went on smoothly, "there's definitely a chance that you could get this back. I don't need two bloodstones, just one."

"I suppose it would be redundant to ask why you want one?" I put in, not wanting all of my bloodstone-addicted sister's attention on our mutual enemy. I had faith, I *did*, but there was faith and then there was blind trust, and that was a currency I couldn't traffic in.

"Probably, but I'll tell you anyway." He looked at the bracelet with a satisfied expression. "I've always fancied the idea of being immortal, but it always seems to come with so many downsides. I mean, look at vampires. Incredibly powerful and long-lived, but their weaknesses are legion. Specializing in killing vampires is like specializing in handling venomous snakes – sure, there's an element of danger, but once that's accounted for it's practically humdrum."

He'd clearly never gone up against some of the regrettably creative bloodsuckers I'd faced, but whatever, he was on a roll.

"And mutation, experimentation, radiation?" Arcade shook his head. "Too risky. My brain is a finely tuned instrument, and I can't risk something going wrong with it in the lab. But a bloodstone shard?" He pulled his cuff back down and cupped his free hand over the bracelet possessively. "Well, there's just nothing else like it."

Honestly, there were other artifacts out there like the shard that promised a long life, but I could see where he'd gotten the idea that these were the be-all, end-all of functional immortality.

"I've been on the sidelines for too long," he went on. "People have started to forget why they feared me, started to forget me altogether! That's not acceptable. I'm tired of being out of the spotlight, ladies, and having the powers of a bloodstone shard at my beck and call will do wonders for my image, not to mention my longevity."

"And you've got a shard," I pointed out. Mihaela's gaze snapped suddenly to me, her lips drawing back from her teeth in a silent hiss. "You've had Mihaela's shard for quite some time now. Why bother trying to get mine? Why arrange this elaborate scavenger hunt, why spend all this time and money, when you've already got what you say you want?"

"Oh, Elsa." Arcade shook his head disparagingly. "For all that you're tough as nails, you're not much of a thinker, are you? Why simply 'take' whatever I want when I can make it into a game? Games are so much more fun than the regular old real world, aren't they? You get to make up your own rules, play for stakes that you design… I can't think of anything else that compares to the fun of running a game like this."

"Mmm. Clearly you need more friends. Or any at all."

He scowled at me. "Laugh while you can. You won't be joking for long, though. You've played the game all the way to the end. The only thing left to do now is determine the winner." Arcade rubbed his hands together. "The winner apart from me, that is. This is the best part of the whole thing! Two near-immortals, pitted against each other… what's not to love?

"I've already told you about the time shift surrounding this warehouse," he continued. "Right now, neither of you can leave here and expect to survive. But I will allow *one* of you to walk out of here, as long as the other is dead. And!" He waggled a finger at us. "No honorably sacrificing yourself for the sake of the other. I'd be so disappointed if one of you did that." His grin came back. "Not that I think either of you will. You're both survivors, in your own way."

He looked at Mihaela. "If you win, I'll give you back your bloodstone shard bracelet."

She eyed him warily. "Why would you do that?"

"Why not? Elsa's is larger and arguably more powerful, and it would be mine for the taking."

"Unless *I* decided to take it."

Well, that was unexpectedly violent. Not like Mihaela at all.

Definitely making a play, then. It was going to be risky, but we didn't have much of a choice.

Her outburst just made Arcade laugh, though. "You could try, you could certainly try! But I've been ahead of you every step of the way so far, haven't I? What on earth makes you think I can't put you in your place on my own?" He turned to me. "And Elsa... you know I respect the power that the bloodstone gives you. If you kill Mihaela, I'll let you go. One shard is enough for me. Hers might not be as powerful, but my primary weapon has always been my brain. I want a bloodstone shard for the effects of its longevity, not for how big it'll make my muscles." He shuddered theatrically. "Awful things, muscles. They ruin the line of your suit.

"Besides..." His voice got low and insidious. Mihaela backed away from the image of Arcade, stepping out of my line of sight. Fighting my instinct to keep her in view was hard, but I kept my eyes on the villain ahead of me. If this was going to work, I had to give her an opening. "Aren't you a monster hunter? The creature you're in there with is no different from any of the other monsters you've dispatched over the years, not any more. She can't stand the sunlight, she needs blood to survive... she's a vampire, Elsa. And vampires make life terrible for regular people. They don't know any other way. Even the best of them can only express their solidarity with humanity through violence. Do you think Blade kills his own kind because he loves the little people? No, he does it because he's a creature made for the hunt, and vampires make more interesting prey.

"Even you." He moved steadily closer to the camera until his face filled the entire wall. "You could do so many things with your talents. Be like your friend Misty and split your time between human problems and super hero problems, or buckle down and devote yourself to taking out your average, everyday serial killers or murderers. But you don't. You don't because that would be boring. It would be a waste of your skills. You have so many skills, Elsa Bloodstone, and you put them to good use ridding the world of monsters, just like your father intended. Why not just keep up the good work? Kill the vampire and get your life back on track."

The worst part was how tempted I felt. There was a part of me that got genuinely engaged by what Arcade was saying, that followed the logic of it and was nodding along. I *was* a brilliant monster killer. Vampires were some of my headiest targets. Mihaela might be in control right now, but I'd seen her out of control too, and it had been frightening. Some people would consider it a mercy to take her out right now. Was I one of them?

No, I wasn't. Arcade was trying to make me into the worst version of myself, just like he'd done with Cullen, and I wasn't going to play along. I knew better. More importantly, I was pretty sure that Mihaela knew better, too. But was I willing to risk my life on it?

"Is that agreement I see in your eyes?" Arcade asked coyly. "I'm so glad. But you know, as things stand right now, it really isn't a fair matchup. So–" He stepped back and raised a gun. "Let's even the playing field."

His gun was plastic, clearly not capable of firing an actual bullet, but I heard something within the warehouse shift in a mirror image of it. Some sort of remote firing system? Was he about to –

Bang! A bullet penetrated my right thigh, hitting so hard that it knocked me right off my feet. It hurt like the blazes. The bullet had lodged in the bone itself, which was crackling and crunching as it worked to push the slug out. The pain was hideous, but I forced it back–

Just in time for Mihaela to descend on me from behind, grabbing my hair and twisting my head back to expose my neck. Her teeth were long and sharp, and her eyes gleamed with cold desperation. "I'm sorry," she said, "but I need my shard." She lowered her lips to my skin.

I kicked my good leg back like a mule and hit her so hard in the side that she flew back. She skidded to a halt with a snarl, but I was already looking for the remote guns. There was the one that had shot me last time. I fired on it and left it a smoking ruin, then heaved myself to my feet and looked for the next one.

Bang! Another shot went off, but I could hear the gun's platform move before the weapon fired and rolled out of the way. The bullet came from the left – there! I shot it out, then turned to my sister. "Stay back!" I warned her, holding my gun at the ready. "I don't want to have to–"

Bang! This one took me in the back, through the

shoulder. Not the arm holding the gun, luckily, but still bad enough that I almost dropped my weapon anyway. How many of these had he set up? I gritted my teeth as I turned and spotted it, high up in the corner, before I blew it out of existence. Now that I saw the pattern of Arcade's placements, I could take the rest of them out. I got one, got two… There should be one more left, where was it?

"Oof!"

Mihaela tackled me from behind, driving me face-first onto the concrete floor. I writhed against her grip, blood loss making me both slippery and woozy, but she kept a firm hold on the back of my neck. The other hand dug into the bullet wound on the back of my shoulder. I couldn't help it – I screamed bloody murder. A second later her hand was in my hair, jerking me up and back, and then–

She hesitated. Just long enough for our eyes to meet, for me to stare up at Mihaela and know she held my fate in her hands. *You've got this.*

Her fangs found my neck. The pain was sharp, intense, and shaming, a prelude to the ultimate indignity of being someone else's dinner. I choked out a hoarse "No!" and tried to throw her off, but it didn't work. Her teeth widened the wound, and blood dripped down my neck in a steady flow as I gradually stopped fighting. My breaths slowed, my flailing movements became shudders, then tremors, and finally…

Finally I didn't fight any longer, and Mihaela let go of me. My head hit the ground with a painful *thunk*, but I didn't react.

I'd been close to death more than once, and of all the senses to go, the last one for me was always my ability to hear. I heard Mihaela get to her feet, then stagger. A second later she began to choke. I heard the scrabble of her fingers against her own neck as she coughed and coughed, trying to clear my fatal blood from her throat. It didn't seem to be working, if the spatters and gasps were anything to go by. I heard the *thud* of her knees hitting the ground quite close by, then the rest of her body collapsing. A moment later she convulsed, then went still. Deadly still.

"How... beautiful." Arcade sounded truly impressed with what he was looking at. "Ladies, ladies, you've outdone yourself. Time to get up now, though." There was a pause. "Time to get up, I said." From somewhere against the wall, a remote gun fired. The bullet hit the ground less than two feet from my head. I didn't move.

"Really? Oh, come now." Another shot, this time one foot away. I still didn't move, but a reluctant tension was building in my muscles. The last thing I needed was to get shot in the head, have to rely on the shard to heal me, then have it taken away by Arcade before I was done.

The next shot was so close to my head, it literally parted my bangs. I still didn't move, but my ears were honed for the *click-click-click* movement of the gun. Before it could fire again, I would–

"Grrrrr."

A rumbling growl interrupted my worrying. A second later, there was the sound of metal being crunched, followed by a cry of "No, you idiot dog, don't–" But it was too late. The Hulk-uahua had been ensconced in a comfy spot just a few feet from Arcade's final remote-controlled gun, and it was far from pleased to have its repose interrupted by more noise.

"Great," Arcade groused. "Just great." It sounded like he was trying a few of his other platforms, but even if I hadn't destroyed the mechanism for moving them, I'd certainly taken out their actual firing capacity. "Damn it."

Now came the real test. How badly did he want *my* bloodstone shard? It was bigger than Mihaela's, more powerful – would Arcade risk coming into the warehouse to get it? Would he continue to hole up in his safe zone, wherever that was, and wait to see what happened? Or would he write the whole thing off as a loss and leave us here, half a second off from the rest of the world? Had our mutual murder been convincing enough?

I had to suppress a wince. It had certainly been convincing as far as I was concerned, if the fang marks in my neck were anything to go by…

A distant creak caught my attention. It was the sound of a door opening I hadn't seen earlier. It must have been hidden by one of the garish cutouts. Shoes clicked against the floor, getting closer and closer, but not quickly. Arcade appeared to be a bit gun-shy.

"I knew the dog was too much," he muttered to himself as he walked our way. "I should have made it a robo-dog, something I could control completely. Wouldn't have lasted long, but at least it wouldn't have turned on me like Fido here. I swear, this is the last time I buy my genetically engineered super beasts from the seconds lot in Latveria."

The footsteps got closer. Closer. He was nearly close enough to touch now, and he'd have to touch me if he wanted to get the choker off. At which point… well, I might be shot in numerous places, slightly mauled around the neck, and down several pints of blood, but for all that he was wearing Mihaela's bracelet, I'd had my shard for a lot longer. I could do this.

I didn't get the chance to. Mihaela, two paces closer to him, made her move first. She leapt to her feet and wrapped Arcade up in a suffocating embrace, biting at his neck – but she couldn't reach it.

"Whoa, what the–"

By the time I joined her in the world of the standing-and-totally-fine-trust-me, Mihaela had pulled her head back from him with a snarl. She still had a grip on him, but it looked like it was hard to maintain – her hands kept slipping off. Arcade looked between us and laughed.

"Ladies! Brilliantly played, I did not see all of this coming. Well, actually I did, but I certainly didn't see every part of it." He focused on me. "I knew your blood was toxic to vampires, but I didn't realize that your sister here already knew that trick. That was some great acting by you two."

"Your approbation means so much, truly," I snarked. "Now how about you give us the bloodstone shard, and we all go on our merry way?"

Arcade laughed. "I wish I could reward your persistence, I really do, but it's not that simple." He gestured to Mihaela, whose hands had finally slid completely off him. "I'm protected by a force field, one of my own design, that makes me literally untouchable. The harder you try, the harder it resists you, so there won't be any snapping of my neck or throwing me to the hound as a chew toy." He looked smugly at me. "I'm invincible, and there's no way for you to get the bloodstone shard off of me. So instead, let's–"

I couldn't help it – I started to laugh. All of the frustration and anger and pain that had been building up in me since this whole heinous trip began were bursting out of me now, making me laugh so hard I cried. I bent over so I could support my still-healing self by bracing against my own knees.

"Elsa," Mihaela snapped, "what is so funny? I can't hold him."

"Yeah, Elsa." Arcade's voice wasn't angry, like hers. There was a delicious tinge of fear there instead, and I knew I had to act fast before he figured out a counter to what I was going to do next. "What's so funny?"

"Oh, it's just…" I got vertical and wiped away a tear. "I do find it hilarious whenever someone throws the 'invincible' line around. No one, nothing, is ever invincible. No one! I should know, I've taken on plenty of 'invincible' monsters in my day, and let me tell you, when the rubbery flesh meets the road, they all collapse in the end. And you?" I smiled at him. "You're just another type of monster, Arcade. One I'm well equipped to deal with."

I looked around for the nearest cutout and found our partially destroyed dinosaur looming nearby. Perfect, just what I needed. I ran over to it and, quick as I could, smashed the wooden beams keeping it from toppling over. One solid kick later – one that I really felt, since my leg wasn't quite done healing yet, *ow* – and it was toppling down on both my sister, who'd gotten with the program pretty quickly and was doing her best to keep Arcade from running, and Arcade himself. *Smash!*

I walked back over at a more leisurely pace. Mihaela had managed to dodge most of the heavy cutout at the last minute and was now in the process of disentangling herself from a string of lights while swearing what was probably bloody murder in Romanian. Arcade, two feet to the left of her, was comfortably held down by the bulk of the dinosaur's neck. He was battering at it, and the bloodstone shard did give him enhanced strength, but he hadn't practiced how to use it. He was trying to lift the whole bloody thing instead of focusing on destroying the part nearest to him and going from there.

Oh, it was positively delightful to identify incompetence in your enemy.

I squatted down on top of him and punched a hole straight through the cutout right above his face. My fist didn't hit him, of course – he was right about the force field deflecting impact that way – but it did expose him enough that I could enact phase two of my plan.

"The thing about a force field like this," I said, reaching over and grabbing some of Mihaela's discarded lights, "is that they're far from impermeable. You have to be able to breathe, after all. Given that it rides very close to your body and you're not wearing an oxygen mask, I assume that indicates that air, at least, can get in and out. That means we could certainly poison you."

"You can't," Arcade blustered. "You don't have the time. My backup forces will be here in–"

"No, see, I don't think you have any backup forces readily available. Otherwise, you would have sent them in to ensure we were dead, rather than coming in and exposing yourself to danger. Your flavor of baddie is positively allergic to personal threat, so the fact that you're here at all informs me that you're at the end of your rope, and that all these goons in the warehouse were your final reserve, so to speak. And, well." I shrugged. "Look at what's happened to them. But you're right, I don't want to go hunt down a gaseous poison right now, or even a convenient stream. Even after we used it, that would leave the problem of the force field."

"Exactly." Arcade tried to smile at me. It was a weak thing, but at least he tried. "Look, I can be reasonable. You want Mihaela's shard, right? Let me go, and I'll leave it for you at a pre-established–"

"No, no, let's not try bargaining, that way is only boredom and lies." I wagged my finger at him. "No, I think I'll handle the problem of your force field right here, right now." I ripped the string of lights in two, making sure the wires were exposed, then repeated the process with another string. The wires were a fairly wide diameter – they'd have to be, given the size of the bulbs they were powering.

"You know what I've found tends to work in cases like this? Elemental forces." I knelt on top of the cutout, right over Arcade's chest. "Wind... water... earth..." I tapped the wires against each other, lighting up the air with a shower of sparks. "*Fire*."

Arcade's eyes were so wide I could almost see back into his scheming brain. "Elsa, let's not be hasty, now. I- I'll tell you how to get into the force field, there's a trigger, it's in the other room, we just need to–"

"What did I say about bargaining?" I leaned in close, so the last few drops of blood from my neck wound trickled down right onto Arcade's face. They pooled on top of the force field in the corner of his left eye, probably obscuring his view. *Good.* "I... don't... like it." I tapped out a few sparks one last time, then applied the wires to the force field.

Nothing happened. After a few seconds, Arcade began to laugh. "Ha! All that build up, only to find out your tricky little plan doesn't work! I bet you want to bargain with me now, don't you, you bi–"

Never has there been a more satisfying place to interrupt a madman's sentence than right before he gets done calling me a rude name. The current coursing through the wires had worked its magic on the force field and whatever was powering it, because it vanished. A second later Arcade convulsed beneath me, wiggling like a fish before he finally stilled, his eyes closed, body twitching.

"Is he out?" Mihaela asked.

"It's possible." Or he could be playing possum, as the saying went. To be sure, I put the wires aside, then cocked my arm back and rabbit-punched him right in the center of the forehead. His rather theatrical twitches abruptly ceased. There. Now he could be unconscious *and* have a mild concussion when he woke up. "Yes, he's out."

Mihaela didn't answer. She was too busy rooting around beneath the edge of the cutout, retrieving her bracelet. She jerked it off Arcade's wrist none-too-gently, then... she just stared at it. Didn't shout with triumph, didn't do a victory dance, didn't even put it on. She simply stared at it.

"It's not going to work like that," I pointed out gently after a few moments of silence.

"What if it doesn't work at all?" she asked. There was eagerness in her eyes, but also a lot of fear. "What if I can never go back to the way I used to be?"

"We'll cross that bridge when we get to it." I set a hand on her shoulder. "Come on, now. Stiff upper lip."

Mihaela nodded, then closed her eyes. In one smooth motion, she slid the bracelet over her left wrist. It fit her beautifully, like it was meant to be there, and the bloodstone shard seemed to shine brighter. We waited, both of us barely breathing. A minute passed. Then another.

"Is it–"

I cut my own question off when Mihaela abruptly began to weep. There were no tears, of course, but her body made all the other motions. Her face crumpled, her chest heaved with air she didn't need, and her back bowed until she was nearly prostrate on the ground. She wept hard, the kind of crying you did when you were faced with a loss you'd never fully recover from.

My heart ached from looking at her, but I couldn't get caught up in it. There were still too many things left to do here. I laid my hand on her shoulder and gave her a gentle squeeze, then headed deeper into the warehouse.

In silence, I checked every single mercenary to make sure they were truly dead – there was no sense in leaving an enemy behind. Then I went over to the Hulk-uahua and held out a hand, clicking my tongue gently. "Hello again, pup. Are you ready to get out of here, hmm? Ready to move on to greener climes? I bet you'd be aces at chasing down a ball, wouldn't you?"

The dog tilted its head at me curiously, then trotted over and licked the tips of my fingers.

"Yeah, I smell good right now, don't I? Mmm, there's more where that came from. Just walk along with me, and you can have all the wretchedly smelly things you've ever wanted to roll about in whenever you want."

The dog put his front paws up on my knee and barked. That was as clear a sign as I was going to get. "Good boy." I picked him up and carried him over to Mihaela.

"Darling, I need you to hold this for me." It took a long

moment, but when she finally lifted her head, I thrust the Hulk-uahua down at her. "You take him, I'll take Arcade," I said. "We're getting out of this place."

Mihaela took the dog on instinct, cuddling it against her chest. "But... the time distortion," she said after a moment. "How will we avoid that?"

"Not sure yet, but the first thing we need to do is verify its existence. I wouldn't put it past a muppet like Arcade to tell us he'd moved a time-distorting portal without actually doing the work." I held out a hand and helped her to her feet, then reached under the edge of the cutout and jerked Arcade out and over my shoulder. He weighed just what I'd expected a morally and ethically empty individual to clock in at – something negligible. "And lucky for us, we've got the perfect test subject."

She tucked the dog a little tighter to her chest. "Surely you don't mean..."

"Of course not the dog." I rolled my eyes. "Do I look like someone who indulges in acts of animal cruelty? I was talking about this piece of work." I headed off toward the door Arcade had entered from, and after a moment Mihaela followed.

The door led into a control room that, for all it seemed fancy on the inside, was clearly a repurposed cargo container. There were screens on every wall showing different views on the warehouse, while others were tuned in to the sites of Ulysses' other bases. Had this one been Arcade's home base all along? How much work could we have saved ourselves if we'd just come here directly, instead of hunting down nonexistent shards all over the world?

On the other hand, this particular stop had been far more of a challenge than I liked to let on. If Mihaela and I hadn't taken the time to build a sense of mutual trust over the course of our adventure, things might have gone rather differently inside Arcade's latest Murderworld. As it was, it had taken every ounce of faith I had to let her get her teeth into me again. I certainly couldn't have done it yesterday.

In the end, it didn't matter if we'd wasted time or not. We had survived, even if things hadn't gone exactly to Mihaela's liking. At least she had her shard back. That had to count for something, even if it didn't turn back the clock and transform her into the forbidding, sixty-something senior she'd been when I first met her.

I walked over and opened the door. Cool, wet night air blossomed around me, replacing the smell of ozone and blood in my nostrils with something far more palatable. The sound of cars driving nearby was clearly audible, and the air in front of my nose didn't waver at all, didn't seem out of sync. Then again, half a second wasn't much time.

"Pass me the flashlight on that table over there, would you?"

Mihaela grabbed it and brought it to me. I turned the light on and pointed it at the floor, then moved it slowly onto the concrete step in front of me. No discernible change. Right then, I'd try a bit farther afield. There was a patch of grass about ten feet ahead, next to a parking lot. I moved the light along the ground, watching every inch of the way for any nerve-racking signs. Nothing.

"Lovely. On to the live test." I set Arcade down and trussed him up tight with the cords I'd scavenged from the dinosaur cutout, then tumbled him out the door and down the step. He groaned but didn't wake. "Oh joy, he's still alive. Good enough for me." I looked over at Mihaela. "Shall we?"

She nodded slowly, then nudged past me and stepped out into the night. It might have just been me, but the darkness seemed to suit her. She seemed far more relaxed in the light of the moon than I'd ever seen her under the brightness of the sun. Perhaps that was just because her secret was out now, and there was no longer a need to hide, but I hoped it foreshadowed better things for her. "Any dislocated veins?" I called down.

"Not that I can tell." She scratched the pup behind the ears. "And this little guy wasn't bothered at all, so I think we're fine."

Score one for the "lie" bin. I hopped down onto the ground, placing one foot firmly in the center of Arcade's back, just in case he got some ideas. "Well then. The first thing to do is contact someone who can get this weasel somewhere secure."

"Why not just kill him?"

I turned and stared at her. "Really?"

"Really. He's… he's a grotesque human being," she

said, her face twisted with loathing. "He has no respect for anyone or anything other than himself and his own ambitions, and he has gone out of his way to induce suffering in others as entertainment for other people just like him. Didn't he nearly kill your brother, Elsa? He has killed so many other people and gotten them killed on his behalf without a moment's qualm." She motioned toward the warehouse, where a great number of bodies were laying in testament to that. "Why should he live, then, when he would so quickly consign anyone else to death?"

There was a lot to unpack there, but firstly... "Don't feel sorry for the mercs," I said firmly. "They made the choice to take money from Arcade. They didn't have to work for him, they chose to, which means they got what was coming to them. And as for him?"

I nudged him with my heel. "Yes, death would certainly be a reasonable price for him to pay after all the crap he's put our family through. But killing someone like this attracts its own kind of attention, and most of it's not benevolent. 'Good'–" and I put that in air quotes so she followed how I truly felt about these sanctimonious skunks "– super heroes will put you on a permanent blacklist the moment you take a matter like Arcade into your own hands, and that can lead to professional problems down the line. And while killing him would earn us some street cred from bad guys, some of the maddest of them would see it as an invitation for them to come after us."

I shrugged. "It's not perfect either way, but if we turn

him in to the authorities, he'll become someone else's problem."

"What if he escapes?"

"It wouldn't be the first time, but like I said: someone else's problem." I kept my voice light, non-judgmental. The truth was, I longed to end Arcade here and now, but it would stir up a lot of controversy that I didn't need. And for Mihaela, who was just entering the supernatural sphere, so to speak, it would be a lot of controversy that I sincerely doubted she could handle on her own.

"Fine," she said at last.

"Good. Now." I spun on my heel. "I'm going to go find whatever is left of our bags and rescue that bloody lamp while you keep an eye on Arcade. Then I'll make some calls, and we'll see who cares to take over this mess."

NINETEEN

It was amazing, the people who came out of the woodwork and wanted to take credit the moment you took out a super villain. I'd barely had my new phone for five minutes – thank you, twenty-four hour Russian supermarket chain – and I was already fielding calls from heroes, governments, and a few shady characters who refused to identify themselves as more than "interested parties". The Russian news corps found us not long after that, and Mihaela and I had to retreat to Golosov with our prize to keep from being mobbed.

Fortunately, our friendly local leshy used the stream to call up a mist that blanketed the entire west end of the ravine in obscurity, then escorted us to a little island surrounded by trees where we could wait out the media's hunt for the "Red-Headed Menace" in peace. I didn't speak enough Russian to know if they were referring to me or to Arcade, and frankly I didn't want to know. I'd picked up plenty of snacks at the supermarket – where my bloodied, brutalized appearance barely fazed the cashier – and spent a few hours sharing handfuls of rusks flavored like jellied meat and horseradish with the Hulk-uahua until the reporters went home.

The winner of my "who gets Arcade" roundtable came and picked him up shortly thereafter, assuring me that he would be locked away in a secure facility for the rest of his natural life.

"Sure he will," I replied, doing my best to rein my condescension in. I'd chosen this crew, after all. I should try to have some faith in them. I didn't, but I should. "But if the unthinkable should happen and he somehow escapes again, please do me a favor and don't call me." Then Arcade, who had woken up enough at this point to make me happy I'd had the forethought to gag him, began to bluster and attempt to shout around my dirty sock.

"What's that, pet?" I cupped my hand around my ear. "You want to be kicked in the fork before you leave, as a reminder that evil doesn't pay?"

He'd immediately stopped struggling and was taken away. After their helicopter flew off, the leshy came out from his hiding place and banished the mist, escorted Mihaela out to join me on the trail, and bowed once before melting back into the trees.

"He ended up being quite a nice bloke, didn't he?" I murmured, trying to catch a glimpse of where, exactly, he'd vanished to. It was a rare beast who could disappear so seamlessly into their background, and while I wasn't about to start hunting leshies, it was a potential learning moment for me.

"Elsa?" Mihaela said. She sounded dead tired. "What are we going to do now?"

If it had been just me, I would probably have spent some time blowing off steam in downtown Moscow. Now, though, I had not one but two dependents along for the ride, and taking care of them had to be my priority. It was a little odd to think of Mihaela as a dependent when she was older than me, but she was still a baby when it came to vampirism. If we parted ways here, I didn't want to lay odds on her discovering a lot of healthy coping mechanisms for handling her transition to bloodsucking on her own.

"We're going to get out of here." And we needed to do it fast. Mihaela's sunblock was gone and the dawn was already here, coloring the clouds above a vivid, violent red. God, I'd had enough of that color to last me a lifetime… or at least a week or so. The last thing I wanted to do was wrangle our group into an airport, or even a private jet, the way we were looking and feeling right now.

Was it worth trying the lamp? Had the genie learned its lesson? I pulled the heinous device out of my tattered bag and rubbed once.

"Ugh," the genie intoned in a hung-over sounding voice. "Don't start. You are seriously driving me bonkers, Bloodstone, you know that?"

"The feeling is entirely mutual," I assured the genie. "And right now, I think the best thing for all of us is to be home as quickly as possible. What do I need to do in order to get you to send us there without shenanigans? Because I swear to all that's holy, if you drop us in the middle of a dinosaur fight again, I will let the dog turn you into a chew toy."

"It's not that easy!" the genie whined. "You think I *wanted* to end up living in a lamp that looks more like a beer can someone ran over in the road? Those dents aren't easy to fix, you know. Look, I home in on conflict, that's the deal, and the biggest conflict in the area is what my magic focuses on. I can't change that, not even if I want to!"

"So you say."

"So I know! C'mon, seriously, I'm too tired to lie to you right now, all right? I need a few days of not being jostled around." It made a suspiciously gross sound. "Who'd have thought a genie could get motion sickness before this trip?"

Interesting. I might be a fool to take it at its word, but I was a fool whose blood-soaked pants were beginning to chafe and who needed more than a few bags of crisps to keep her engine running smoothly. Perhaps I could make things easier on it with regards to getting back to Boston. I thought about it for a moment, then called home.

Adam picked up immediately. "Bloodstone Manor."

"Adam, I need you to start a conflict."

To his credit, there was barely a pause. "Are we talking 'minor argument over the temperature of the tea' type conflict, or a 'middle eastern peace deal' conflict?"

"Minor, definitely minor, but still violent enough for the genie to home in on."

There was a moment of silence before Adam said, doubtingly, "Do you really think that will work?"

"At this point, I'm willing to try it."

"Very well." He hummed thoughtfully for another moment, then said, "Call back in five minutes," and ended the call.

I looked at Mihaela, who was still holding onto the dog like a lifeline even though its wriggling was beginning to get pronounced. "I think he needs a potty break," I pointed out, and she nodded and set him down. Sure enough, the Hulk-uahua lit off for the nearest bush to sniff and do his business.

"You should name him," I suggested.

She startled. "What? No, I can't have a pet, my apartment, it…" Her new reality caught up to her all at once, and she sagged for a moment before continuing, "I don't know where I'm going to live, or how I'm going to make a living. And the search for a new situation could take weeks, maybe more. It would be very uncomfortable for a dog to wander around like that."

I rolled my eyes so hard they nearly got stuck behind the lids. "Have I done something to give you any sort of impression that you wouldn't have a place in my home, at this point? Do you remember how big the manor is? Don't you agree that it's big enough to accommodate another person and her puppy until the bloody end of days, even if that puppy is capable of transforming into a monster that could put Cullen's Glartrox form down if it wanted to?"

"I... Well, I had thought you would want your space."
She smiled, and it finally had a hint of genuine amusement
in it. "After all, you did get rather more than you bargained
for when you agreed to help me, and I browbeat you into it
in the first place."

"Nobody makes me do anything I don't want to do,
darling," I said airily. "Arcade learned that. And I do want
my space. I've got three floors and over five thousand square
feet of space in the manor, and that's not including all the
amenities like window blinds that will not let in a hint of
light, and a butler who also happens to be Frankenstein's
monster and is impervious to blood lust, super-strength
temper tantrums, and crying jags." I'd had a few of all of
those over the years, or variations on them, and Adam had
been the rock against whom all my wretched moods had
broken and washed away. "At any rate, consider this your
official invitation to stay with me until you figure out what
comes next."

"That could take a while," Mihaela muttered.

"That's fine. Besides," I added cheekily, "I know a few
people in the Legion of Monsters, so if you decide using
your new abilities to be a super hero is a potential career
path–"

"Ha!" Mihaela said with a snort. "I can't think of any way
that wouldn't end poorly. I'm no hero."

What did she think being a hero was? "You have been,
actually. This entire trip, you've gritted your teeth and put
up with discomfort and danger in order to achieve your

goal. Maybe the goal was misguided, but the fact is you were willing to do the work to find out. You plunged into situations that would have given anyone else pause without a second thought. When you got hurt you learned from the experience instead of giving up. You *kept going*, Mihaela, and you didn't throw the towel in when things became difficult. That's just about the most heroic thing I can think of, and it's a trait that all the best heroes I know have in common."

She wavered, appearing to be somewhere between considering my suggestion and calling me a madwoman. I decided to give her an out so she could think about it without any pressure of timing or expectation. "That's been five minutes, don't you think?" I called up Adam and waited... and waited... and waited...

Finally, he picked up.

"Done yet?" I heard something shatter in the background, and what sounded suspiciously like something else being set on fire.

"Ah... yes, the genie should be able to transport you all to the manor without problem. Do come quickly, if you please. I've possibly outdone myself with this idea."

Well, that wasn't ominous at all. "We'll be there directly." I ended the call and looked at myself. I had one knife, no ammunition, and a grenade that I wouldn't be setting off in my own home, thank you. "This could be a bit dicey, so you might want to set the pup down," I advised Mihaela.

"Lasha," she said.

"What?"

"His name. It's Lasha." From the expression on her face, if she could have been blushing, she would have. "It's the name of my favorite Olympian."

"Oh really?" I rubbed the lamp, warning the genie that we'd be ready to go in a moment. "What's his sport?"

"Weightlifting. He's a super-heavyweight."

How incredibly appropriate. I laughed helplessly, and only managed to stutter out my directions to the genie once I'd calmed down. A moment later, we were dropped into a warzone that looked suspiciously like my subterranean range, except for the mass chaos going on.

Adam was crouched in the control room, looking out of his depth as lines of fire scored the walls all around us. I grabbed Mihaela's hand and dragged her and Lasha over, joining Adam as the spot we'd been standing in when we arrived was incinerated.

"What is all this?" I shouted as I traded the lamp for the gun he offered me.

"I needed to create a conflict! There are always cockroaches scuttling around in the mudroom, so I gathered some and equipped them to do battle with each other," he explained, looking remarkably sheepish for a monster with next to no ability to change his expression.

"Do battle how? With bloody rocket launchers?"

"No! Little laser backpacks, part of a prototype we were given to try out by... It doesn't matter. Needless to say, when I activated them, they came on at a very intense frequency instead of the lower, less fatal one I'd intended."

I goggled. I couldn't help it, the whole thing was just so surreal. "You're telling me you armed a bunch of roaches with laser backpacks and set them loose in my weapons range with no way to shut the things off again?"

He stiffened, which given that he was already a literal stiff was saying quite a lot. "That was also unintended. It turns out the program has a failsafe on the off switch that can only be user-operated, so while I could start them up, I cannot shut them down short of eliminating them all, and I wanted to wait for you to arrive before beginning that."

"So thoughtful," I snarked. "Fine. Let's–"

Mihaela tugged on my sleeve.

"What?"

She pointed around the corner at the range, which ... had become suspiciously quiet. "Look." Her smile was broad.

I looked. Lasha the Hulk-uahua was in the process of chomping the last laser-packing cockroach between his massive drooling jaws. As soon as he'd mashed the little beastie and its weapon of mass destruction into bits, he changed back into his unenhanced form and trotted over to Mihaela, who lovingly scratched him behind the ears. I gave him an appreciative few scritches as well.

"Well, that's bloody useful," I said, and stood up to look around my range. It was still smoking in places, but the fire suppression system had done its job and sprayed the danger spots down with foam. It would be a terrible mess to clean, and speaking of terrible messes, Mihaela and I were no treat to look at right now either. There was a lot left to do, and a lot still to figure out, but right now there was only one thing I wanted. I was determined to have it before anything else happened. And there was a lot that still needed to happen.

I needed to figure out a way to take out that beastly ooze monster back on Bloodstone Isle before it started gobbling up hapless fishermen or migrating to other islands. I needed to check in with Azizi and my contacts in Glasgow, just to make sure my recent work in both places had stayed comfortingly dead. I needed to figure out what leshies liked and send a bunch of it to Golosov Ravine, as a final thank-you to the one who had been so unexpectedly helpful. I needed to make sure Misty wasn't still incendiarily upset at me, and see if she couldn't help me make some connections for Mihaela in the hero community. I knew monsters well enough, but it never hurt to have some of the cape-and-tights squad on your side. I could also use a bath.

Yet all of that paled compared to what I really, truly, desperately needed more than anything else right now.

"So." I rubbed my hands together and looked at my companions, my roommates, my *family*. For the first time in a long time, the thought of dealing with another connection to my father didn't fill me with dread. Instead, I was… actually happy about it. How remarkable.

"Who's up for a spot of tea?"

ABOUT THE AUTHOR

CATH LAURIA is a Colorado girl who loves snow and sunshine. She is a prolific author of science fiction, fantasy, suspense and romance fiction, and has a vast collection of beautiful edged weapons.

twitter.com/author_cariz

MARVEL HEROINES

Showcasing Marvel's incredible female Super Heroes in their own action-packed adventures.

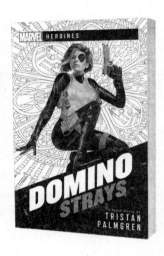

Sharp-witted, luck-wrangling mercenary Domino takes on both a dangerous cult and her own dark past, in this fast-paced and explosive adventure.

Rogue's frightening new mutant powers keep her at arms-length from the world, but two strangers offer a chance to change her life forever.

XAVIER'S INSTITUTE

The next generation of the X-Men strive to master their mutant powers and defend the world from evil.

Two exceptional mutants face their ultimate test and the X-Men's worst enemies when they answer a call for help, in the first thrilling Xavier's Institute novel.

Marvel's X-Men heroes return when a remarkable student rushes to save his family from anti-mutant extremists, but ends up in a whole heap of trouble...

MARVEL LEGENDS OF ASGARD

Mighty heroes do battle with monsters of myth to defend the honor of Asgard and the Ten Realms.

When Frost Giants invade Asgard, the young Heimdall and Lady Sif embark on a perilous quest to save Odin, and all the Realms in this heroic fantasy adventure.

The God of War must plunder the burning realm of Muspelheim for a lethal relic, at the risk of triggering the apocalypse and cursing his name forever.

MARVEL UNTOLD

Discover the untold tales and hidden sides of Marvel's greatest heroes and most notorious villains.

All of Latveria is at stake when its ruler, the infamous Doctor Doom, attempts to steal his heart's desire from the very depths of Hell.

When S.H.I.E.L.D. loyalists threaten to expose the Dark Avengers, Norman Osborn's infamous super-villains will stop at nothing to keep their secrets.